James Barr Walker

Experiences of Pioneer Life in the Early Settlements and Cities of the West

James Barr Walker

Experiences of Pioneer Life in the Early Settlements and Cities of the West

ISBN/EAN: 9783337338213

Printed in Europe, USA, Canada, Australia, Japan

Cover: Foto ©Andreas Hilbeck / pixelio.de

More available books at **www.hansebooks.com**

EXPERIENCES

OF

PIONEER LIFE

IN

THE EARLY SETTLEMENTS AND
CITIES OF THE WEST.

BY

JAMES B. WALKER.

CHICAGO.
SUMNER & CO.
1881.

PREFACE.

EXPERIENCE OF A PIONEER IN THE FRONTIER SETTLEMENTS AND
CITIES OF THE WEST.

The chapters that are to follow will contain a true statement of incidents occurring in the life of a man who lived from childhood to old age in the forests, villages and cities of the Great West. The history will be an egoism, of course. It can be nothing else. Those who read the first chapters will be interested in the last. The first, although widely different in spirit and purpose from the last, are a part of the whole, without which sketches of the life of a western man would not be complete.

Few persons living in the world have passed through so varied an experience as the writer of the chapters which are to follow. This I am sure will be the opinion of the reader who follows the series to its conclusion. But I will not anticipate. The common incidents of life are not often impressed upon the memory; but sometimes incidents which would seem minor to others are of deep interest to the individual who experiences them. Such incidents are not omitted in the following narrative.

CONTENTS.

6 CONTENTS.

PIONEER LIFE.

CHAPTER I.

THE CABIN AND THE CLEARING.

My father and elder brother both died before I was born. I have never known what may be peculiar in the love of a brother or sister. I have no record of my father's history except a marriage certificate preserved by my mother, and some masonic regalia, indicating that he was a master mason. My widowed mother returned to the home of her father, and soon after removed with my grandfather's family from the city of Philadelphia to a new farm in a region which was then the western frontier—twenty miles from Fort Pitt—now the city of Pittsburg. My first recollections are of a log cabin—the "clearing" in the woods, and the struggle of a family from the city to live in a new settlement.

The region west of the Allegheny Mountains was then called the "Indian Country." The names of

Brady and Poe, and others who led the pioneer settlers in the border warfare with hostile Indians,
were the honored names with those who came first
into the new settlements.   In the neighborhood
gatherings of the men, and the visits of the women
to each other's cabin, tales of peril with the Indians,
or of adventures in hunting the game which then
abounded in the forests, were familiar, and often ex-
citing subjects of conversation.

Among my first recollections is a story told of
one of the earliest settlers, whose cabin was occupied before the incursions of hostile Indians had
ceased.   The husband had gone a day's journey to
Fort Pitt, to obtain food necessary to the subsist-
ence of his wife and child, which he left alone in
the cabin to watch and wait, in fear, until his return.
Before he left, the cabin was made to look forsaken
—as though the family had suddenly removed from
it.   Cooking utensils and such other implements
as they possessed were hid in the woods.   No fire
was kindled.   The slabs, split out of logs with the
axe—called puncheons—which had been laid down
as a floor, were taken up and thrown confusedly
around—principally piled in one corner of the building.   Under these an excavation was made in the
ground, and some bed clothes thrown down, where
the woman and her child might be concealed if she
saw signs that Indians were in the vicinity.   Here
this brave pioneer woman had slept, or rather
watched one weary night.   Early the next morning
as she looked out stealthily through the chinks of

the cabin, she perceived Indians lurking upon the edge of the clearing. She hastened with her infant child to her place of concealment under the floor. The Indians, when they supposed they had satisfied themselves that the cabin was forsaken, came in and examined the premises to see if any thing was left worth appropriating. While they remained, the woman lay nursing her child to keep it from movement and noise. Once or twice the movement of the little one, it seemed to her, would surely betray her; but the talk and tramping of the Indians prevented their quick ears from catching the sound from beneath. In a short time they hastened away, fearing, perhaps, an ambush or attack by the settlers. The husband returned, heard the story of his wife's peril, and removed his family to the nearest "block house," or frontier fort, and hastened to give warning to the pioneers that Indians were prowling upon their border.

The first families in Western Pennsylvania and Kentucky subsisted in a good measure, during the first years, upon corn bread, and the game which they procured in the forests. The deer, the wild turkey, and other game were plentiful; and almost every family had a rifle or two hanging over the cabin door, on buck horns, by which they supplied themselves with venison. The skins, which they seasoned and tanned themselves, were made into moccasins and breeches for the men and boys, or they were bartered at the nearest market town for supplies of ammunition and whiskey for the men, and occasionally a quarter of tea for the women.

Soon after the removal of my grandfather to his cabin, a company of three hunters called to see the new-comers. As yet there was no door in the cabin. A bed-quilt was hung up where the door should have been, until a single board was brought twenty miles to make a door. This board was the only one ever used in the cabin. The hunters, (without the ceremony of knocking,) put aside the quilt, perhaps with the muzzle of their guns, and walked in. The incidents which followed, rendered vivid by frequent recital, are still distinct in my memory. They were dressed in the hunter's costume of the times. A cap made of a fox or raccoon skin, with the tail attached behind; a hunting-shirt (as the outside garment was called,) which consisted of a butternut colored linsey-woolsey frock, with a small fringed cape; pantaloons of dressed deer skin; a leathern belt, with a large knife attached, and moccasins tied with leather strings upon their feet. As these three men entered the cabin, they were saluted with a loud scream by my mother and aunts. The women had heard of the Indians with terror, and supposed that they were now to be scalped or carried captive by these supposed savages. There was a second floor—what was called a loft—in the cabin, reached by a ladder. The young women sprang up the ladder and crouched together trembling, and perhaps praying for deliverance. After the hunters had a little recovered from their surprise, words of inquiry and explanation, spoken in their own language, assured the affrighted women that their scalps were safe, at least for the present; and after a little delay to compose themselves they ventured down the ladder, and shook hands with the grinning hunters.

A sorrowful tale was told in the frontiermen's settlement of a frozen hunter found near the decayed trunk of a fallen tree, against which he had laid his rifle. There were marks of his fingers upon the tree where he had attempted to detach dry bark and material to make a fire. His lint or flint had failed him. He had probably lost his bearings in the woods; or he may have followed some valuable game away from his accustomed track. The night had come on, and with it intense cold. Feeling chilled and drowsy as those do who die by freezing, he had lain down beside the fallen tree. The death chill had imperceptibly stolen over him, and he slept his last sleep under the stars in that trackless forest. There were sorrowful hearts in one lonely cabin during that winter. When the snow was gone in the spring, the hunter's body was found and interred by the few settlers of the border. Long afterwards the story of the "lost hunter" was told, and his finger marks were shown upon the tree, where failing to kindle a fire, he had laid down to sleep the sleep that knows no waking.

My grandfather's family consisted of two young men and two daughters beside my mother. All these labored by day and by night to reach a self-sustaining condition in their new home. Within

the period of three years the desired end was gained
and the deprivations and sacrifices of pioneer life
were greatly abated.   During those first years the
woods around the clearing were often lit up at night
by the blaze of burning log heaps; and from the
cabin door my grandfather and uncles could be seen
revealed in the light, or flitting like spectres
through the lurid smoke, rolling the logs and piling
the brush upon the blazing heaps.

I remember that a German neighbor, who lived
on the adjoining farm, and who had "settled" before
we built our cabin, had the first wheat flour in the
neighborhood.   My grandmother having dieted for
a long time on corn-bread and potatoes, either borrowed, or she received a present of two cupfulls of
wheat flour, which, no doubt, was to her more savory food than are costly confections to the debili-
tated victims of fashionable life.

Our people were of the Scotch Covenanter stock,
and at that time there were no churches of their
own persuasion in the region.   At the distance of
about six miles a frontier Presbyterian minister, Rev.
Mr. Bracken, was endeavoring to gather the pioneer
families into a congregation.   The meeting house
was of logs, and the floor was not yet laid down.
The congregation for a time sat on the cross logs
which were designed to sustain a floor, when material could be procured to make one.   A little incident which occurred about this time evinced the
unsophisticated character of the youth in the woods.
The younger members of the family frequently

walked to meeting, while those who remained observed sacred time with a degree of strictness and reverence unknown in this day. Nothing was read but the Bible on the Sabbath. I was permitted to indulge in no excited movement, nor even free laughter during the Day of Rest; and in after years, although reverence and faith were, in a general sense, lost, there was still something in my mind that reluctated against Sabbath profanation.

On one occasion as a party journeyed on foot to the church, they were accompanied by my youngest aunt, who had scarcely reached womanhood, and a youth who was one of our neighbors. The young woman accidentally lost her garter, which becoming known to the party, the young man took out his jack-knife, stepped aside into the forest, and separated the pensile bark from a bass-wood bush; and having cut a band of it about the length of the lost garter, he tendered it, with kindly suggestions, to my youthful aunt. The incident was reported in the family circle before sun down on that Sabbath day, and the loud and prolonged hilarity that followed, at the expense of aunt Mary, could be restrained by no rules of Sabbath decorum. Whether it were reprehensible or not, the casuist may determine. For myself, I have no doubt the intention in the act was as pure and more benevolent than that of the royal gallant, whose like courtesy is perpetuated from age to age by a brotherhood of knights, whose escutcheon bears the significant device, "*homo soit que mal y pense.*"

The early times families had not the facilities to
supply themselves with raiment which those possess who now emigrate to the West. The people
clothed themselves almost entirely in material of
their own manufacture. Flax was sown, prepared,
spun and woven in our own family; and when a few
sheep could be kept on the farm, wool was mingled
in the fabric, and an article called linsey was produced, which was commonly worn, both by men
and women.

When wool became more plentiful and flannels
were manufactured, there were no fulling-mills such
as existed in later years. Necessity was the mother
of invention more frequently in early days than now;
and one of the methods of fulling flannels was suf-
ficiently primitive; while at the same time, it was
excessively exhilarating to those engaged in it, and
those who witnessed it. The woolen web was saturated with soap and water and thrown down in an
emulsient mass upon a clean space in the centre of
the cabin floor. The men of the neighborhood,—
especially the young men—rolled their pantaloons
up to their knees, and with bare feet sat in a circle
on the floor around the woolen web in the centre.
At a given signal each one commenced kicking vigorously upon the web, and his kicks were met by
equal ones from the opposite operator. It became
a matter of muscular endeavor by each one not to
be kicked back on the floor by his antagonist; hence
quick, prolonged, and spasmodic kicking was paid
out upon the web in the center, which was occa-

sionally plied by the laughing house-women with additional soap and warm water. The result was that the flannel was thoroughly fulled, the operators thoroughly saturated with sweat, soap and water; and a general, and somewhat vociferous laughter was induced, which shook the sides of all present, and promoted appetite for the homely but wholesome meal which followed. Gatherings for the purpose of fulling by this primitive process were called by the pioneers, "kicking frolics." Since then I have seen fulling mills pushing and pounding the woolen web with their wooden instruments, but I think I never observed the process without smiling when the old recollection of the "kicking frolic" was suggested to my mind. And I think it doubtful whether any fulling mill ever did the work more thoroughly than it was done in the cabins of the first settlers in the "Indian Country."

As the people found means to clothe themselves in fabrics of their own manufacture, the old and worn apparel which they had brought with them from their former residence, could be cut up and made into clothing for the youngsters. I remember well a suit which my aunt manufactured for me out of a worn garment which belonged to my mother. Buttons were scarce in those days, and the expedient was adopted of cutting slices off from the corks of bottles, and covering them for button-moles. When the job was finished, I was dressed in my new suit, and sent on an errand to our nearest neighbor, John Henry. I have a distinct remembrance of a feeling of pride, strong to exultation, that possessed me, as I entered the cabin door. My excitement was so apparent that the family noticed it, and some of them made a remark which I remember to this day, that little James ———— was proud of his new suit. I have had various suits since then of various text-ures, but I have no recollection of a feeling of self-gratulation so strong as that which possessed me, when clad in that new suit made out of my mother's old one.

Schools in the early years of the settlement were few and sometimes distant from our dwelling. The first school which I attended was kept by an old gentleman whose name was Ashton. He had been a militia officer in the time of the Revolution. He married a young wife, and removed from the old settlements into the new, where he taught a school in the same room in which he and his wife lived and lodged. His successor was a young man of fine personal appearance, but a great rascal, who made it his business to try the hearts. and the virtue of the young women in the country around. The pleasantest face in our neighborhood was that of Sally Otto, a daughter in a German family of the better class of pioneers. The first pleasant impres-sion ever made on my mind by woman's face was made by Sally Otto. I remember standing—a little boy—at her knee, and looking up at her pleasant features, while she talked, and her large blue eyes beamed smilingly upon me, as I tried to answer her questions.

It was not long before it was whispered in the neighborhood, that the school-master was to be married to poor Sally Otto. I write "poor Sally," because these were the words of affectionate regret used by the neighbors, when Sally's hard fate became known to them. They were married—he in a coat borrowed of a young man who had come in from the old settlements—she in the rustic garb of a pioneer maiden, with what little adornment my aunts and other friends could grant her. Soon after their marriage she was removed to a remote neighborhood, where her husband again taught a school, and where he proved unfaithful to his marriage vows, and broke the heart of poor Sally Otto. Even in his recreancy she clung to him with imploring affection, until he left her to do a villain's work in other places. The remembrance of her benign countenance and her sad fate has frequently recurred to my mind during a life time; and seldom without claiming the tribute of a sigh. The young and the fair in the rural districts should be admonished to trust nothing to the professions of prepossessing strangers. "A man may smile and smile and be a villain." Remember Sally Otto.

In a few years our family became acquainted with many families in the older settlements near Pittsburg. About the time that the family removed to the West, an elder sister had married in Philadelphia, and removed to Fort Pitt, (afterwards Pittsburg.) Her husband was a mechanic and purchased lots in the new town, which afterwards, with other accumulations, made him a wealthy man, of whom we shall hear more hereafter. During the visits of the family to their friends in Pittsburg and the adjacent neighborhoods, they found suitors and were all married but the two younger. My mother married a second husband and removed to his home upon the Allegheny river, eight miles above Pittsburg. About the same.time that these changes were taking place, my grandfather was visited by an agent of the first iron and nail factory established in the West. It was located at Pittsburg; owned by Mr. Cowan, and subsequently purchased and enlarged by Whiting & Co., of Boston, Mass. My grandfather had been a worker in iron in the city of Philadelphia, and now his services were sought to aid in the construction and working of the new mills. He accepted the invitation; left the farm; and removed to what was then the borough of Pittsburg.

I should not be true to my memory of this period if I did not relate, that on the night when my mother was married, previously to the removal of the family, I had a dream which so impressed me that it has often been suggested by incidents in subsequent life. I dreamed that a large ball, so large that it filled the room, was revolving in the cabin where I slept. It rolled on its axis with some noise. I observed it intently and noticed upon it lines and traces as of chalk, indicating paths of travel. I was then a lad some seven or eight years of age, and knew nothing of the rotundity of the globe ; and, there were no geographies or maps in the family or in the schools of that period. When at a subsequent time I learned that the world was round, and revolved on its axis, and noticed its figure in the geography, it recalled my dream ; and I thought of it with some degree of curious inquiry in my mind. At a later time I was discussing the philosophy of dreaming with a most excellent man, now deceased, president of one of our western colleges. We agreed in adopting the prevalent exposition of the subject, that the "stuff of which dreams are made" is the ideas and fragments of ideas which had previously existed in the mind. Of these are composed the pictures, sometimes fantastically and sometimes regularly constructed, which the mind sees in dreaming. We supposed various ways in which the archetype of the dream might have been thrown into the mind. We were satisfied;—and yet something seemed to say to me,—*that is not all!*

Most men are fools enough to believe in dreams;
But wise enough to keep their inward thought
A secret from each other.

CHAPTER II.

SCHOOLS AND SCHOOL DISCIPLINE.

My grandfather's family having removed to the borough of Pittsburg, my time was divided for four or five years between such school studies as were common in that day, and labor in the nail factory. During this period the first Sabbath-school taught at the West, was opened in an upper room of a store on Wood street. Of this school, at my own request, I was permitted to become a member. There were doubts at the time, whether the Sabbath-school were not a charity institution, and whether on that account it was proper for me to attend. Our family, although in humble circumstances, were self-sustaining; and would have resented as an insult any intimation that they would receive a benefit of any sort without rendering an equivalent. During a visit to Scotland and the North of Ireland at a later period, I found this feeling of personal and family independence prevalent everywhere among the Protestant laborers of the "old country." It was supposed likewise that it would be a violation of the sanctity of the Sabbath, to attend a school upon that day. And as the Sabbath-school was first conducted it would still seem so to many good people.

The Superintendent of the school was Mr. Lowry. He was a member of a good family in Pittsburg, which has since been distinguished in the Presbyterian church for its devotion to missions and other benevolent efforts of that denomination. We were taught in the school to read, write and cypher, in the first rules of Arithmetic; our books, paper and other requisites being provided for us. The first strokes that I ever made with a pen were made in the Sabbath-school, under the tuition of "Squire Lowry." I well remember his kind expressions as he leaned down over my desk, and taught me to make straight lines and crooked ones; or *strokes* and *pot-hooks*, as they were technically called. These early forms of the Sunday-school were soon superseded by more Scriptural instruction. Verses of Scripture were learned by the pupils, and for a certain number committed to memory, a New Testament was given by the teacher. I was one that recited the required number and procured the first Testament I ever owned. And many of the verses learned at that period are more distinct in the memory of an aged man to-day, than that of any other portion of the Scriptures. I have taught Sabbath-school myself since then, and the large portions of Scripture thus early stored in my memory, have been a blessing and an unction to other minds as well as my own.

During these years a Sabbath-school missionary came from Philadelphia and preached to the chil-

dren in Rev. Mr. Swift's church, on Diamond Alley.
He had the 13th part of the 119th Psalm, Watt's
version, printed, and desired all the children present
to commit it to memory.   I did so, and although it
lay dormant in my mind for years, yet subsequently,
traveling on business through many counties of the
State of Ohio, I sang on horse-back hundreds of
times—when no one but God heard:

> " O that the Lord would guide my ways,
>   " To keep His statutes still;
> " O that my God would grant me grace
>   " To know and do His will,"—&c.

The teacher of the day-school that I then attended was doubtful about my committing to memory one of Watt's Hymns.   He was a rigid adherent
of the Associate Reformed Scotch Church, and
thought it sinful, as the same church still does, to
sing any but "inspired psalmody," as they called
Rouse's version of David's Psalms.   To commit one
of Watt's hymns, the good man no doubt supposed
might give me a bias in favor of profane singing.
He perhaps did not understand as well as christians
do now, the relation of the introductory dispensation of Moses to that of Christ; and that, if the
psalms of the Old Testament were inspired to suit
the principles and the worship of the darker dispensation "that made nothing perfect," they would
be deficient in the superadded truth and grace which
came by Christ under the Gospel.

The instruction and school discipline under master McClurgan, would seem peculiar at the present
day.   Our reading books after Murray's Introduc-

tion, were the New Testament succeeded by the
Old.   Passages of David's Psalms, and some pages of
the Assembly's Catechism were learned each week,
and recited on Saturday forenoon – the afternoon
being a holiday.   The discipline was rigid and solely
by corporeal infliction ; great care being taken to
ascertain correctly the degree of malfeasance, and to
administer castigation in proportion to the offence.
The old man used a rod, and for grave offences,
what was called the "taws ;" which consisted of
several thongs of leather fastened upon a round
stick for a handle.   A small edition of what is called
in sailor phrase –"the cat-o-nine-tails." I passed
under the rod several times, but, more fortunate
than many of my companions, I experienced the
infliction of the "taws" but once.   That occasion,
of course, I shall not forget.

The master was hostile to the use of marbles, and
those who engaged in the game when they should
have been at school, were deemed culprits liable to
the penalty of the "taws." · Being permitted to
leave the school-room for a brief space, on some
errand, I unwisely made an effort to replenish my
store of marbles, by a game with a youngster whom
I found on my return near the school-house.   We
were engaged with great earnestness, when I noticed
my companion looking up with apparent surprise.
I turned in the direction of his gaze, and,—alas for
me !—the master was standing demurely behind me,
looking with quizzical countenance and simulated
interest upon my exploits in the marble ring.   He

had achieved a strategy, and by a detour reached the scene of our engagement. I may not give the precise words, but I shall give the spirit of the scene which followed. There was a cessation of my performances, of course; and for a moment I stood at a loss what to say or do in the premises. The old man assuming a peculiar look, remarked—"That was a good shot Jamie;—ye seem to be quite a proficient in this business. When ye get through with the game, if ye have no objections, perhaps we had better walk back to the school-house." I did not, however, wait to get through with the game—nor to make objections—nor to walk back with my teacher; but making my exit suddenly, I hastened back with all speed, and arrived at the school-room some minutes before he returned. As I took my seat, I remarked to a pleasant young girl, (Sarah Trovillo,) that sat nearly opposite:

"Sarah, as soon as the master comes I shall ketch it."

"What in the world kept you so long?" said Sarah.

"I wanted to win back my marbles from Sam. Ross."

I had done what the foolish victim of the gambler generally does, trusted to winning back my losses, until my time and my stakes were both gone.

I had only time to devise and execute with some assistance, the expedient of putting my copy-book under my jacket to save myself from the sharp pain that I knew was coming, when the steps of the

teacher were heard upon the stairs.   As he entered,
everything was as silent as a graveyard.   I was considered in the school, a favorite with the old man,
and probably many were anxious to see whether
the known penalty of the "taws" would be fully
inflicted.   But the autocrat of that school-room
would have thought it as great an offence to be
influenced by favoritism as would Sir Matthew Hale
in his duties as Cromwell's chief justice.   The heads
of the scholars were bent over copy-books, slates
and testaments; but glancing down the long desk
on one side of which sat a row of boys, and on the
other, a row of girls, I could see most eyes turned
ascant in the direction where I sat.

The teacher entered, took his place as usual, and
ordered attention to lessons which they all gave
but with their eyes still upon me.   In a short time
the rod fell before me on the desk.   The master was
in the habit, when he noticed any neglect or transgression by a pupil, of throwing his rod to the culprit, who had to carry it back, and stand to be
adjudged and punished according to his demerits.

I carried up the rod, and the old man took down
the taws, and after lamenting my depravity and expressing his regret that such an one as I should
transgress in such manner—taking me by the collar
with his left hand, in the other he wielded the terrible taws.   The first two blows, rapidly inflicted,
sounded upon the paper under my jacket with a
sharp crack almost like pistol shots.   The school
was convulsed with laughter.   The old teacher, with

some apparent surprise, suddenly suspended the infliction. He did not at once understand the unusual sharp sound so different from the sound of the taws upon the backs of other delinquents. Perhaps he thought that the blows might be too severe for the slender, delicate boy under correction. But peering into my face, where a suppressed laugh was struggling with the effort to appear awfully hurt, he began to comprehend that some mischief had been practiced. The copy-book was soon discovered and dislodged, and then the castigation followed with a will that left in my mind no doubt of its thoroughness. I returned to my seat, and although Sarah Trovillo gave several indications of sympathy, I did not raise my eyes to look at any one for some time. The old teacher subsequently seemed unusually kind to me, and I believe that was the only grave transgression, by which I ever grieved the heart of my good old school-master, Hugh McClurgan.

During most of this period, before Sabbath-school literature existed, my library consisted of "Goody Two Shoes," the "Ballads of Robin Hood," a "Token for Good Children;" and in later years a Song Book and Æsop's Fables. I could recite at one time some of the ballads of the "forester bold," and most of the poetry in the old Dilworth Spelling Book. And I had essayed, about the age of thirteen, to write, in Robin Hood measure, my first poetry, addressed to an absent uncle. I remember, as I write, the following verse:

Remember still I am your friend,
Remember uncle dear,
I have no father to defend
Me in my youthful year.

This is juvenile and doggerel, of course, but first efforts are remembered not so much for the value as for their place in the history of the mind.

CHAPTER III.

THE FACTORY BOY.

The rolling mill and nail factory in which my grandfather labored, was owned by a Boston company—Whiting being the principal name. Workmen were brought from Massachusetts. They were mostly young men, and were known collectively by the sobriquet of "the yankees." My business, with that of several other boys in the factory, was to heat the nail plates in a furnace, and carry them to the men who operated the machines. There was a set of doggerel verses composed by somebody about the factory that characterized, and sometimes caricatured, many of the laborers. I remember some of them. I was flattered by the following description:

> There's little J—— ——r
> He picks up the poker,
>   Flies round like a ghost in a throng;
> With his hat cock'd a-side,
> And his shirt neck untied,
>   He carries his plates all along.

Of one of the finest and freest young men the rhyme said,

There's generous James Fails,
He shells out the nails;
  Nor thinks that the time it is long:
He can take a good drink,
And at it never wink;
  But pass it all off with a song.

Poor Fails!—fine looking and generous to a fault, if he had lived in other times and under other circumstances, he might have been a successful man and an honored citizen; but there were no temperance societies in those days, and I feel as sure as I do of anything unknown to me in the past, that the devil that dwells in alcohol, increased his power over the young man, until with lost character and impaired health, he sank to a premature grave.

The boys in the factory were in the habit of earning a little money in leisure hours, by packing the nails in kegs for the workmen. On one occasion I was bringing the empty kegs down a high flight of steps, when by some mis-step I fell over the side upon a heap of cut iron plates below. I was taken up lifeless and conveyed home by two of the men. After a time I was restored; but a point of sharp iron had penetrated my neck and made a wound, the scar of which remains to the present day, as a reminder of factory life and labors.

The "Yankees" were often attendants upon the first cheap theatre established in Pittsburg. Some of the earliest players were the Drakes, who plied their vocation in the villages upon the Ohio and Mississippi rivers between Pittsburg and New Orleans.   As the audiences could not be large in those days, some effort was made to attract the factory men.   On a certain night a song entitled "The Nails" was to be sung, and the men generally purposed to be present.   As the verses were said and sung frequently in the factory, I remembered them, and recall some lines at the present moment :

> "To sing of nails, if you'll permit
>   My sportive muse intends, sir;
> A subject that I now have, pat,
>   Just at my finger ends, sir.
>
> We've spikes, and spriggs, and sparables,
>   Both little, great and small, sir.
> Some folks love nails with monstrous heads,
>   And some love none at all, sir.
>
> The bachelor's a hob nail,
>   He rusts for want of use, sir;
> The misers are no nails at all,
>   They're all a pack of screws, sir.

As all proposed to go to the theatre that night, I was very anxious to be of the company ; but my friends were averse to my wishes.   They spoke of theatres as the "Synagogues of Satan."   Play-actors they called "mountebanks," and considered them the associates of gamblers and loose women, an opinion of which I had an opportunity to learn more at a subsequent time.   I secured the aid however of a friendly yankee, who interceded for me with success.   He guaranteed my safety, good behavior, and admission fee ; and I was allowed to accompany him to witness the performances of the evening.   Either from a penchant for roguishness, or to save the half fare, he persuaded me to adopt

an expedient, which,—possessing in those days a
slight vein for the comic and adventurous,—I was
nothing loth to do.   It was in cold weather, and the
yankees .wore great coats or cloaks.   The tickets
were delivered at the foot of the stairs, which they
ascended to the circle in which they sat.   The expedient was, that I should conceal myself under the
great coat of my friend—cling with my hands upon
his shoulders, and let myself down full length.   As
my feet did not reach the bottom of his great coat,
no part of me was visible ; and I, being a slender
lad, and the man who received the tickets not looking after those who had passed, the fraudulent
device succeeded, and I emerged from under the
great coat at the head of the stairs, and that night
witnessed the play.   By that and one or two subsequent visits, while yet a small lad, my moral convictions—adopted from my family—in regard to the
evils of the stage were greatly abated ; and from
the stand-point of present observation, I can see
that a Superintending Providence alone, in subsequent years, prevented me from identifying myself
with the votaries of the theatre.

I remember little of the subject of the evening's
entertainment.   My attention was specially attracted to a sentence in a strange language, in
gilded letters, written over the drop curtain—
" *Voluti in Speculum.*"   I knew nothing of its import ; nor did the men in the factory ; but the
sparkle of the gilding attracted my attention ; and
years afterwards when I was studying the Latin

language, the significance of the sentence " *Voluti in Speculum*," was sought out, and translated by the aid of Ainsworth's old Latin dictionary, which student's used in the first western colleges.

During some years subsequent to the war of 1812, silver money was seldom seen. When it began to circulate, it was cut into small pieces. A Spanish quarter was cut into five pieces, each passing for a sixpence. A half dollar made five pieces, each passing for a shilling. The "fractional paper currency" was mostly what was called, in low phrase, "Shinplasters." Every shop-keeper who desired to do so, issued little, poorly printed, bills, promising to pay at his bar or shop from five to fifty cents. It happened that a gentleman visited the factory one day—probably to ascertain the process or profits of nail making. After spending some time in his round of examination, he took from his pocket a whole silver half dollar, and gave it to me. I was richer in mind with that silver half dollar than I ever have been since with an accumulation of thousands. A man's sense of wealth, I have learned, does not consist in the abundance of the things which he possesseth—*but in his satisfaction with* WHAT *he possesses*. I have accumulated somewhat in my lifetime, but the sense of satisfaction was greater at the beginning than at the end. Silver scarce—to possess a *real round* half-dollar was, in my circumstances, of course, something of an acquisition. It was shown round among the hands generally, and I was congratulated upon my good fórtune. In consulting with friends at home what disposition should be made of the "specie," my grandfather thought that as the money came from a gentleman who had examined the machinery, and seen all the men at work;—and as his gift was probably an expression of his gratification in view of the whole thing—the money should be expended, for a treat all round in the factory. I demurred in regard to an expenditure of the whole sum; but appropriated one-half of it for half a gallon of whisky, with which the men generally drank my health in the health destroying beverage.

Two incidents occurred in these years by which I felt sensibly in the influence both of faith and unbelief. Some of the men were in the habit of assembling in the office of the company on winter evenings and talking of the various topics that come up in such companies. Henry and Robert Steele, sons of the First Presbyterian minister in Pittsburg, were clerks in the establishment, and were usually in the office in the evening. They were both skeptical; because, perhaps of the inconsistencies which they perceived between the private life and public profession of their parents. I was present one evening when Robert Steele expressed his doubts of the truth of the christian religion. He made several statements giving reasons for his opinions. Others assented to the reasonableness of his views, and cited other difficulties which had occurred to them in regard to the christian faith. I was startled and alarmed. The expressed doubt seemed to take pos-

session of my mind; and while I feared to entertain
them, I felt exceedingly perplexed and unhappy
the remaining portion of the evening. I had been
taught to reverence the Bible. The only man that
I had ever heard spoken of as an infidel was a blacksmith, living on my way to school, whose house I
would have been afraid to pass in the night. That
I should have a doubt in my own mind was therefore a cause of self-upbraiding and unrest. But,
as in the parable, the devil had cast seed, in the
night, and went his way; so in this case, as in most
other cases, the evil seed sown that night lived,
even contrary to my own will.

I felt likewise the effect of faith in those years;
and this at a time subsequent to the experience just
stated. The one seemed for a time to displace the
other, without any process of reason in the case. I
was taken every Sabbath day to the Presbyterian
church, where, although I was generally listless, on
one or two occasions my mind was deeply impressed. I felt, consciously, spiritual rest and was
happy in spirit, and averse to anything I thought
wrong. I was in the same mental state that I have
known, since then, many youth and even children
to experience, when there was earnest prayer and
the presence of the Holy Spirit in a congregation.
If, at such times, children and youth were instructed
to see God in Christ, as Lord and Savior,—would
they not be permanently established in the kingdom of God? Such cases—old and young—are
symbolized by the man out of whom demons were

expelled, but the mind being cleansed of evil and not occupied by truth, the demons of evil returned with seven-fold power. There is, in many such cases, repentance towards God, that turns the soul from sin, and gives rest to the mind; but faith in Christ that enthrones the Savior as the Lord of life, is not exercised, because that vital gospel truth is not perceived. This state of mind occurred once or twice while I was a lad, but only for a few days. No one knew my doubts, and few knew my spiritual peace. My young companions who did know, I remember, spoke of me as "getting good." When this peace—and something more—passed, the natural state of doubt and carelessness returned—increased rather than abated.

Two incidents occurred, during my factory and school life, in these years, by one of which I narrowly escaped disability, and by the other sudden death.

A boiler for the steam engine was being manufactured or repaired; and the riveting was done by workmen who needed some one, small enough to go into the boiler; and willing and strong enough to hold a bar braced against the head of the rivet on the inside, while the workmen made it tight by hammering it on the outside. I did the service for part of two days, at the end of which time I had become so deaf that I could not for a season hear ordinary conversation. I was withdrawn from the labor, of course; and for a time it was feared that my sense of hearing had become seriously impaired.

Subsequently, the auditory nerve slowly regained its sensibility; yet a slight dullness continued for some time; and the previous acuteness of the sense has never been entirely restored.

My grandmother had deceased soon after we removed to town, and my youngest aunt had married, and was keeping house in my grandfather's residence, with her husband, William Graham. He was a factory man, and is still living. They were good people, but the care and regard to my reverence for the Sabbath, and other religious observances, which my mother and grandmother had strictly enjoined, was not exercised over me, as in earlier years. It was contrary to general rules to violate the Sabbath; but other interests attracted attention from me, and I suffered for transgression a penalty that nearly closed my life.

I would not give a true sketch of the "pictures in Memory's hall," if I did not state the impression of a dream, which I immediately related to my aunt, who interpreted it as foreboding some impending evil. I dreamed, two or three nights before, the following incident: that I was a truant from school, and traveling in a road to which I was not accustomed, when a black snake suddenly sprung into my path and bit me. I awoke, with the vivid and unpleasant sensation produced by the dream upon my mind. The following Sabbath, I and two other lads from the factory left the city to gather hickory nuts at a distance of two or three miles from town. One had climbed a tree to shake the nuts from the branches, while the other and myself stood below. A dead limb was detached from the tree by the climber which fell directly upon my head. I remember nothing subsequently for two days except a single incident: I was carried home by some friendly persons, and after a season consciousness and reason returned. This closed my labors in the factory, which itself was soon after suspended in consequence of a failure of the proprietors.

After a few months in school I removed from Pittsburg, in the family of my uncle Graham, to a small village on the western border of the State, near the Virginia line. My uncle had some relatives in the neighborhood, and had located there with the design of keeping a country store. He took his small stock of goods, his family and myself down the Ohio river in a keel-boat. Goods for the West and South in those days were mostly purchased in Philadelphia, and the transit was by means of wagons, drawn over the mountains by six horses to Pittsburg, thence down the Ohio river in keel or flat boats to places below. The keel-boat was propelled up and down the shores of the river, by four men using long poles, by which they moved up stream at the rate of some ten miles per day, and down the stream about three times that distance. The flat boat floated upon the current with produce for New Orleans. The keel-boat landed us at Georgetown, six miles from which place was Hookstown—or as it was characteristically called at that time—"the Devil's half acre." In this place

we opened shop in a small house, selling whisky
by the gallon, and other commodities less detri-
mental to the people, in one end of the building
and dwelling in the other.

I would have no one infer that my uncle was a
bad man who sought to injure his neighbors. He
was, and is now an industrious, honest, kind-hearted
man. He was, perhaps, the only man in the township that drank no distilled liquor himself; but not
to sell it in country retail shops would have been an
un-heard-of procedure. A short time ago, not
having seen any of the family for many years, I
called on my uncle's youngest daughter, who was at
the time, unwell. The old gentleman was at her
house. As I looked upon her features I remarked,
"She looks very much like aunt Mary did when she
was young." "*Does she?*" said the aged man,
rising suddenly to his feet, and looking into her face
with an awakened expression. My aunt had been
dead many years; but "it stirred the blood in the
old man's heart, and made his pulses fly," as he
thought he saw again something of the expression
of her who gave him her young love, and was his
faithful companion till death.

CHAPTER IV.

THE STORE BOY ON THE FRONTIER.

Hookstown, or "the Devil's half acre," was not exactly a frontier town, in the sense of its being a new settlement. The region around had been settled for some years; but it was on the borders of Virginia, and the usages of the region and most of the inhabitants, were of the "rough and tumble" kind, often found upon the border of slave states. The village was a small one. I resided in it two years, and never heard a sermon, nor saw a minister of the gospel, but once, when I was taken to Presbyterian service about five miles distant. There were sober families in the region, but the epithet given to the town characterized, with more truth than taste, the quality of most of the surrounding population. In Hookstown and vicinity occasional inebriety was the rule, and abstinence the exception. The taverns, of which there were two, were the resort not only of the neighboring farmers and their sons, but they were places where the rowdies for some distance around were accustomed to congregate. The landlords lived by the sale of liquor. On all public occasions, and at all social gatherings, the bar-rooms were filled to overflowing. On these occasions, such incidents as swapping horses—reciprocal treating, and, in the evening songs and "hot stuff" (as a heated drink mostly of whisky was called) were the order of procedure, often till a late hour of the night. The form of trading horses, when the owners did not agree, was usually to appoint one man to represent each owner. These would retire—examine the animals, and come to some agreement, as to the terms of exchange. When they came in, the landlord, or some one that represented him, would state the conditions in whisky, in case of the agreement or disagreement of the parties. The formula was as follows:

> " Two rues two half pints;
> "Two stands two half pints;
> " A rue and a stand a half pint,
> " And the ruer pays it."

Perhaps the uninitiated ought to be informed that the words "rue" and "stand" meant to reject or accept the conditions of the trade, made by the referees. But trade,—or no trade,—the conditions were such that whisky flowed freely; and generally down the necks of all present. It was therefore the desire of every one frequenting the bar-room to get up these attempts at horse trading as often as possible. One of the landlords usually kept at least one horse in his stable, and a friend at hand, to get up trades by which he often gained considerable sums by actual exchange, and always something by the sale of whisky.

The worst fighting usages of border life were practiced at Hookstown. It was a place where the rough fighters, or "bullies" as they were called, frequently met each other, and grappled in those barbarous conflicts, which were often more brutal than the combats of the ring, where professional pugilists contend for the prize belt or the stakes of their beastly abettors. These rough fighters were the heroes of their neighborhood; and when two of them met who had not tried their prowess, it was always expected that a fight would ensue. And fighting men generally were related to each other by whipping or being whipped, almost as universally as a herd of animals contend until the brute strength of the males in the flock is determined.

These affrays by the low whites in the slave states and upon their borders, had not only the animal characteristics of contending for the mastery by brute force, but in some cases the men used their power more barbarously than do unreasoning animals. They attacked each other with their fists, their feet and their teeth, and used every effort to gain the mastery, and make their opponent cry— "enough." This word—"enough!"—was the sign of vanquishment, and the signal at which all bystanders thought it their duty to immediately rush in and separate the victor from his opponent. Some would endure almost to death before the sign of submission was uttered.

I have, on one public occasion, seen three couples, at the same time, upon the ground,—each sur-

rounded by a ring of excited men. They were beating, and sometimes biting and gouging each other.
The men in the ring around them cried—"*No man
touch*"—"no man touch!"—until one or the other
of the parties cried "enough," when the ring broke;
and then several men would dash in to separate the
combatants. When they were parted—(I hesitate
to write what truth requires)—the faces of one or
both would be beaten and bloody. Often a finger
would be bitten to the bone. An eye closed; and
sometimes an eye gouged by the thumb of the ad-
versary, almost out upon the cheek. Thus bruised
and bleeding, a bucket of cold water would be furnished them, in which they bathed and washed their
disfigured features and broken flesh.

It sometimes happened that the finger of one of
the fighters was clenched in the teeth of the other,
before much personal injury had been inflicted by
either. This was considered "dishonorable." The
bitten man would cry "enough," and be released;
but in such cases the fight was not understood as a
finality; and was generally renewed at some succeeding public gathering, until one or the other was
the acknowledged victor.

There were several in the neighborhood who bore
visible marks of mutilation received in these savage
encounters. Among others was the school master
of the place, from whom I learned to be tolerably
proficient in some of the more advanced rules of
arithmetic. He was a protestant Irishman, and had
been accustomed to the rude conflicts that in former

years commonly took place at fairs in North Ireland,
. between the protestant and papal population.   In a
fight during our residence in Hookstown, he had a
portion of his upper lip bitten off.   I was present,
and witnessed the battle.   A stranger was at the
tavern harvesting for Smith, the landlord.   The
school master was with the company, after dinner,
on his way to the harvest field.   Something was said
by the stranger—probably prompted by Smith or
others—which the teacher considered disrespectful
to himself, or to "Ould Ireland,"—as he called his
mother-land.   The insult was returned, and a fight
immediately ensued.   Each one appealed to one of
the company and asked him to "show fair play;"
and then, in rabble phrase, they "pitched into each
other."   McFarland, the Irishman, had some skill
in the act of self-defence, and struck his antagonist,
who was a stout man, several hard blows before they
closed upon each other.   After tumbling for a time
on the ground, each one damaging his antagonist in
every possible way, my school master lay undermost; but he had clasped the neck and one arm of
the other, and drawing him close to his person, was
striking heavy blows with his right hand.   At this
point, their faces being drawn together, the stranger
bit a piece out of the upper lip of my teacher.   He
probably designed to seize his nose, but failing, he
caught his lip, and took a piece clean out.   The
Irishman did not "holler enough" as some in the
ring desired him to do; but by desperate effort, he
succeeded in turning his antagonist, and dealing

upon his face and person such crushing blows, that the stranger cried "enough," and at once several men "pitched in," and separated the school master from his subdued antagonist. So soon as they were "parted," McFarland ran to Smith, the landlord, and uttered words which I recollect distinctly, both in sound and sense. He asked—"Smith am I disfigured?" Smith answered—"I can't tell—it looks like a bad bite." The school master gave one bound towards his opponent, and uttering the words, "Ould Ireland forever," would have beaten the life out of him, if he had not been seized and restrained by the men present.

The teacher was a tolerable practitioner on the flute, and rejoiced in the execution of such tunes as the "Battle of the Boyne," and "Croppies lie down," which in the north of Ireland, will always heat the blood of a Catholic to fighting temperature. But after this incident, so long as I knew him, he was unable to use his flute; and both his features and his voice had been damaged.

There was another occurrence in connection with this man that seemed like a retributive providence. The father of McFarland had been killed in Ireland, in an affray between Catholics and Protestants. The assailants—two brothers—eluded the law officers, and escaped to America about the time that McFarland came over. Soon after the above incident occurred, these two homicides came to Hookstown, with packs on their backs, as peddlers. They supposed they were in a land where no man knew

them or knew of their crime. McFarland recognized them at once, and was possessed with a spirit
of revenge. They knew nothing of his presence in
the place or in the country. He counseled with a
family in the neighborhood, how he should assail
them and avenge his father. He was dissuaded
from an assault at that time; and soon after the
Pittsburg paper contained intelligence of the death
of two brothers. They had gone in to bathe, at what
was called the "old wharf," on the Alleghany river
above the city, and both had been drowned. There
was very deep water immediately off from the
wharf. Many times I and others had endeavored
to dive from boats at the landing, and bring up
some evidence that we had been at the bottom.
Into this deep water,—of which probably neither
of them was aware,—one of the peddlers had
stepped, and while struggling for life, the other had
endeavored to rescue him, and both had sunk together. They were found, one grasping the other;
but both of them dead.

The school master married in Hookstown and became more sober in his habits. I was told that he
labored industriously and saved sufficient money to
purchase a farm in the State of Ohio, on which he
or his posterity, are probably living to the present
day.

I suppose, it is true that most children before the
age of sixteen, have their favorites among the boys
and girls in the school room and upon the play-
ground. And perhaps these early attachments are

as free from selfish alloy, as any that are known to
the human heart. They are not always between
such subjects as would select each other after selfishness and reason had become more mature ; but
they are unaffected by mercenary and sensuous influence, and seem to be induced by some sort of
mutual affinity of mind for mind.

Among the first memories of most persons is one
of the pleasant little boy or girl who awakened
their first heart interest. The sweetest keys of the
poet's lute, are usually attuned to their early loves.
" Highland Mary " and " Annibel Lee " will live in
song forever; and so of others. Some passages of
this kind I remember; the authors of which are
unknown. Says one—

> " I often think each tot'ring form
>   That limps along on life's decline,
> Once bore a heart, as young, as warm,
>   As full of idle thoughts as mine.
>
> And each has had his dream of joy—
>   His own unequaled, pure romance,
> Commencing when the blushing boy
>   First thrilled at lovely woman's glance.
>
> And each could tell his tale of youth,
>   And think its scenes of love evince
> More passion—more unearthly truth,
>   Than any tale before or since."

And again :

> " There's a magical Isle up the river of time,
>   Where the softest of airs are playing,
> There's a cloudless sky, and a genial clime,
>   And a song as sweet as a vesper chime
>   When June with the roses is staying.
>
> And the name of the Isle is the Long Ago;
>   And Memory's treasures are there;
> There are brows of beauty, and bosoms of snow,
> And forms and features we used to know;
>   And a lock of a young maiden's hair."

I, like others, had my favorite among the little girls of the Hookstown school. And on occasions when the youth were invited by the neighbors to cut apples, or to make apple butter, the evening was spent as the larger children in the country usually spend such evenings; and in going and returning my favorite and I were not often far apart. What she thought of me may be gathered from the following quaint lines, which she had selected from some quarter, and passed to me in the school:

> " Most worthy of admiration;
> Almost to adoration;
> And held in estimation,
> For a fine education,
> And a good reputation;
> I have a strong inclination
> With your approbation
> To become your relation."   MARY.

But time, which changes all things, removed me from the village back to Pittsburg, and not long after removed Mary, in the blossom of her youth, to the land of the departed. Before I left the village, myself and another youth visited a large rock which lay on the margin of Mill Creek, about a half mile distant. On this, with a nail and a stone, we cut our names and the names of our favorites. Many years afterwards I had business in that portion of Pennsylvania. It was not far out of my route, and curiosity led me to the locality which had been the scene of my boyish experiences. Mary had been dead some years; and I wandered to the rock and searched for the names, which in early days had been slightly cut with the nail upon its surface. Every trace was obliterated. No memorial remained of the heart-life of the school boy, and store boy, in the "Devil's half acre."

But there are pauses in the business life of the busiest men ; and during one such pause the following lines were written, somewhat in the spirit of Burns' "Address to Mary in Heaven :"

> Sometimes in the pause of busy life,
>   When my mind is very still,
> There looks on me in Memory's glass,
>   Without the call of will,
> A fair young face from the land of youth,
>   And when she comes I sigh
> And my thought is held as with a spell
>   Of an unseen spirit nigh.
>
> Long, long ago, in boyhood's time
>   She was my earliest love;
> But ere the flush of maiden prime
>   She joined the choir above;
> Her presence gives a sign of peace,
>   All selfish thought is gone,
> I hear her silent words awhile,
>   And then I am alone.
>
> In the spirit-world hereafter,
>   I shall meet an angel friend,
> Whose presence I shall know by thoughts
>   That with my thinking blend;
> She will tell me in life's pilgrimage
>   She oftentimes was nigh,
> And looked on me, in Memory's glass,
>   Till I answered with a sigh.

Men generally fail who embark in a business the details of which they do not understand. So did my uncle. He traded in a small way until he had neither capital nor goods left. He trusted his neighbors—trafficked in produce; and, although he drank no intoxicating liquor himself, he was, for a time, partner in a distillery; and supplied the taverns with whisky. The end, of course, made haste. He was a member of one of the Scotch Presbyterian churches ; and had accumulated, by his labor, a little fund with which he purchased goods, when he left Pittsburg. At the end of two years he returned to his former labors, a poorer and a wiser man. By skill and industry he subsequently gained a competency, and yet lives to be grateful for it. The region around Hookstown has changed in character since then ; but mostly by the death or removal of its first inhabitants.

CHAPTER V.

THE PRINTER'S APPRENTICE.

Having returned to the city I was apprenticed, by my own choice, to learn the art and mystery of printing. The Pittsburg *Gazette* was the first newspaper established west of the Alleghany mountains. At the time that I commenced my apprenticeship it was owned by Eichbaum and Johnston, and edited by Morgan Neville. There was likewise a bookstore in connection with the establishment. With this old firm and for this old paper I commenced setting type, and continued in the office for about five years. My mother and her husband had removed from the farm into the city, and were members of the Scotch Secession church, under the pastorate of Dr. Bruce, where I frequently attended worship. About this time there was some controversy among the older people in the congregation in regard to the method of singing David's Psalms, and the tunes that should be used. Some of the old people had previously been offended by the clerk (or Clark as he was called) "giving out" two lines instead of one. The clerk had stood before

the pulpit and read one line at a time. The congregation would sing that, and he would read another—beginning to sing in a peculiar nasal tone
before he reached the end of the line. The reform of reading two lines instead of one succeeded;
and the old precentor having resigned, a younger
man stood up in his place, and introduced a new
psalm tune called Winter—a sweet, simple melody;
—but it was offensive to the old members who never
had heard a new psalm tune in their lives. They
could not sing the songs of Zion in an unknown
tune; and they looked as sad as the Hebrews by
the streams of Babylon, when the new tune was
used. This will perhaps seem to the worshipers of
our day something like bigotry, or ignorance, or
both. Perhaps these sincere worshipers erred both
in the method and the matter of psalmody; but in
the sight of God, who would have his people "sing
with the Spirit and the understanding"—"making
melody in their hearts unto the Lord," their worship was surely more acceptable than in churches
where men and women sing with the same motive
that they do in the opera, and where melody is
made *in the organ unto the congregation*, instead
of "in the heart unto the Lord." Such psalmody
is an *art offering to the congregation*—not a heart
offering to God.

About this period Methodism began to prevail at
the West; and the youth of the more staid denominations were often restrained from attending these
services. Methodist usages in the early period were

certainly peculiar—unwisely so perhaps; but it is certain that the denomination was more spiritual and efficient then than it is at the present day. The men, for the most part, wore a coat of the Quaker form, and the women all wore the Quaker, or, as it was called, the Methodist bonnet. To be a Methodist in those days was to come out from the world in a sense nòt understood at the present time. When a young woman was converted, all ornament was laid aside. The bonnet of the worldly style was put off or burned, and a demure, plain dress, such as we occasionally see a young Quakeress wear, was the badge of Methodism.

In their meetings, which were held only in the plainest chapels, the preacher generally became earnest, and responses were shouted at the top of the voice by those in the congregation; and during prayer, sometimes five and sometimes twenty, or more, were praying aloud at the same time. And it frequently occurred that during an enthusiastic meeting, one or two would fall and "get the power." To "get the power" was to lose physical strength and fall suddenly to the ground. The subjects of the power were generally women. When they had fallen, all motion of the limbs would seem to cease. The breathing would become slow but easy—the pulse almost dormant. They seemed to hear nothing of the movements about them. The face often looked radiant, and during the suspension of external sense, they frequently professed, upon recovering the normal state, to have seen glories that surpassed utterance. Some of those who "got the power," were too honest and devout to dissemble in a matter so serious. Their loss of the external and awakening of the internal sense was, no doubt, in some sense, real, and partook more of the character of the devotional experiences of the first christian assemblies, than the rational christianity of our time is willing to admit. Like miracles, necessary only in the beginning of a dispensation, to establish its authority, the more fully developed reason and better culture of the politic and more worldly churches of the present day, do not need an impartation of "power." It would not take long for a person who knew the day of his death to determine which were the better experience, the extravagant emotion of the early day, or the formal and fashionable order of later periods. Such an one would be likely to prefer the former, and say there was a "more excellent way" than either.

I sometimes went to Methodist meeting. On one occasion I went home to pray for an hour at my bedside. On another occasion I remember urging skeptical objections to an elderly man, who was an active Methodist, until I seemed to stagger his faith, and I left him embarrassed and perplexed. But I had no complacency or sense of triumph in the achievement. I felt deeply troubled with the thought that perhaps I had shaken his faith; and that night I prayed earnestly and long, that if the Bible were true, God would in some way show it to me, and if I had injured the good man I prayed sincerely that the evil might be corrected. I had some reason afterwards (although we never spoke again on the subject) to think that the arguments I had suggested had done evil. I know nothing of his later history, but I fear he made shipwreck of the faith. For this I can make no reparation or atonement in the government of God. And if the evil is not arrested or compensated for by Christ's sacrifice, what will be the result in my case? My own repentance did not recover him to obedience, and could not counteract or compensate for the current of moral evil which I then originated in the will of that man. Will the currents of life which Christ originated by his life and death, at some future time meet and counteract this evil, and (as *He* does not need) the good be imputed to me?

About this time I began to be enamored of the Muses, although my partiality did not seem to be appreciated by those who had the young ladies in charge.

The *Saturday Evening Post*, of Philadelphia, was, I believe, the first literary newspaper published in this country. It was exchanged with the *Gazette*, and when I could obtain it, I read it with great avidity; and my highest ambition, just then, was to see something of my own composition in print.

The first production that I ever offered for publication, was a parody on something that had appeared in the *Post*. It was rejected with a notice to correspondents, that the editor thought he had read it before. It was the production of a youth, and somewhat extravagant and juvenile, of course ; but it was entirely original. As these first efforts were "driven like nails into the mind," perhaps they ought to be inserted. Here is the parody :

[For the *Saturday Evening Post.*]

MESSRS. EDITORS :—Having a good deal of work to do about the farm lately—clearing up some new land and grubbing out a place for a potato patch, I hung my triangle on the branch of a dog-wood tree. Being out hunting the steers last week I came across the instrument and brought it home again. Looking over the *Post* lately and seeing some beautiful verses on Imagination, I imagined it was spring, and then imagined the following invitation to your correspondent, Isadore :—

O, Isadore, loveliest, come to me,
And we'll sit in the shade of our great elm tree;
And we'll list while the mocking-bird carols along
At the hour of noon-tide his varied song.

Or, come when the sinking god of the day
Has dappled the clouds with a lambent ray;
And we'll talk till the shadows of twilight pervade,
And spread o'er the woodland, a mantle of shade.

Or, come when Luna, pale queen of the night,
And the chrystalized dew shall give thee light;
'Tis elysian pastime to spend a sweet hour
By moon-light and dew-light—alone, in our bower.

Oh come when your cheek is all in a glow,
Like fervid wine be-dropt in the snow;
And hold your breath lest Zephyrus should sip
The honied dew from your fresh young lip.

Come!—no matter when—by day or by night,
With a throbbing pulse and an eye of light;
And I'll sing the words, if you'll sing the tune,
Of the " Banks and Braes of Bonny Down."

Failing on one style and in one direction, I tried another. I offered to one of the city papers a piece of pure sentiment, which was never published. I

thought the editor, of course, a great dunce, and
stated my resolution to some of my companions,
that I should sometime have my poetry published,
if I had to start a paper for that special purpose.
And as a matter of fact these first efforts never
were permitted to appear in print until inserted in
a paper under my own control.

In these years a young girl in the city—Miss Eliza
Hunter,—whom I had never seen, wrote verses
evincing poetical taste and talent. Her teacher
had them published in the *Gazette*. I read them
with interest and admired the mental gifts and imagined personal graces of the poetess. A freak of
foolish adventure induced me to address a note to
her through the post office, proposing to lend her
certain books, (if she had not read them,) most of
which I expected to borrow, if the offer was accepted. The books were to be delivered (if she desired
it) in such way that neither of us should recognize
each other in the transaction. I received a note
soon after accepting my proposition, and proposing
on her part, that on a certain night, the books
should be delivered at a certain hour, at the door
of her teacher's residence, to a person that should
answer to her name. The books indicated were
mostly obtained; and at the time designated I called
and inquired for the poetess. She was not at home;
and it was not known to her friend when she would
be. It was night. I recognized her teacher in my
interlocutor; but I did not observe him so intently,
as I presume he did me.

I never saw the poetess until forty years after, when one day in summer I was riding with my wife on a visit to a relative near a village where she resided. A lady was approaching us on the sidewalk whose name I inquired. It was Mrs. Dr. Barker—forty years before—Miss Eliza Hunter. I had the driver rein up the horses, and asked pardon of the good looking elderly lady, for inquiring if she remembered a note signed "Carlos," and the tender of books in her school girl days. She looked a little surprised; but said, after a moment's hesitation, that she did, and asked me to call. I have not seen her since.

A little difficulty between myself and a fellow apprentice originated in this affair. Thomas Collins, son of a deceased lawyer, in Pittsburg, and who had been for a time a cadet, at West Point military academy, was an apprentice in the same office. He had a good looking overcoat—a comfort which I did not possess. It hung in the office, and on the night in question, as he was not using it, I appropriated it for half an hour, to convey the books as designated. When he learned the fact his wrath waxed exceedingly hot. He feared he should be identified as the hero of the foolish adventure. Collins was a good, gentle youth, and afterwards a fast friend; but it was some time before he was reconciled to appear on the street in his own overcoat.

The first steam-boats that moved upon western waters were constructed at Pittsburg about this time. Oliver Evans and Henry Holdship were principally engaged in the enterprise. I had a ride on one of the first steam-boats that floated in a western river. My employers had some interest in the craft, and all hands had a holiday the Saturday afternoon on which she was to make her trial trip, and by some means I managed to get on board. She proved to be a slow boat, unable to make head-way against a strong current. We ran down the Ohio river in fine style to what was called in those days Smoky Island, about five miles below Pittsburg. The passengers were exulting and hilarious; but when the boat was turned and headed up the stream, the cast of countenance on board became gradually less self-complacent. Her machinery worked on, but the boat made no head-way against the current. After various devices had been used with little avail to make her go ahead, she was turned out of the channel to take advantage of dead water; and by this expedient she was constantly in danger of sticking fast on the bottom. The boat left the dock soon after noon, and did not make the five miles down the river and back until after dark.

I had a friend in later life, William Patterson, a banker of Mansfield, Ohio, now in heaven. He resided in Steubenville, on the Ohio river, about this time, and had an experience on this boat, or one which commenced business about the same time. He was an intelligent and devout man; and not in the habit of telling exhilarating stories; but his first ride on a steam-boat he never forgot.

The young people of Steubenville determined to have a social time,—and a large pleasure party, of which he was a prominent member, embarked on board the first steam-boat that reached the town, on her return trip to Pittsburg. But the party never arrived at their destination. The river was in good stage, but the current in many places was too strong for the power of the boat. The gentlemen excursionists used every expedient to aid the engine by an application of their physical strength. They used poles on the sides of the boat. They took the yawl ahead and endeavored to aid by a tow line. In one or two instances they seized the limbs of trees overhanging the stream;—but all effort failed and the pleasure party,—having, undoubtedly, had more exercise, and recreation, and exhilaration, than such a party would have on a better boat at the present time,—voted the effort to reach Pittsburg by steam-boat a failure, and returned to their homes, believing that steam-boat navigation on the Ohio, was what the best civil engineer in Europe affirmed it would always be on the Ocean,—an impracticable achievement. Steam-boat travel subsequently on river, lake and ocean reached a degree of speed, comfort and splendor the acme of which was passed twenty years ago. Before the competition of the rail-roads the boats on the Ohio and Mississippi rivers, and on the lakes from Buffalo to Chicago, were fitted up with a degree of comfort and splendor, which is not seen now-a-days. The fixtures and furniture were far

superior to anything seen in Europe ; and the speed
was nearly one-third greater than the best boats
on the Rhine.   I have, since my first experience on
a steam-boat, crossed the Atlantic four times from
one Continent to the other without a stoppage of
the wheels from port to port.   And on the Channel
—on the Rhine—on the lakes of Europe—I could
not refrain from a feeling of suppressed enthusiasm
for my Fatherland and the Great West in particular
when I compared the best European boats with the
old Sultana, and her compeers, on the American
lakes and rivers.

During my apprenticeship I had some literary
advantages, which in the latter part of the period,
I endeavored to improve.   There was a book store
in connection with the establishment to which I
had access.   There was likewise a subscription reading room of which the father of Mr. Eichbaum was
librarian ; to this I was admitted when none of the
members were present.   About this time, likewise,
Mr. Kirkham, author of a school grammar, that subsequently circulated largely in the West, got out
an edition of his book.   He was very frequently in
the printing office, and was kind enough to loan me
several volumes, and commend them to my attention.   One of them was Cobbett's Grammar, which
I read, and he expounded at leisure opportunities.
I have always been grateful to this traveling gram-
marian for his kindness.   I remember some of his
topics of conversation to the present day, and about
all I knew of grammar, when I subsequently became

a school teacher, was what I learned from Cobbett's grammar, in the printing office, by the aid of Mr. Kirkham.

A debating society existed at this time in the city, composed of young men, with one or two of whom I became acquainted. By their introduction, I became a member of the club. They were mostly clerks or mechanics. Every one of them was a man of some native ability, and subsequently each one, with perhaps two or three exceptions, achieved for himself an honorable place in society. One of the members—a mechanic—was subsequently sheriff of the county. Another, Mr. George Darcey, whose family, poor but industrious, had resided in a small house belonging to my step-father, was subsequently state senator from the city district; and, when I last met him—treasurer of the Pittsburg and Fort Wayne Rail Road. Another member, Joseph Barker, became mayor of the city. One a druggist's clerk, accumulated a large fortune in South America; another, a grocer's clerk, became one of the wealthiest wholesale dealers in the city. I, the youngest of them all, and the only one that failed as a member, passed through a life more varied and I think more useful than any of them.

I never succeeded in making a speech or arguing a question before this society. The members were mostly better informed than myself; and I was in such positions anxious and diffident. Having attempted to discuss the question of the evening two or three times, being able to get no further in my

remarks than—"Mr. Chairman—you know * *
that is" * * * I was ashamed and vexed with
myself; and determined to make a last effort. I
thought out and matured my remarks for the approaching discussion. I designed to achieve a triumph that would make up for all past failures; and
some of the members, who had read some things
that I had written, were sure I could do so. When
the evening came, I expended the only sixpence I
had for a cup of beer, supposing it would give courage and aid to banish diffidence. The eventful
moment for my delivery approached. I remember
it distinctly, and almost feel it now. While the
member that preceded me was speaking I could
actually feel, if I did not hear my heart thumping
against my sides. I rose in order, and addressed
the chairman. I was able to utter mechanically
some two or three of the sentences I had prepared.
But, alas! I again lost the chain of consecutive
thought; and repeated like one talking to the stars
—the old words with some additional expletives:—
"Mr. Chairman! * * * You know * * that
is * * consequently—therefore—but"—. I sat
down; and my efforts at public speaking closed for
some years. In after life, years after, I became a
public man, my heart beat energetically, when I first
rose in new circumstances to address an audience.
But diffidence, which accelerates pulsation, often
aids in impression, and since then I have seen audiences both in church and state more effectively
controlled by my words, and by others whose speech

was generated by a like impetus, than I ever saw one controlled by a self-sufficient or phlegmatic speaker. It is when the impulse is generated by emotion originating in the conscience or the heart, that the mind moves with sublime and controlling power.

But time lapsed. My apprenticeship closed, and finding no employment in Pittsburg I concluded to set out for Philadelphia as a traveling printer. A little company of friends assembled on the night preceding, at the residence of my mother, to bid farewell. On the following morning, when I awoke, my mother was in my bed room praying. I did not then know that she prayed habitually; but she told me subsequently—when the crisis in my life was passed—that she had made supplication for me daily from the day of my birth; which no doubt she continued to do, including her other children, until the day of her death.

CHAPTER VI.

THE TRAVELING PRINTER.

There were no rail roads in those days, and stage coaches between the East and the West were slow and expensive. Men journeyed over the Alleghany mountains mostly on horse-back or on foot. Western merchants often rode, and sometimes walked the distance between Pittsburg and Philadelphia. Their goods were, as before stated, conveyed to the West in wagons, drawn over the mountains by five or six horses, and thence by keel-boat down the Ohio river, and again by wagons into the interior, of the new States of Ohio and Kentucky.

On a morning in August, a robust young man, who was a carpenter, and myself, started to accomplish the journey over the mountains on foot. Our wardrobe, tied in a handkerchief, was carried in hand, or on a stick upon our shoulders. We were about ten days in accomplishing the distance of three hundred miles. My companion was athletic, and suffered little, comparatively, from fatigue. Ever day I was weary with travel. We would oc-

casionally sit down in a shade to rest. At such
times, foot sore and weary, I would throw myself upon the ground, and almost immediately "nature's sweet restorer, balmy sleep," would come to
my relief. But the next sensation was always an
unwelcome one,—sometimes painfully so:—it was
that of a call or shake from my companion, arousing me to endure again the labors of the road.

On one such occasion, we followed a little path
that led off from the mountain road to a spring near
by. The spring was known to mountain travelers,
who generally stopped to rest and drink ; and often
to bathe their swollen feet in the cool brook, which
ran from the spring. Here we tarried a little longer
than our usual time. A draught of the limpid
water, distilled away down in the crystalline alem-
bics of the mountain, and a slumber on the bank
of the murmuring rivulet, protracted a little longer
than the usual time, refreshed and strengthened me.
When I arose we took another cool draught, and
set out again upon the mountain road. As we journeyed on, I composed in my own mind, the last of
the following stanza. Subsequently, in writing for
a friend a poetical description of the journey and
the spring, I prefixed the preceding lines. They
would not have seemed egotistical to the friend for
whom they were designed ; and now that they are
copied when the eye is faded, the natural strength
abated, and the dark and curling hair has become
white as snow—their introduction here will be for-
given :

PIONEER LIFE

A traveler on the mountain,
 In a warm mid-summer day,
Sat down beside a fountain
 That gushed beside the way—
'Twas a cool sequester'd fountain,
 Where the birds and breezes play.

He was a youthful traveler,
 And delicately fair ;
With eye as bright as diamond light ;
 And dark and curling hair ;
His hat lay by him on the sward—
 Bosom and brow were bare.

'Twas a pleasant spot, and a pleasant thought,
 That Memory treasures still,
Flow'd through his mind as he lay reclin'd
 By that flowing mountain rill—
The rest was sweet, and nature kind,
 And numbers flow'd at will.

The numbers flow'd at will, dear friend,
 And I write them here for you ;
The rest was such as Mercy gives ;
 The spring was honey-dew ;
Or nectar drops, when angels seem
 To bathe the lips in a fever'd dream.

The sweet repose ; the shaded spring ;
 The carol of the birds,
The Muse gave form that Memory set
 To music in these words :—
 * * * * *

Know ye delight when the spirit droops
 With the sorrows fatigue can bring :
I do !—for I sat on the mountain side,
 And drank of the mountain spring :
And laid me down on the cool green sward,
 Where the brook ran murmuring by,
While the feather'd songsters overhead,
 Carol'd a lullaby—
And the cool, pure breeze that linger'd nigh,
 And whispered among the boughs,
Seemed kind as the light in a woman's eye
 When kissed by her chosen spouse.

Having arrived at the city of my birth, I first expended a portion of my little fund of money in a visit to Peal's Museum, of which I had read in Dilworth's spelling book; and where I expected to gratify a longing desire of many years, to see the wonders of art and natural history stored in that old first American Museum. Having satisfied myself in this particular, I sought out and called upon the friends of our family, to whom I had been kindly commended by my mother. In these visits I had the first experience of what is frequently the dehumanizing effect of wealth upon the natural heart. Some of our relatives were in fashionable society, but the larger number were in the better and happier association of the middle class—generally industrious citizens. The ladies of the wealthy family, with a single exception, after they had learned that I was "only a journeyman printer," gave those indications which are easily understood, that my position was not such as would qualify me for introduction to some of their company; hence, I was invited to call at certain specified times:—times, of course, when their fashionable friends would not be present. I do not know, at the present writing, that there was anything improper in this, considering the tyranny that the forms of fashionable society exercised over all its victims; but a "journeyman printer," of course, felt himself to be as good as anybody in the city, and had no disposition to call upon the family at the times designated, or at any other time. Wealth does not always eviscerate the

soul. Culture and character and conscience often
co-exist with fortune; but after some experience in
various classes of society, I am sure that characters
deserving contempt;—or rather compassion,—are
found more frequently in fashionable circles, than
among the industrious middle class of the country.
Selfishness and vice prevail in their worst forms at
the two extremes of society. The mean is the
gold: One extreme is tinsel; the other tin.

My more humble friends received me with kind
hearts, and manifested a sincere interest in the experiences of their friends at the West. In their
minds the "Indian country" was still associated
with Indians and bears and barbarians of the border. To find a young man from Fort Pitt, civilized
and social, surprised them into a state of mind that
was quite gratifying to me. I found among some
of them real heart-friendship. Some were caring
for the orphan children of deceased friends;—and
in their circle of association I heard of some families of little means that were assisting neighbors
poorer than themselves. There is more real charity
exercised by the better class of laboring people ·
and shop keepers towards their needy neighbors
than the world supposes. The kindness of the virtuous poor to each other, is neither known nor appreciated as it should be. There is little kindness
in *fashionable* circles for each other, except that
which is selfish or affected.

Some months of labor were spent in the printing
offices of the city. Most of the time in the office

of Jasper Harding, near the Girard bank. In this office the workmen received, each Saturday night, little more than sufficient money to pay their boarding bills; and the sum earned beyond this was paid by orders on clothing stores, and such like devices, by which unscrupulous dealers could charge such rates as their avarice dictated; and the journeyman printer had about the same chance for a respectable living, as the needle woman has who makes shirts for the shop keepers of the city.

Wearied and disaffected with such style of life and labor, I sought other employments. Among the efforts which proved unsuccessful, was an attempt to enlist in the service of the South American Republic, then contending with Spain for independence. This endeavor was suggested by my friend, Collins, who had finished his indenture, and come to Philadelphia, soon after my arrival. He had, like myself, failed to get remunerative employment; and, as he had spent some years at the military academy, he supposed we might both succeed with the consul of the New Republic, in getting a passage to South America, and a lieutenant's commission in the army. The consul was a portly, pleasant looking gentleman, and seemed somewhat inclined to favor the application of Collins, as his military education was deemed a fitting preparation for the service. But as for me, neither precedents nor papers were in my favor. There was nothing about me or my antecedents that indicated fitness for the work of the warrior. With proper courtesy, therefore, my aspirations to command a squad of peons was dismissed, and that of Collins held under advisement. But as my friend was a diffident young man, he never returned to urge his application; and moreover, he did not desire to leave for parts unknown, without a companion.

Collins had wealthy friends in the city, and soon found employment as a teacher, which he followed for some years. I soon after left the city for New York. We never subsequently exchanged but one letter; and I have never seen Collins but once since we then parted. We were resolved to struggle manfully to gain—what we supposed we had ability to accomplish—an honest living. Correspondence was expensive in those days, each letter costing from twelve to twenty-five cents. Laboring men could not afford to have many correspondents besides their near relatives. We had agreed, however, if fortune frowned or favored—if either of us should deem it expedient to commit suicide or matrimony, that one should inform the other, as the facts might be.

Some years afterwards the following letter was addressed, *verbatim*, to Collins, still in Philadelphia. After place and date there was inserted,

T.—I'm married—J. B.

To which a response was returned immediately in the following words:

J. B.—I'm not yet; but soon shall be.—T.

I know that brevity is said to be the soul of wit, and the fashion with the generals since the time of

Cæsar; but if there have been any more laconic epistles in connection with matrimonial matters than the foregoing, I have not read them.

Once since the days of other years ˙I have met Collins. He is now an old man; and has a clerk's place in the Post Office in Pittsburg. Being recently in that city, I took pains to learn his address. I called at his dwelling and awaited his return from labors much too laborious for him. I was anxious to see, if after a separation from youth to age, he would recognize me. He came into my presence, an aged and a sad man. He stood before me and surveyed me some minutes with interested scrutiny. Occasionally saying, "I ought to know you, sir." "I do know you"—"But, who is this?" The effort at recognition, however, was a failure, and I had to give him the name of his old companion. Then followed the exclamation—"is it possible!" and a strong clasp of hands. Poor Collins—diffident—intelligent —educated—kind of heart—he is nearing the close of life with a dependent family, and yet dependent for a living on the salary of a clerk. Once he possessed some means by inheritance, but having invested it in the suburbs of Pittsburg, the title proved to be imperfect, and by the wiles of dishonest men, he lost his little all. His eldest daughter was a young lady of amiable qualities and the light of his house. She had recently died, and her father carried to his daily toil, the heart of a stricken mourner. He said he had given one hundred dollars for the lot in the graveyard where his dear

daughter lies buried, and it required one year of
close economy in his family to save the money
which procured the deed. That little lot in the cemetery, where, when his labors are done, he hopes to
rest by the side of his daughter, is the only inheritance he has on earth. Poor Collins.

During the time I was in Philadelphia, my friends,
of course, were somewhat solicitous that I should
find immediate employment which they knew was
difficult to obtain at that time. My good mother,
especially, was anxious for my welfare ; and strange
as it may seem to others, and as it seems to me, I
am, in writing these lines, more sensible of her
anxiety for me at that period, and more affected by
the remembrance of her labors to procure friends
for me ; and by her motherly gifts and advice, than
I was at that time. I think the longer a man lives
in the world he becomes more impressed and grateful by the recollection of a good mother's interest
for him in the days of his youth.

My dear mother had a sore trial in connection
with her solicitude for her absent son. It so happened that a person of my name—(a druggist, I
think)—committed suicide during my sojourn in
the city. By some means the report reached my
mother, with the additional conjecture that it might
be her son. Her distress for a season was painful
for her friends to witness. She conjectured causes
for the event. What disappointments or sufferings
could have caused an act so unlike anything she
could have anticipated. Although it was a mere

rumor, she could not be comforted, until the history of the case was obtained. When I heard of this incident, and many times since, when friends have described her state of mind at that time, my heart has been deeply affected by the thought of what my dear mother must have suffered in consequence of her maternal attachment to her son.

A little incident which memory preserves affected me, and affected a companion much more than myself. Walking one evening in the autumn in the pleasant streets of the city, my companion was a young man from Pittsburg, who had come to the city before me. We boarded in the same house—had known the same families in our youth, and of course, we sympathized with each other, and talked over reminiscences of the past. On that evening Alexander K. seemed pensive, and thoughtful. To walk and talk of our old homes, and old friends—lady friends especially—seemed more than usual a special interest with him. (Allow me to assume Dermoody as my *nom de plume*, and I can give the reader the spirit of our talk for a few minutes.) A conversation I shall never forget.

"Dermoody," said he, pressing my arm closer, "you know Sally Brown."

"Yes."

"Well, this night she and I were to be married."

"Is it possible?"

"Yes, this night—this night Sally Brown was to become my wife."

"Why did you not mention this before?"

."We were to keep our secret till the event was past—but it's all over now."

"Has she been untrue?"

"No; nor I—but the thing is impossible. She sees it. I see and feel it. Dermoody, it would be madness to marry Sally Brown with no prospect of a comfortable living. I can't do it."

"It is postponed, then."

"No; the engagement is given up. She thought it best. But, Dermoody, it is hard for me. I could work day and night for that girl. But it's all over now! I think she is crying to-night. Oh, if I only could see her. But I have no money to go home; and it would do no good, if I had. I have no heart either to write or to work." (His voice grew tremulous and he said,) "Dermoody, whoever gets Sally, I *know she'll remember me!*"

With other words of home and friends, we walked on, and ever after, during the little time I was with him, I spoke to him less mirthfully but with more kindly interest than before.

My friend K. was married long ago, and Sally, too—better, I think, than though they had married together. Does she remember him? Surely; and he remembers her; but both, probably, with the conviction that their early purpose was better unfulfilled.

Before I left the city I spent a day or two in visiting places of public interest. There was an exhibition at the Asylum for deaf mutes, and having procured a ticket, I attended the exercises. I remember that the gentleman who handed me the ticket, inquired why I wished to be present; and that I had some difficulty in assigning a reason. Feeling alone in the world, the incident commemorated in the following verses impressed me, as it might not have done at another time. A class of mutes was reciting. The features of the young girl to which the lines refer, bore the impress of a pure, affectionate and thoughtful mind:

> "Her deep expressive eye had caught
> Its lustre from the Spirit's gem,
> And on her brow the light of thought
> Flashed like a Spirit's diadem."

She noticed my look of interest, and it then seemed to me not only recognized, but felt it. Her eye dropped from mine, where she, no doubt, read sympathy for her situation, and a slight color suffused her cheek. Years afterwards, in hours of relaxation from professional study, I recalled the event, and gave the impression permanency in the following lines:

THE MUTE GIRL.

> She was a fair young girl; and all I've seen
> Of woman has not left within my mind
> So pure a picture. Her beauty was not such
> As I have seen in portraits: It seem'd to live
> Upon her face: And when her mind had caught
> Her teacher's thought, her soul would seem to come
> In beams of intellect to her dark eyes
> And light her features with a sentient glow
> Of meaning I could read   *   *   *
>
> I felt my heart
> Was sympathizing with that silent girl:
> She felt so too. For when she had perceiv'd

My earnest look, her glance grew fix'd a moment
Soft'ning down into a tender inquiry
Which asked, if I had lov'd or pitied her—
And then she turned her eyes away and blush'd!

O, Nature, it was lovely thus to place
A sacred spring within the virgin' breast,
Which in the bosom of that voiceless girl
Who knew no causes why her cheek grew warm,
Would thus vibrate and tremble to be touch'd,
By the slight impulse of an ardent glance.

Unknown to that dumb girl, was art's device
And the dissimulation of the world,—
Her heart was a hid fountain, and its springs
Of pure and fresh affection were concealed
From the intrusion of the common herd
The flatt'rer's breath—the impiety of men—
The words of malice, pride and guilt, which soil
And harden other hearts, came not to hers.

I then was very young, and thoughts like these
Came to my mind:—that if I could unseal
That maiden's ear, and pour into her mind
A living language;—softened by the deep
And touching pathos of a kind regard
From her heart-treasure I would thus bring forth
The Pure affections of her virgin soul,
Like rich and fragrant unction upon mine—
Ambition then I'd leave to selfish men—
(Who toil and struggle anxiously to gain
An increase of anxiety)—and live
In wedlock with that maiden. And I'd store
Her mind with a rich furniture, and by
The tenderest loving kindnesses and care
Unite her heart of heart unto my own.

I'm older now, and fancy more subdued;
Yet to my thoughts to-day there came the form
Of that fair voiceless girl; and I have prayed
She may have happiness that angels know—
That in the silent dwelling of her soul
Sweet peace and joy may dwell continually.

CHAPTER VII.

THE CLERK AND THE SCHOOLMASTER.

Having arrived in the city of New York, with but a small fund of money, and finding no immediate employment, I called upon Mordecai Manuel Noah, then editing a daily paper in that city. I found he had the reputation among the laboring printers and others in the city, of being a "good-hearted and liberal man." When I inquired for employment, he replied courteously, and not with the repulsive and misanthropic "no" that greeted me when I made the same inquiry at some other offices. Some words of his led me to state my antecedents, —present needs,—and my willingness to do anything honorable by which I might get a start in the struggle of life. He employed me as an under-clerk in his office; not so much, as he said, because there was need of another hand; but as a personal favor in view of my needs until a better place could be obtained. Here I remained a few weeks, copying letters, mailing papers, and doing other miscellaneous writing, until by some legal process, the paper passed out of his hands. He subsequently

established the *Ark*, and managed it for a time; but
my employment closed with the close of the old
office. My patron, however, (for such he seemed
to be) at my suggestion, gave me a letter of recom-
mendation to Mr. Booth, just then a star actor,
managing one of the city theatres. He asked the
manager to give me a chance to exhibit my thes-
pian qualities. Upon presenting my letter, I learned
that supernumeraries were abundant, and applica-
tions numerous, and no opportunity for my entree
upon the boards seemed probable.

The Booth, to whom I was introduced, was the
father of the notorious murderer recently executed.
While in Mr. Noah's office I had some opportunity
to learn the habits, and character of professional
players. They met and talked in the office, and
more freely in the absence of Mr. Noah. I am perfectly sure that if my application had been successful, meritorious aims and a virtuous life would have
been abandoned. "Evil communications corrupt
good manners," and allowing for extraordinary exceptions; such as Mrs. Siddons and Mrs. Richie,
there is no virtue on the stage. The evil of theat-
rical exhibitions might, perhaps, be abated; but so
long as the habitues of the stage are what they are,
no reform will ever take place. The evil is not all
with the actors and their female associates. So
long as respectable men and women in the presence
of their families, give enthusiastic demonstrations
in behalf of profligate men, and such women as
Rachel—known to be the mother of illegitimate

children, and the mistress successively of men of the town—when virtue thus smiles on vice, it indicates a taint at the heart, and parents so doing invite the infection into their families. Such parents and children may be virtuous; but their virtue stands in caution, not in conscience.

My washerwoman during my stay in the city, resided in an alley back of the city hall—the same, I think, which now passes the side of Stewart's dry goods palace. We usually called for our clothes in those days—generally on Saturday night or Sunday morning. During my visits to this family I saw the needs of the poor in an aspect which had not presented itself at the West. The inmates were Germans, and used various expedients to live;—among others, that of buying wood by the half cord, and splitting it into small parcels, which they sold to the most impoverished people in the neighborhood. One Sabbath morning I saw little ragged, hungry looking children call with a sixpence and receive a few little pieces of wood—not sufficient to kindle a fire in the stove of a thrifty family in the country. It was but a few steps to Broadway from this scene of poverty and need. Three minutes' walk changed the scene. Men and women in rich attire (few rode in carriages in those days) were passing on the streets. Some of them leading children clothed in warm raiment. They were probably going to the churches, which were, at that time, mostly in the lower part of the town. Being so near the confines of need myself, prob-

ably the contrast affected me more than it would
do now. The worship of Christians clad expen-
sively, and even deformed in person by the extrav-
agances of fashion—in immediate proximity to the
ignorant and destitute poor, produced reflections not
favorable to city life, nor to city style of piety.
Experience in late years has induced views that
are somewhat more charitable. Still, at the present moment, I am sure that those who pray, "Be
ye warmed and filled, and do not the things that
are needful to the body," are hypocrites. Not that
all the poor are worthy—many of them are evil and
vicious. Not that every mendicant should receive
alms without inquiry: but it is the business of
Christians, when both classes cannot be supplied,
to have the Gospel preached to others rather than
to themselves; and to pray for a blessing upon
their efforts and their alms—not for a blessing without efforts and alms.

My means being about exhausted, I crossed the
ferry at Hoboken on Sunday morning, with the
purpose of walking to Albany, and of embracing
any chance that might offer by the way, to engage
in any employment that would supply present ne-
cessities, and give an opportunity to commence life
in some new direction. Before I left the city I had
sold a camlet cloak, much worn in those days, in
order to pay my washing bill and supply some articles that I needed. The day was chilly—snowflakes
were falling, and without my cloak I felt uncom-
fortably cold. I have always been hopeful in all

circumstances. Not more than twice in my life do I remember a moment of despondency; but on that Sabbath — alone, on foot — going, I scarcely knew whither—with little money, and too thinly clad—I felt, for once, near the end of my resources, and that I was shut up to a higher power.

There were at that time large Lombardy poplars standing by the roadside, near Hoboken, on the way to Hackensack. I stopped and stood for a few minutes under one of those old trees, and offered up heart-felt prayer. If I had been asked that day whether I believed the Bible, I should have replied that I was in doubt, and could not believe. Yet under that tree, I prayed as sincerely as I have ever prayed. I did not ask my soul whether there was a God, or whether there was reason in prayer. I did not inquire whether I believed or not. I prayed to God for aid and guidance; and whether the opinion is orthodox or not, to this day I believe God heard and answered my prayer.

In a few minutes I walked on, and had not proceeded far before I was overtaken by a farmer traveling in the same direction. We talked by the way familiarly, and I stated my desire for some employment; proposing to teach a school, or to do any other service to recruit my spent resources. He informed me that a schoolmaster was wanted in his district, about three miles further upon the road, at the little village of New Durham. The principal man in the management of school affairs lived there, and he proposed to introduce me when we should arrive

at his house. It happened that the family were absent at church. The snow was still falling, and I
was rather pleased than otherwise that the family
were away. It was so comfortable to sit by the
cheery fire, and to look out upon the falling snow ;
and to smell the savory dinner, boiling in the pot,
(no cooking stoves in those days), that I really
feared they would return soon, and reject my application at once, so that I should have again to take
the cheerless road. I remember no hour in my
life when I felt a deeper sense of comfort than I did
that Sabbath day, sitting within, before the open
fire, and looking out through the window upon
the falling snow.

The farmer, Mitchell Saunier, soon returned. He
had, if I remember rightly, learned from the neighbor who left me at his house, that a candidate for
schoolmaster was awaiting his return. I was invited to dinner, and complied earnestly with the
scripture injunction to "eat what was set before
me without asking any questions." Mr. Saunier
was not a religious man, nor was there, I believe, a
male member of any church in the neighborhood.
The fire, and the dinner, and the hope of employment, aided me to present myself favorably to my
patron ; and by the time we were done eating, it
was understood that I should exhibit my hand writing at once, and as the weather was getting better
we could employ the afternoon in visiting families
in the neighborhood, to ascertain the number of
scholars they would send. I had commenced to

write in the Sabbath school—practised under Master McClurgan ; and had become a good penman in the shop at the Devil's Half Acre. Writing was the only scholarly accomplishment of which Mr. Saunier could judge. His eye aided him as to my competency in that acquirement ; and when I sat down and wrote some lines of good copy hand, accompanied with divers flourishes, the matter was settled as to my qualifications, and we started at once to canvass for scholars. The effort was a success ; and the succeeding Wednesday I began my school as teacher of the New Durham Academy. There was a fine school building, and the name of Academy had been given to it under my predecessor, Mr. Randall, who had taught the school for some years. He was a man of fair ability, and had recently deceased.

I was greatly pleased with the change in my temporal prospects ; but with the success came a measure of solicitude. I feared I should have a larger job on my hands than I wished to bargain for. It so happened, however, that the pupils who attended the first term were not advanced scholars in any department of study. There was an exception or two, but I deemed it an excellent method to review first principles, and to become rooted and grounded in these before proceeding to more difficult studies.

By doing my best, both as a student and an instructor, I achieved in a short time the reputation of skill and learning as a teacher; and I was not forward to give all the information I possessed

on the subject of my own scholastic advantages.
Indeed, being rather social in regard to subjects
generally, and rather taciturn in regard to this, it
was supposed by some, that, being now "only a
schoolmaster," I was ashamed to mention my previous advantages in contrast with my present
position.

A circumstance happened about this time which
greatly increased my reputation, and consequently
came near destroying it.   It was stated in the
Almanac that two stars of the first magnitude were
approaching each other in the western horizon, and
that on a certain night there would be a conjunction
of their rays.   I knew little about the stars, but I
knew the evening star, and had learned, by obser-
vations through a month, what other star was approaching it in a direct line.   The people did not
pay much attention to astronomical tables in the
Almanacs; and when I pointed out the stars to Mr.
Saunier's family, and announced the night when
they would unite their rays, I had not the most remote intention of setting myself up for a wiseacre,
any farther than I had by observation learned the
two particular stars that would, on a certain future
night, form a conjunction.   The event, I presume,
was talked about in the school; and when it occurred as predicted, my reputation for a knowledge
of astronomy beyond the comprehension of common people, was established at once.   A young
gentleman of the old aristocratic family in the village (Mr. Doremus) called upon me immediately,

and two families from the city of New York, who had their summer residence in the neighborhood, on this or on some other account, sent their children to school. They had been instructed in some of the best schools in the city, and were proficient in some of the advanced studies. It required more than all my knowledge and tact to "master the situation." I had previously purchased keys to the arithmetics used, and a key and Exercises for Murray's English Grammar; and there was nothing in the class books that I did not understand. But I knew nothing of the prevalent *methods* of instruction; and had never in my life parsed a sentence according to the forms of the schools. My methods of teaching, therefore, were often original, and quite surprised my new pupils. After a short experience they thought fit to withdraw;—their parents either doubting my capabilities, or supposing, perhaps, that it was not best to mix up in the minds of their children, systems of instruction so different in character.

Subsequently, in connection with my day labors, I taught a night school in the winter. A number of young men attended, some of them wishing to study various branches not often heard of in common schools. I instructed them, however, in my way, in all branches, common and uncommon, that they wished to study; and the knowledge which I then gained, in connection with what I had previously obtained in the printing office, has been of more practical advantage to me in the duties of life, than four years of subsequent collegiate study.

As a matter of fact, the years spent in college study of the dead languages is of little benefit to the pupil. Translations are so bungling in style, and so blind in idea, that the student often learns to be satisfied with an obscure perception, and an imperfect expression of thought. Distinct and discriminating statement is hindered rather than furthered, unless the study be pursued much beyond the college curriculum. So far as mental discipline is regarded, much of the talk of professors on this subject is mere selfish verbiage. Mental discipline is that which gives self-possession, clear apprehension and logical acumen. The study of the dead languages gives neither. If one-half of the time spent in the study of language in our colleges, were added to studies in the English language, law, natural science and natural history, the change would be a large advantage to students.

The older residents of Bergen county, N. J., are mostly the descendants of the Dutch families that first settled on the North River. They had at that time still some peculiar usages, especially upon the holidays. At such times it was customary for the young people, together with such married persons as were so inclined, to assemble without invitation at the public houses in the villages and engage in dancing during the afternoon and evening. At such times ardent spirits and less harmful beverages, were freely circulated. The best families were not often represented on these holiday occasions, but respectable young people of the country around were present, often in large numbers.

I was sometimes present and engaged with others in the free and easy usages of the descendants of the Dutch. Two such occasions I shall not forget, and "the truth of history" requires that I should note them here. I shall tell the truth as due to conscience :—of course, "nothing extenuate or set down against myself in malice."

In those days, when everybody drank brandy, most persons of those called temperate, felt, at times, the exhilarating influence of intoxicating liquors. I think I never was so affected by liquor that strangers would notice its effect upon my "walk and conversation." But I have been exhilarated by it, and prompted to conversation and conduct, that in my more thoughtful moments I would have eschewed. I learned by experience that the moderate drinker is not a safe man to trust with the management of affairs that require close thinking. No man *after* he has taken a glass of spirits will mature his thought so perfectly, nor look to results of his actions so carefully, as he would have done without it. No one knows how many of the failures in business and of the unexpected defects in moral conduct are to be attributed to this cause.

I have not been many nights out of bed after ten o'clock during a whole lifetime. My grandfather taught me to have faith in Franklin's maxim :

"Early to bed and early to rise
Makes a man healthy and wealthy and wise."

I have lived in the light during a lifetime; and observation has taught me that there is something wrong in the heart as well as the habits of those who may be called *night birds:*

> Keep regular hours,—the wise and good
> Live mostly in the light;
> While vice, and crime, and fashion hold
> Their orgies in the night.

I have retired from lectures before they were closed, and from social gatherings before supper, rather than violate the order of nature, or encourage others to do so. On two occasions, however, my attendance upon the gatherings mentioned above was prolonged till near the middle of the night, when my desire to go home became so controlling that I set out alone about midnight on my return to my lodgings.

On one such occasion I traveled from Bergen to Hoboken, and thence over Wehauken Hill—a distance, I suppose, of about eight miles. I desired to reach the residence of Mrs. Ross, a patroness of my school, with whom I was boarding at the time. I had either to go by the road, which would prolong the distance three miles, or to go over the hill without road or guide, which few would have attempted in daylight. I had less caution than I would have had if I had drank nothing but cold water, hence, I attempted to reach my bed by the shortest route. The hill is precipitous, and it was then covered with trees and undergrowth. How long I struggled over precipices and through underbrush I do not know. I did not lose the road,

because there was none. I did not lose myself, for
I was never more self-conscious in my life; but I
lost my latitude and longitude, and at daylight,
having emerged into a farming region, I found
myself about two miles from the residence of Mrs.
Ross, in a more thoughtful mood than when I
started from Bergen. I had but little time to rest
and think before breakfast. The son of my hostess,
who was one of my scholars, had not yet returned,
and the narration of my night walk, and the attempt to abridge my journey by scaling the precipices of Wehauken mountain, was, to them, a
matter of marvel. I did not think it wise to make
it a subject of much talk afterwards.

On another occasion, I wished to leave a rendez-
vous called the turnpike gate, about midnight, and
return home, a distance of some three miles. I had
gone there in a light market wagon with a young
man who lived near my boarding place. No one was
prepared to leave at that hour; and I was unwise
enough to perpetrate what I designed as a joke—
to take the horse and wagon of my friend, and
start for home alone. I did not get off, however,
without the movement being noticed. The owner
of the vehicle, and one or two others, hallooed and
pursued; but I put the horse on his metal, and
followed by shouts and baying dogs I reached, in
advance of my train of followers, the residence of
the owner of the horse; and, having made the
excited animal fast to the hitching post, I put myself in a secure place for the balance of the night.

I fear that the freak occasioned language that was neither complimentary nor classical. I was not anxious to meet my friend for a day or two; and when I did see him, I had the gratification to learn that the salutation was quite different from what it would have been if we had met before I reached the hitching post on the evening aforesaid.

During my service as a teacher, I had periods of mental struggle on the subject of faith in revelation. There was a Dutch Reformed minister, who preached a sermon once in two weeks in the school building. I had met him, and had stated my doubts concerning divine revelation. He urged some views in behalf of inspiration, which, to me, seemed feeble. This, with his positiveness in regard to things for which I thought he ought to show a reason, strengthened my doubts. He lent me, however, a volume of the history of Jerusalem, which contained Gibbon's account of the Emperor Julian's attempt to rebuild that city, and the reason assigned for his failure. I was not satisfied with the exposition of the historian. It seemed to me that the determination of the Emperor, the enthusiasm of the Jews, and the means and men engaged, could not be defeated by gaseous explosions as supposed. Other considerations led me reject, as of no value, some of the arguments urged against revelation. Still I could not believe. But my desire to know—" *What is truth?*"—was sometimes intense.

I remember, when alone, taking the large Bible

used by the minister, which lay on a desk in the corner of the school-room, and removing it to the centre of the school-room and then retiring a few paces, and praying to God that if the Bible contained a revelation from Him, He would give me evidence of the fact by some voice or sign that I could understand. There was, of course, no manifestation. Perhaps I ought to have known that it was folly to expect visible interposition. Yet the Bible spoke of such being given in the old time, and I had interest enough to make the effort. I affirmed my sincerity and called upon God. Was that prayer answered? I only know I felt easier in my darkness after I had done what I could to get light.

After about a year and a half of service as schoolteacher—by economy—boarding around, and management in other ways,—I found my purse and wardrobe in much better condition than when I arrived. I tarried a short time longer to collect arrearages on bills; and meanwhile, to pay expenses, I repainted the dwelling of Mr. Saunier, lettered the kegs of the tavern with such labels as *Whisky*, *Brandy*, *Gin*, *Wine*, etc. I kept bar on muster day, and became an expert in compounding "gin-slings," "toddy," "egg-nog," and the like beverages for the victims of alcohol. I aided the town assessor to make out his books; and after a very miscellaneous service of some weeks, I bade farewell to many friends, and accompanied by one of them to the city of New York, I set out again for the wide West, with some more knowledge of the world, and better prepared to turn circumstances to good account in the battle of life.

With a gentleman who taught school at Hoboken, Col. Taylor, I had frequent interviews during my stay at New Durham. He was an educated man of ability and literary attainment. In his association I was often profited and interested. He had been an officer in the regular army, but for some reason had resigned, and was now gaining a scanty living by teaching a grammar school. He would sometimes become intoxicated, and was a man of fearful passions when excited. While in the army he had married a Southern lady of delicacy and culture, whose heart he had broken by his bad habits and passions. He suffered intense self-reproach, but too late to save the lost, or to reform confirmed habits. Before I left for the West he sent me the following lines, which I find to-day among my old papers. His life was a failure, but his regard for me was generous, and I felt it. He had better anticipations of my future than I had myself. After some introductory lines Col. Taylor wrote:

The day we part shall in my memory dwell;
But I salute thee with *a last farewell!*
O, shun the siren Pleasures every lure,
As heat be ardent, and as light be pure,
To some great object give thy brilliant powers,
Let humbler minds riot in festive bowers.
The bar at which true genius loves to flame
To perseverance offers wealth and fame.
If still more arduous labors thou would'st find
Go, well prepar'd, instruct the public mind—
The patriot, too—but let me not presume—
For thee the olive-palm and laurel bloom:—

Adieu,—Dermoody—when in distant climes,
Forget not Oscar and these off-hand rhymes.

Tarrying recently for a week in the city of
New York, when more than three score years
of age, I had the curiosity to cross the ferry at
Hoboken, and visit the scene of my former experiences. The former village of Hoboken had become
a city. The old road around Wehauken Hill for
three miles is traversed by street cars. I looked
for the old Lombardy poplars; they were all gone
except a few straggling ones, which looked old and
decrepit. The precipices of Wehauken arose above
the cars, and looked as though no ordinary labor
could surmount them. Mrs. Ross was long ago
called from earthly labor. Her farm had been sold
by speculators for town lots. Her children were
dead or dispersed. I met her grandson, who was
familiar with my name, as he had often heard his
uncles and aunts speak of their former teacher.
He looked at the aged man before him with awakened interest. The academy building, and the old
residence of Mr. Saunier, were gone. Nothing was
as I had known it but the old stone house of Mr.
Doremus, which was occupied by another family.
I could find but one of my old pupils. She was
one of the most ungainly, but is now probably the
most respectable and influential of them all. After
dinner, and an hour's talk of the days of other
years, I left a package of useful tracts upon her
centre table, and returned again to the cars.

Sic transit gloria mundi.

CHAPTER VIII.

EDITOR—POLITICIAN—STUDENT AT LAW.

Having reached home and visited friends in the city, I hastened to the residence of my mother, on a farm seven miles from town, on the Alleghany hills. My step-father, for some years of his life, had labored in a white lead factory, and was subject to a disease of the stomach, produced by inhaling the poisonous vapors of the metal. His disease had sometimes produced spasms, from which he recovered with difficulty. He had recently kept a drug store in the city, but declining health induced him to retire to his farm in the country, where he was confined mostly to his house as an invalid.

My mother seemed pleased with the person and presence of her returned son, as did also my step-father, and they readily assented to have a gathering of a few of the young people from the farms in the neighborhood, to renew old friendships, and spend a social evening. With the young people in the neighborhood I had been familiar, and with some of them—it is proper to say—a favorite. I had, during the years of my apprenticeship, often walked seven miles, after the labors of the day, to spend an evening at what was called a country frolic; where the rustic plays and dances of the "merry, gentle country folk" were enjoyed by those present in a sense that those constrained by the forms and fashions of life never experience.

My parents did not encourage the ruder pastimes that sometimes characterized the neighborhood. But few were assembled this evening, and I was to call at farmer Phillips' to accompany his daughter Eliza to the little company. The young woman had that morning scalded her foot severely, and could not go. She was anxious to accompany me, as she had often done years before; and she would now have endeavored to ride over to our house, but her good mother interposed, reminding her that she had had various ominous warnings, which indicated that Providence did not favor her going. I returned alone, leaving her a few yards from her dwelling with a sad and longing look. The young people were mostly assembled when I reached home; and kindly greetings were cordially and familiarly exchanged. I had improved in social qualities by absence. The friction of society will polish individual habits.

But the evening that began in gladness, closed in tears. My step-father, who, perhaps, had partaken more freely than usual of the refreshments which my good mother had prepared for the company, was seized with one of the spasms produced by the poison of lead. In a few hours his soul,

released from its earthly tenement, entered upon
the untried experiences of the world to come.
Some remained to weep around the dying bed of
their friend and neighbor. My mother kneeled in
the presence of us all, and uttered a sobbing, heart-
felt prayer. The scene was one that cannot be
forgotten. I had never heard my mother pray
until that night. Women, except in the Methodist.
churches, prayed only in secret in those days. But
her joy of heart had suddenly been succeeded by a
great grief—and she prayed aloud.

After a season of mourning, and some labor in
arranging with the children of the deceased (two
of whom were children of my mother by her
late husband) a plan for the future of the family,
I again left the city.

My uncle, during the time that he was shop-keeper
in Hookstown, had purchased a contract for a tract
of land in the State of Ohio. He had not been able
to obtain a perfect title, and I set out to visit the
parties and procure a deed of the land. On the way
I was detained by an attack of ague and fever, and
after a protracted season of illness, I reached Ravenna, a new county town on the Western Reserve, in
the State of Ohio. Here, after I had succeeded in
the business for which I was sent, I engaged in a
new printing office, having, by the assistance of
friends, bought half the interest of the "*Western
Courier.*"

General politics had scarcely any influence in those
days upon the local elections of the new counties.

The northern counties of Ohio were settled almost exclusively by New England people. The little paper advocated the interests of John Q. Adams for the Presidency ; and as I was from Pennsylvania, and professedly a Democrat, it was arranged that I should take charge of the literary department of the *Courier*, while a young attorney—C. B. Thompson — managed its politics. Our paper was the only one in the region. It was the organ of the village politicians who managed the political machinery of the county. There were some Jackson men, mostly from Pennsylvania, in the district. We desired to issue an address in favor of Andrew Jackson, and I was chosen to write it. It was the only address printed in Northern Ohio advocating the election of Old Hickory. It was a curiosity in its way. The names of parties seem to have changed sides since then. The coalition with the South demoralized the Democratic party. There should be a Democratic party, opposed to monopolies—to class legislation, and class education—a party from the people and for the people, opposed to the money power and the lobby power in legislalation. The Democratic party then professed to be the party of morals and of progress. So I understood its principles, and strenuously urged, in my address to the people, the doctrine of General Jackson's letter to Monroe, urging him to select for office "men of known probity, virtue, capacity and firmness, without regard to party."

The General was elected, but he abandoned the

principles he urged upon President Monroe. But as I had no expectations, I continued to be a Jackson man in the old sense, after the General had himself left the Jackson platform.

Our paper made no opposition to the administration, and I fell quietly into the political association of the town. We confined ourselves mostly to State and County politics. The machinery for managing elections was operated, as before said, by office-holders and village politicians. My experience was instructive, but somewhat surprising to a young man who had not become accustomed to the management usual among those who are adroit in local politics.

The principle study of the village junto in those days was concerning the best way to manage the farming population, and make them subservient to the aims of the office-seekers. "Coffin hand-bills" had been a staple document with those opposed to General Jackson. They represented some militia men being shot for desertion. But one old Justice of the Peace in the country had concluded that the men deserved to be shot, and was using his influence against a candidate for County Treasurer, who had circulated the bills. He had a large circle of friends, and it was necessary that he should be "brought into the traces" before the election. It was arranged, therefore, that the Sheriff should call and see him, and make his visit at such time that he would be invited to stay all night. He was to "intimate that the Squire had been a little in advance of others in his opposition to the hand-bills; and that all could see now, since the election, that his views were right. It was likewise thought best to put into the paper the name of his son Bob, as a candidate for some county office. It was understood, of course, that he would not get the nomination at the convention to select candidates, but it would commit him and his father to stand by the nominees in such form that they could not "back out."

There was another difficulty, the shape of which I do not exactly remember. I can give outlines: A conscientious deacon proposed to split the ticket, because a man who was somewhat immoral had been nominated for a responsible place. The thing had to be "managed," and a certain lawyer, whose brother-in-law was a minister, undertook to "fix the matter with the deacon." The moral intentions of the deacon were not carried out; but by what means the thing was done I never knew.

When there is but a single newspaper in the new counties of the West, it is potential in determining political issues. I endeavored, in one case, to accomplish an end in an independent way. Oliver Snow was one of the first settlers and wealthiest farmers in his neighborhood. He had a daughter who had contributed original poetical articles for the *Courier*. Nothing had appeared from her pen for some time. I was anxious, in my sphere as editor, to be the patron of genius, and wrote a paragraph inviting "Angerona"—alias Eliza Snow

—to send something for the poet's corner. There
are more poets in the world than there are books
of poetry; and better passages have been published in the corner of a newspaper than can be
found in some duodecimo volumes. I only remember a word or two of my invitation to Angerona
to renew her correspondence. I said: "Has Angerona hung her harp on the willows, or quarreled
with the Muses, or why, in the name of Poesy,
do we not hear from her again?" Soon after,
Oliver Snow, her father, came into the printing
office to see the new printer, who had noticed in
such appreciative language the productions of his
daughter. I had on a ruffled shirt that day—an
item of apparel not uncommon at the time ; and I
did the amiable for the old gentleman in my bland-
est manner. The consequence of which was, that
as Mr. Snow passed out through the front office, he
remarked that the new printer seemed to be a
"real gentleman." To which, of course, my partner smilingly assented. This visit was followed
immediately by a contribution from Angerona.

I had not yet seen the poetess, but I was interested in the family, and wished to commend myself
to their attention. I took the responsibility, therefore, of putting her father's name in our paper as
an independent candidate for County Commissioner.
Tickets were printed and circulated in his region
of the county. The regular nominee was Owen
Brown, of Hudson, father of John Brown, of Harper's Ferry, "whose soul is marching on." Mr.

Snow was not elected, but he received a large vote, and a little effort would have carried him in.

I desired to see the poetess, and accompanied John Pierson, Esq., (subsequently Judge Pierson, of Iowa,) who was to deliver an address to the farmers of her neighborhood. The address was given in a large barn on the Fourth of July. The lady auditors were seated on the first floor, in front of the speaker; and the· gentlemen—the young men especially—in the haymow, back of the speaker—opposite the ladies. A friend indicated which was Angerona; and it was plain that Angerona knew which was "Dermoody"—a cognomen I had chosen for myself.

That evening there was a dance at the village tavern. Angerona was pious. She did not dance; nor did she stay to witness the amusement of those who did. That night Mr. Pierson and myself tarried at the dwelling of Oliver Snow. I did not see much of Angerona afterwards; and our intercourse closed entirely by my removal to college. I should have seen more of her, but I offended the poetess unwittingly, and I am not sure that she ever forgave me. I wrote a little scrap in verse, and inserted it in my paper. It was entirely a matter of the imagination; but she was too pure to conceive of such things being written even in poetry, without having some objective reality. Here are the offending lines:

My love, the gift you gave me
Has bound me with a spell,

As pleasing as the witcheries
Of which old fables tell;
The loveliness subdues me;
Thy gentle voice I hear,
And the cadence of thy whispered words
Still murmur in my ear.

There is a charm about thee
Of modesty and youth;
There is a meaning in thine eye
Of constancy and truth;
And I'd sooner trust thy single vow
Than all the prayers that said
At Lama's shrine, or Mecca's tomb,
My own delicious maid.   DERMOODY.

These simple lines did not suit Angerona; and she sat down immediately, and sent the following for publication in my paper:

Say, who on earth would not despise
A paltry thing which thousands share;
A friend in fractions who would prize,
Or deem the piecemeal worth a care?

Say, who, that would not scorn to aim
For that which all besides possess'd;
Say, who would ever wish to claim
A heart which many else had bless'd?

Then talk no more of friends to me—
I will not share a friend in co,—
I now a single friend will be,
Or friend, oh, never let me know!

Poor Angerona! intelligent—gifted—pious and unsophistocated in the ways of the world; and receiving the Old Testament to be the rule of duty, as well as the New, she became, a year or two afterwards, a convert to the Mormon's, who made their first settlement in Ohio, not far from her neighborhood. She thought their miracles, their simple habits, and their faith, were a reproduction of primitive Christianity; and believing in the obvious cases of healing, she became a victim to the base imposture. Her family followed the faith of their favorite daughter, and they all emigrated with the Mormon's to the West, where she is now a spiritual wife of the impostor Brigham Young—a fractional wife of the polygamous patriarch in the Valley of Salt.

The followers of the Mormon's were generally sincere country people. I have met them in different parts of the world since then. In Glasgow, Scotland, an honest servant girl in a hotel, who had been perverted by the propagandists of their faith, was about to emigrate, with a company, to Salt Lake. Knowing that I' was an American, she took an opportunity to speak to me of the Mormon's in America. I did what I could to dissuade her from her purpose, but she was immovable. Everything—she said—in the Bible was like the Mormons. Nothing was like the religion of the churches in Glasgow. The Mormon preachers traveled without purse or scrip. They preached from house to house. They often healed the sick. They preached the Gospel to the poor; and if some of the older men had several wives, so had Abraham, Isaac and Jacob. One man she knew had been healed of disease by laying on of hands. He felt the cure the moment it was affected. He had continued well, and could work ever since. It was therefore impossible for her to doubt.

So she talked. It was in vain that I spoke of the Old Testament with its polygamy, as introduc-

tory, and imperfect in doctrine and morals, compared
with the New.   It was in vain that I spoke of the
natural effect of the mind upon the body, by acts
of sudden and strong faith.   She could see no
value in my words.   She was a poor girl—intelligent beyond most of her class.   I desired to save
her, but she did not understand my arguments;
nor would they have affected her if she had.   She
assented to everything I said in regard to the
purity and obligation of the New Testament.
That, she professed to believe ; and she said the
Mormon's practised it ; but the churches in Glasgow
did not.   If I had been asked at that time if I
thought this young woman was a Christian, I should
probably have said the dispensations of Providence
are often mysterious—let us judge charitably.

I had always, from my boyhood, been possessed
with the notion—that perhaps every selfish mind
possesses more or less—that I was adequate to a
higher sphere of life than that in which I was
moving.   Such inward promptings led me to commence the study of law, while, at the same time, I
was engaged in printing the paper.   I spent part of
each day in the office of Hon. Jonathan Sloan.   He
was subsequently elected to Congress, and I continued the study with my partner, Mr. Thompson.
I anticipated that when I had finished my studies,
a partnership would be formed, embracing all departments of our business.

I was able now to do something for aspirants to
county offices, and to one man, at least, I gave the

assistance necessary to his success. S. D. Harris,
General of the county militia, was the old County
Surveyor, and had been Auditor for a series of years.
An effort was made to oust him, which I resisted.
I wrote his defensive articles for him, and assailed
his opponents. My conscience did not always
quietly acquiesce in the part I took in the contest:
But the General was elected, and did not in all
respects "forget Joseph."

The drinking usages of those days would surprise the people of the present time. (I mean the
better class of people). The General and I had
frequently drank together before the election; but
I am sure we never met subsequently in a public
house ; that we did not take alcohol in some of its
forms. And as I boarded at a hotel, and he spent
a good share of his leisure time there, our drinking
(always at his expense when the courtesy exceed-
ed two treats per day, which I thought should be
the maximum of indulgence,) may be supposed to
have been a pretty extensive patronage of the bar.
Strange as it may seem, I never had, and never
contracted, a taste for ardent spirits. I drank because it was universal social usage ; and friendship and good fellowship were supposed to be
indicated by the invitation to partake of the poisonous beverage. But tobacco I always *es*chewed ;
and alcohol was always distasteful to me unless
thoroughly saturated with sugar. I drank a native,
still wine (Lunell) on the *Col de Bam* pass of the
Alps that, to one wearied by travel, was refreshing,

and had a pleasant flavor ; and sparkling Moselle may be drank occasionally by invalids, especially by dyspeptics, like Timothy, with profit ; but no man of either sense or conscience, should ever permit the "leprous distillments" of ardent spirits, or the defilement of filthy tobacco to pass his lips.

Thus time passed in the village until the winter holidays, at which time, as usual, a ball was projected, of which I was one of the managers. The others,—whose future I shall note,—were my partner, C. B. Thompson,—John Whittlesey—Charles Clapp and Ely Campbell. Such assemblages were common in new country towns ; but there were those who said that evil omens gathered over the dancers on this particular occasion. A portion of our company seceded, and got up a dance for themselves in an opposite hotel. Lucy Robinson, my companion for the ball, whose residence was several miles from town, lost the flower-wreath that bound her hair. Not many weeks subsequently she was taken ill, and after a lingering sickness, she "slept the sleep that knows no waking." The tidings made me sad for a little while, and I often said in thought, alas ! poor Lucy !

The managers for the evening were to lead in the first set ; and first of those stood the manly form of my partner in the office, Charles B. Thompson. He moved but a few steps, when his dancing-shoe rent in such form that he could not proceed. The program was broken, and the set went on without him. The next morning Mr. Thompson

was not at breakfast—he was ill. Slightly so, at
first; but his illness increased, and after a few days
he retired from his hotel to the residence of his
sister (Mrs. Dr. Swift) where, after several weeks
of illness, he died.

· His mother, who had come to watch by his sick
bed, was a Christian woman; and was anxious
that her son should speak with some minister of
the gospel in regard to his spiritual interests.
There may have been others, but I knew of but
two professors of religion in the village; and there
was no resident minister. One was procured, however; but although the sick man respected religious institutions, he had no heart for such converse,
and indicated his apathy by turning himself away
in his bed. I think, likewise, the minister was one
in whom, when well, he had but little confidence.
There came, however, almost immediately afterwards, a sudden change in the spirit of his mind;
and his awakened interest on the subject of religion surprised me more than his previous apathy.
He seemed to wake as from a dream, and look at
religious subjects as a new revelation. He would
say: "How could I live in the presence of the
Bible, professing to be a revelation from God?—
How could I constantly hear preaching of Christ's
life and death?—How could I live in the presence
of all these things—even assent to them—and yet
not regard them?" He was now exceedingly anxious
that Rev. Mr. Storrs, president of Hudson college,
should be sent for. When that good man came,

Mr. Thompson still continued to express surprise at his former apathy. He thought of himself as one that had been asleep, and was interested in dreams rather than in the realities he should have considered.

I do not know what Christians thought of his exercises. They produced no effect whatever upon my own mind. The last night I watched by his bed,—waking from a troubled sleep, he said he had dreamed that he was struggling through a sea of ice. His fever had suggested the opposite sensation. But a few more nights of fever and wandering thought, and Charles Thompson departed to learn the realities concerning which he had been thoughtless in life, but thoughtful when irrevocably summoned to die.

There were sad hearts in the village when Thompson died. There was one who mourned as though she had lost more than a friend. There was one — a brute in the legal profession — who seemed to be gratified by the event which afflicted others. A competitor at the bar had gone.

Of the other four managers of the New Year's ball: Ely Campbell, a jeweler, grew wealthy. He established the first bank of Ravenna. Subsequently he removed to Wisconsin, and engaged more extensively in the money trade. During the mania on the subject of spiritualism, which prevailed in the country at that time, he accepted the doctrine, (as did skeptics generally)—became disgusted with earthly things,—and shot himself dead in his own counting-room;—to wake up, as he imagined, in an exalted spiritual sphere.

Charles Clapp, the most amiable of us all—a young merchant from Boston—married Miss Clapp, the leading belle of the village. Religious interest increased with the growth of the town; and in a revival which occurred in subsequent years, he made a profession of religion. In the Miller excitement of 1843, he embraced the doctrine that the end of the world was at hand. He expended his time and his money to further the delusion. I traveled some distance to visit him at Akron, hoping to lead him to forsake, or, at least, to doubt the error to which he had committed himself. But it had fastened upon him as a mono-mania; he could see nothing except in the light of his own convictions. He had been led astray by a minister in whom he trusted; and when the set time for the destruction of the world had passed, he abandoned as lovely a family as there was in the State, and joined a settlement of Shaking Quakers, where he is now the principle man in the community. His sorrowing wife said her husband was certainly a good Christian—why was he suffered to fall into error? Why?

John Whittlesey, son of Hon. Elisha Whittlesey —for many years third Auditor of the national treasury, was a merchant's clerk. He subsequently became a merchant,—married, and lost his first wife. I did not see him for more than thirty years; and then I married him a second time, to a lady residing in the city where I was then living.

CHAPTER IX.

THE NEW COLLEGE AND THE NEW LIFE.

After the death of my partner, my legal studies were closed. The entire management of the paper devolved upon me; and other pursuits and studies were not possible, without relinquishing the labors of editor and printer. I set type during the hours of each day, and wrote editorials and packed and mailed the papers as I could find spare hours. It was necessary for me either to relinquish the study of the law, or to dispose of my paper; the latter I concluded to do. I might have been admitted to practice without much further study; but I felt that some further knowledge of Latin and mathematics was desirable; and more especially, the sense of diffidence—and the recollection of former efforts at public speaking—led me to seek some more private opportunity to train my mind in extempore talk and argumentation before appearing at the bar, where a failure would be a disaster from which it would take years to recover. With these views I left Ravenna to spend a year at the Western Reserve College,—a new institution that had just been opened at Hudson, in the same county in which I published the *Courier*.

The appearance of things at college quite surprised me. Nothing of the like is seen now-a-days. I had thought of collegians as genteel young men, well dressed and well bred; and had some misgivings in regard to my age, supposing the young men would all be my juniors. There were about twenty, in all grades of advancement, from those who had a very imperfect knowledge of common school studies, up, perhaps, to the Sophomore class, and several of the number were older than myself. I gained some assurance by noticing that one of them tacked on his door a notice: "Lost—one pare of tongues." All of them, when I first entered the institution, were from the country, or the country villages adjacent. Several of the best of them were young men endeavoring to educate themselves. Their garments were mostly home manufactured; and if they had been acting in obedience to a law which prohibited conformity to the fashions of the world, they could not have been more diversified and rustic in their appearance. A few years subsequently, the aspect of things changed in this respect. The new colleges of the West, when farms and villages were not much advanced, gathered young men who, in polished society, would have seemed uncouth in appearance, and rustic in manners; but under their homely exterior were often hidden mental and moral qualities greatly superior to those of some who might be disposed to disparage them.   Among the students was one who now holds the highest judicial position in the State where he resides.   Others have an honorable record in professional and public life.

Some of the Professors in the new institution were among the ablest men in the country—East or West.   The school had commenced, as that of Oberlin and many others in the early period of Western progress, with a single instructor. When I arrived there were three,—President Storrs, who had just entered upon his duties, and Professors Nutting and Wright.   Mr. Storrs was brother of Dr. Storrs, of Braintree, Mass.   He was a man of piety and ability.   Prof. Wright is now a State officer in Massachusetts.   He is one of the best scholars in the country, and has distinguished himself both as an editor and an author. At a later period Beriah Green, of New York; Dr. Hickox, President of Union College; and Prof. Barrows, recently of Andover, were teachers at Hudson.   These are distinguished men in their profession.   Most of them are still living to tell the story of their early labors in a Western college; one—the devout Storrs—has "fallen asleep."   These professors have labored since then upon more polished material, but not upon material of more intrinsic value.

In such association I began my college experience.   My surroundings were new in more respects than one.   Since my boyhood I had not had a companion who professed to be a Christian.   I had

many associates, male and female; and the lines
of Moore had been verified in my experience:

" Go where we will,
The heart will find something to twine around still."

But with the exception of Angerona, of whom I
knew but little, I never had an associate that. was
even professedly pious.

Now, however, my circumstances were altered.
Some of the teachers and many of the students
exerted themselves personally to procure the conversion of those whom they considered impenitent
students. They did not speak to me directly on
the subject 'of religion, but they did to others; and
the presence of such an influence was new and
distasteful to me. My influence and opinions, I
presume, were no less so to them. I was a *rara
avis* among them. I had aided the collection at
the county seat to pay the fine of a man who had
attacked and beaten one of the students, (William
Russell), who had prosecuted him for breaking the
Sabbath. I had, in my paper, opposed the movements of the men (many of them connected with
the college) who first introduced the temperance
reform at the West. Claiming, as all moderate
drinkers then did, to be in favor of temperance, I
opposed the total abstinence pledge. All this was
known at Hudson, and I learned subsequently that
there was some doubt in the mind of at least one
of the Professors, whether it were wise to admit
me to the privileges of the institution. But unworthy as I was, I had one of the best friends

that any young man ever had, in President Storrs.
He had, previously to his going to Hudson, preached
in the village of Ravenna, where I published the
Western Courier.   He knew me well;—my gay-
eties, and follies, and errors; but, for some reason,, he was always my friend—whether I was
thoughtless or thoughtful—until he died.   I appreciated his friendship; and if he had needed the
friendly offices of such a one as I was, I am sure
I would have talked for him,—or fought for him,
if necessary,—so long as strength lasted.

I was admitted to the institution; and having
stated what studies I wished to pursue, was permitted to recite in such classes as would enable me
to attain my purpose.   I found a boarding house
in the hospitable dwelling of Owen Brown, father
of John Brown, of Harper's Ferry.   Thus favored
and associated, I began student life at the Western
Reserve College.

So soon as I was fairly initiated in the routine
of affairs, I endeavored to make the old College
Society—the Philozetian—subservient to my aim
of preparation for public speaking, and public proceedings of a political nature.   I was probably per-
sistent in this effort, beyond what was proper; and
hence, many of the other young men, who had
different views of matters, and different aims in
life, resisted encroachment upon old usages and
forms of proceeding.   Secular aims succeeded,
however, with the majority; and the more devout
young men withdrew, and, with permission of the

faculty, formed another society. The two societies, I presume, have their place in the institution
till the present day.

About this time the report was published in the
newspapers, originating probably in the New York
Herald, that the Poles, who were at that time in
insurrection, had achieved a decisive victory over
the Russians, and that their independence would
be the result. We of the Philozetians, thought
it expedient to make a patriotic demonstration in
honor of the occasion. So, at a certain hour in
the evening, most of the college room windows were
illuminated with tallow candles. The bell, which
was a steel bar, made in the form of a triangle,
was rang energetically, and sent its sharp, stinging
tones through the surrounding neighborhood. The
students assembled in the chapel, where another
gentleman and myself were to make speeches for
"Poland and Liberty." The faculty had been ap-
prised of the meeting, and, I believe, did not forbid
the assemblage ; but the people of the village and
neighborhood had heard nothing of "Poland and
Liberty;" at least, they had heard nothing of our
proceedings in regard thereto. They heard the
bell ringing furiously at an unusual time, and they
saw the blaze of light proceeding from the college
building, and concluding, very naturally, that the
college was on fire, a crowd of them rushed to the
rescue. I do not remember who was speaking when
the first excited men entered ; but our exercises
were suddenly interrupted by the rush of the well-

meaning villagers to extinguish the fire, which they supposed was consuming the building. If their coming did not extinguish a fire in the building, it extinguished the enthusiasm of the speakers,— put out the tallow candles; and closed, rather unceremoniously, the evening's proceedings.

The religious influence about me was active. It was in the early period of the wide-spread revival of religion in the West, in which Charles G. Finney was one of the most active laborers. I had some difficulty in exhibiting courtesy and attention to the persuasions of those who addressed the students on that subject. In some of them I had but little confidence, but to the words and prayers of President Storrs, I was always respectfully attentive.

One morning, after the President had led in prayer in the little chapel, I can recollect the thoughts that passed through my mind as I went to breakfast. They were the first of a series of exercises which lasted for months; vivid to me; but unknown to those about me. The President had prayed that the students might all possess certain principles, and fulfill certain duties to God and men, which my reason assented to as proper; but I felt unwilling to be and to do what I assented to as right. I did not inquire with myself why this was so; but the consciousness of the contradiction between knowledge and will was unpleasant to me. I had never *felt* it before.

Another inquiry kept constantly recurring to my

mind, with an intensity that I had not before experienced. *If Christianity were discredited or
destroyed, what would be the result?* Such inquiries were often accompanied with doubts and
objections to the Bible, that I had never thought
of before; and which, perhaps, others have never
thought of. Most of these related to the Old
Testament; and although disposed to solve them
in my own mind, it was not possible, with the
views that I then had, for me to do so; and to
this day, with the views commonly held of the
Old Testament, the difficulties would remain.

But the doubts and difficulties that still possessed
me when I recurred to certain subjects, did not in
the least abate the uncomfortable conviction that
I was not willing, and did not even desire to be
willing, to do the good which my reason and conscience approved. The doubts remained, but the
inward conflict, although held in abeyance at times,
was not overcome, but increased.

After weeks of solicitude, I began to seek in the
library for books to aid me to determine what was
truth and duty in regard to the ever present subject of thought. It is somewhat strange, perhaps,
but the arguments of Chalmers and others, concerning the reliability of the inspired witnesses and
kindred discussions, had no influence whatever to
remove difficulties, or determine my mind to right
convictions. One volume, however, which finally
fell into my hands, was clear and satisfactory.
And in settling one point, it aided to settle many

others.   It was "Paley's Horæ Paulinæ."   It satisfied my mind, beyond the shadow of a doubt, that
Paul was a real character ; that most, if not all the
epistles attributed to him, were written by him ;
and that they contained a true account of his
beliefs and experiences.   No fair mind can read
Paley's treatise and avoid the same conclusion.
This point settled, was a solid centre of reflection.

For many months this state of inquiry and interest continued.   It did not seem to me that my
mental exercises were in any wise supernatural.
They came in the ordinary way of suggestion ; and
as yet the internal interest was not shown in any
wise in the external life ; and yet, actions which a
year before I should have done with unconcern, I
felt now to be of doubtful propriety.

The Fourth of July holiday was at hand, and the
faculty of the college gave the students some days
of recess.   There was to be a ball at town centre
on the evening of the holiday, in which the faculty
did not think it wise that the students should par-
ticipate.   At least, we presumed that to be their
opinion from the fact that in giving the recess, they
desired all the students to continue recitations, or
to visit their homes until after the holiday.   There
were but few of the young men whose parents did
not reside within a day's travel, and I always supposed that the unusual provision was to remove Mr.
Loomis, who was my room-mate, and myself, from
scenes which they thought would be morally injurious to us.   For reasons that I do not remember,

the usual demonstrations were made during the day, but the dance was postponed to a succeeding evening, at which time we had returned to college. Dancing in those days was prohibited in the churches, as were other social amusements, much more rigidly than they are at present. My mind had come into the state, in which I felt a growing desire to be a christian; yet, I saw no evil in social amusements. I supposed, however, that one or the other must be abandoned. There were those in the college, as I afterwards learned, that knew, or supposed, that my mind was unusually interested in religious subjects; and on the evening of the dance there were a few invited to meet socially at the house of one of the professors. There were prayers and hymns, interspersed with our talk; and at the usual hour we retired to our rooms, while those who remained undoubtedly offered prayer in our behalf.

In returning to my boarding house I had to pass the house of mirth. I had concluded not to be present that evening; but the illuminated hall—the music and the movements of the dancers, observed through the open windows, attracted my attention, and I stood for several minutes, until the desire to mingle with the company gathered strength. I could give no reason to myself for my perplexity on the subject; and concluding that I was a fool for feeling as I did, I started for the ball room.

For reasons entirely inexplicable to me, when I entered, instead of enjoying the spirit of the scene and the congratulations of friends, male and female, I felt a solemnity that I could in no way dissipate. I was vexed with myself, and in order to disperse the gloom and awaken feeling in sympathy with the scene about me, I retired to the refreshment room, and drank a glass of brandy, which could be had in a private way, by those inquiring for it.

When I returned to the ball room I went through a set in a contra dance with a young lady who, long ago, passed, as I hope, to the land of peace. After retiring and sitting a few moments, I noticed that she was looking at me with surprise. I recollected myself, and found I was talking to her on the subject of religion. I was chagrined; and as soon as I could courteously do so, I retired from the room, a mystery to myself and to my companion.

That night and for sometime afterward I was unhappy and perplexed. There was an element of conscience and solemnity in my mind that did not usually belong to my thought. I do not remember whether the thought of God was a prevailing one or not. I did not feel that I had been a great sinner; but I felt I had been ungrateful to God. The death of my partner now affected me more than it did at the time of his decease. I felt that my heart was sinful, rather than that my life had been so. I tried to control my mind and avoid all wrong thought, but could not satisfy myself. "When I would think good evil was present with me." I felt this in the depth of my soul. I burned some books, not so bad in themselves, as some books are, but because I thought them unprofitable. I found a Bible belonging to the family where I boarded, and read it in preference to other things. Its teachings were now subjects of interest and inquiry, and fixed my attention. No one, however, who called at my room during this period ever saw me reading the Bible. Several passages seemed duplicates of my own experience: One I remember expressed my state of mind, and my heart rose in supplication in the words of one that had felt just as I did at that minute, "*Lord I believe, help thou my unbelief.*"

I struggled hard to regulate my thoughts and imaginations, some of which I now felt were offensive to God; but I could, by no act of will produce the good in myself that I desired. I shall always remember one day, when I had determined with stronger purpose than usual to keep my heart with diligence, I set out for recitation, and by the way I was shocked to find my mind full of imaginations that I had determined should be cast out. It may not be believed—it seems so incredible—yet it is true, that I was angry with myself; or rather with my heart; and stamping on the ground, I uttered an oath, which I do not remember that I ever did before, and that I have never done since.

During all these long months, no one had spoken to me on the subject of religion. There was no special interest on religious subjects in the college or the church at this time; and it seemed to me that christians, who once seemed so much interested, now endeavored to avoid the subject in my presence.

At length I received a note from Joseph Barr, who afterwards died on the way to Africa, as a missionary. He invited me to call at his room in the evening. I presumed that he desired to talk with me, on the subject which was now seldom absent from my mind. I went at the hour designated; but Mr. Barr was not there. I waited; but he did not come. I was disappointed and vexed with his delay, and determined to know the reason why I was invited and neglected. I remained in the room until nine o'clock, at which time students were ordinarily required to retire. He came after the hour. My spirit of reproach and controversy had left me. He soon spoke to me of the subject which absorbed my thought. We talked till a late hour—perhaps the middle of the night. He prayed two or three times; and asked me to pray. I uttered some words, not in the christian form of supplication, and stopped, but did not rise from a kneeling posture. It seemed to me that a cramped, hard pressure was on my breast, and I struggled as though I was separating myself from some physical burden. Mr. Barr prayed again, and ceased; and I seemed to get rest, and rose to go home. He went with me. We did not talk much, but I exclaimed several times, "How strange!" In reply to the question—"What is strange, Mr. W.?" I remember only that I felt as though the stars and all things praised God,—and replied—"Everything looks so light and pleasant."

He left me at my boarding place. My mind continued for some days to grow more peaceful and happy, and thenceforward I lived in conscious peace for many months.

I did not think anything about the doctrine of the Trinity. I did not think of the questions concerning the divinity of Christ. The idea of God in my mind, was that of a Holy, present Father, whose attributes I saw in Christ. Preachers seemed to talk in a new language. I think I had not then fully believed in Christ, as I do now. I remember the first sermon I heard on the subject of the Savior after I had "ears to hear," I wept, and laid my head on the front of the pew to let my emotion flow off in tears. One marked change in the state of my mind was that while before I saw no God in anything that occurred about me, I now saw God in all events. In everything that occurred, from the least to the greatest, I saw the hand of God; and it is so to this day. In all things that occur in connection with individual or general history, I see the presence of God. And while, in many cases, I can see no exposition of particular providences I am sure there is a reason, and that God is in the incident, be it what it may.

During this period I was not afraid of death; and often said so to others. When I retired at night my mind was in a state of pleasant peace. In the morning the mental enjoyment had abated; but with the first waking thoughts it gradually returned. I did not ask myself whether I had become a christian. The first incident that led me to realize the difference between present and former states of

mind, was the pleasure begotten by hearing it stated
that a young woman, (now Mrs. Simeon Porter, of
Cleveland,) had become a christian, and was rejoicing in hope.   This I knew would before have given
me no pleasure ; but now my interest and joy were
great.   I had occasional throbs of sorrow, but they
related to the cause of Christ.   An aged minister,
Mr. Hughs, in Beaver county, Pennsylvania, had
fallen into sin.   Probably no one in the college knew
the man.   I should not think so much of the incident now ; but then, for days, whenever I thought
of it, I felt a deep sense of humiliation and regret
for the dishonor which had been brought upon the
cause of Christ.

My faith at this time was not in creeds nor in
passages of Scripture.   I had a sense of reconcilia-
tion with God.   There was one thing, however,
which at a period somewhat later, seemed to me to
be a ground of reasonable assurance, both in regard
to the faith of the New Testament, and in regard
to the character of my own exercises.   Peter and
James and John and Paul speak of the experiences
of themselves and others who believed the truth
that they believed and taught.   It was faith in those
truths which produced the purposes, experiences,
hopes, and fears of which they speak.   Now these
same purposes, experiences, hopes and fears, I found
in myself which are described as existing in them.
The conclusion, therefore, was a logical necessity,
that the same truths were in existence, and were
believed by them as they were now believed by me:

because the effects of faith were the same in them as they were in me: Hence, the truth believed was the same.

This sameness of experience was extended to what seemed the paradoxes of the gospel. I had known what it was to feel that "when I would do good evil was present with me." Now I could see what John meant when he wrote, "They cannot sin, because their seed remaineth in them." "Sorrowing, yet always rejoicing." "We know we are of God and the whole world lieth in wickedness." Others might dispute about the import of such passages. I could see that they were the utterances of minds exercised by the faith of Christ in peculiar circumstances. Doubts there might be about the histories of the Old Testament—about variations in the narrative of gospel events; but of the sameness of the objects and subjects of faith, which produced the same experiences in those who accepted and obeyed, there could be no doubt.

Thus through exercises protracted and intense, and perhaps peculiar, I awoke to the consciousness of being a disciple of Christ; and with this consciousness came the sense of duty. "Lord what wilt thou have me to do."

CHAPTER X.

VARIOUS COLLEGE EXPERIENCES.

The time that I designed to remain at the new college was now more than past. My means were exhausted. My purpose to devote my life to the profession of the law did not stimulate me as formerly. If I had such purpose at all, it was a purpose without a will. In this state of mind I consulted president Storrs on the subject of my future employment. He advised me to continue by some means study for another year, saying that probably Providence would meanwhile reveal more distinctly the path of duty. I assented, but as I had little money left it became necessary to devise ways and means, by labors of various kinds, to meet my expensive bills. Some of the best of the young men were paying most of their expenses by their labor. This is one of the advantages of new colleges in a new country. This I now prepared to do.

A voluntary association of students had formed a club to board themselves at cheap rates. I was elected steward, and received my board for my services. We rented a vacant house, and hired a

widow lady to cook for us. Some of the boys furnished provisions from their father's farms. Others
procured sufficient money by various expedients to
pay rate bills. I transacted the business of the club
—procured supplies; and did some things in ways
that would seem peculiar to people now-a-days. I
remember well an incident that had some effect
upon my feelings at the time, and was an amusing
recollection for years afterwards. It was difficult
to obtain female assistance in the labor of the house.
This, however, became necessary, as a large number of the students had joined the boarding hall.
We heard of a young woman ten miles distant, who
could be obtained to aid in the culinary department. I borrowed a horse and rode to her father's
residence. She willingly assented to come, and it
was proposed that she should sit upon the horse
behind me, and thus ride through the woods to
Hudson. The blanket was taken from under the
saddle, and so arranged that she, without hesitation,
bounded into her seat from a stump, and off we went
over new roads and rough roads for our destination.
There were places in the road where it was necessary for me sometimes to aid her to keep her place,
and necessary for her to grasp around me with unusual tenacity; but we got home safely,—I vacating
my place that she might ride alone into town. The
approaches of a young maid in the earlier years of
Peter's discipleship led him to deny his Master. I
kept in mind my profession.

But clothing as well as boarding had to be pro-

cured, and in addition to my management of the
boarding hall, I labored in a printing office which
had been recently removed from Cleveland to Hudson.   It was the first religious paper published in
the state.   In subsequent years I was, in the course
of Providence, to become owner and editor; but
now I labored, twice a week in the press room,
working off the edition of the paper, of about one
thousand.   Beginning after supper—I, with another
student, using the old inking balls,—would usually
get through our labors about the middle of the
night.   If we began later, we did not finish our job
till near morning.   Thus, by various labors I succeeded in paying expenses for the most part for
about two years; which were perhaps as happy
years, if not so useful, as any subsequent years of
my life.

The happiness of these years, especially the first
portion of the time grew out of a will in perfect
˴submission to the will of God, and a heart that reluctated against all sin — even against acts of a
doubtful character.   I was in harmony with my
own conscience; and labored as I had opportunity
in various ways to promote the good of others.
Sometimes myself and another student walked five
miles to attend a Sabbath-School.   One evening in
each week I attended a meeting for prayer and conference in the neighborhood near by.   Here I met
with John Brown, afterwards sacrificed at Harper's
Ferry, for his honest and prayerful but misdirected
efforts to emancipate the slaves.   The character-

istics which marked his subsequent life marked the
man at that time. He was sternly opposed to all
wrong and all sham; and yet there was, in worldly
matters, a spirit of speculation and daring about
him which led him to attempt large, but impracticable things. The first meeting to consider the
practicability of a railroad from Cleveland to Pittsburg, of which I was secretary, was assembled in
the church at Hudson, and was organized principally by John and Frederick Brown. We were
ahead of the time, but the project was subsequently
accomplished. He planned a city on the Cuyahoga
river at Franklin—bought a farm which he surveyed
into city lots and sold them to such as would buy.
One of the best deacons in the church of Hudson
mortgaged his farm and bought lots of Mr. Brown.
He was a friend; and I remonstrated with the
Browns for making the sale. They were honest in
the opinion that a town of no mean dimensions was
to arise on their purchase. I got a promise, however, that they would take back the lot and release
the mortgage. The purchaser did not assent to
the arrangement; and hence, one of the best of
deacons lost half his estate, and died some short
time afterwards, a wiser and perhaps a holier man.
Subsequently John Brown, who had formed a partnership with Simon Perkins, a wealthy citizen of his
county in sheep growing, devised a scheme to control the wool market of the entire union in behalf
of the farmers, whom he thought were defrauded
by eastern purchasers. He went to England to

consummate his plan. He failed, of course, and removed with his family to Kansas, where he and his
sons fought the good fight of faith and liberty,
which to him were one and indivisible. In the Kansas struggle he lost part of his family and most of
his property. This intensified his hatred of slavery
which became in some sense a mania—a mania which
ultimated in the tragedy of Harper's Ferry, and
linked the name of John Brown, until the end of
the world, with the history of emancipation in
America.

During this period of study and faith, Theodore
D. Weld, a man of marked character and one that
left his mark upon the student mind of the West,
visited the college. He had for his patron the same
man, who had rescued William Lloyd Garrison from
prison in Baltimore, and aided him in his anti-
slavery efforts. Arthur Tappan—a name that ought
not to die—did more and better than any other
man in the nation, in the initiation of the religious
reforms of the half century in which he acted. Mr.
Weld passed first through the West lecturing on
the importance of manual labor in Academies and
Colleges; and for a season thereafter almost all the
new institutions of the West, endeavored to furnish
labor for students who desired to aid in their own
education; and many self-reliant boys who procured for themselves an education in those days,
have done well, since then, both for God and their
country. "Brave boys were they." Some of them
long ago finished their course and have gone to

their reward. Others lived to see the country pass through its baptism of fire and blood in the civil war. A few still live with their armor on; and when the fight is over, and old opponents have joined the ranks, "let not him that putteth on the harness boast himself as he that putteth it off."

Mr. Weld subsequently visited the West as a temperance lecturer. He traveled West and South, and collected the statistics of intemperance, and the opinions of jurists and officers of prisons, which he used with great effect in initiating the temperance movement of that day. He performed a similar mission, (sustained first by Mr. Tappan, and subsequently by philanthropists at the West,) in introducing the anti-slavery reform in the Western States. This was the martyr age of the reform movements in America. Before it closed, Mr. Weld was married to the eminent Quakeress, Angelina Gremke and retired from public effort. The first struggle was for liberty of speech on the subject of slavery. When that victory was gained, the power of further achievement was secured. It was the beginning of the end. And that battle was fought by men, of more moral courage than was that of any other that succeeded it from Sumpter to Appomattox.

A single incident will give the prevailing spirit of those times. The mob spirit was everywhere rampant, and sometimes triumphant. The only instance in which I found it necessary to retreat from the field, was at Aurora, a town about eight miles

from the college. Here was a large brick church
and one of the oldest religious societies in the State.
The population in the township, with few exceptions, were opposed to the discussion of the anti-
slavery question.   I was invited by the people of
the church to speak to them on the subject of Sab-
bath-Schools and Slavery.   The pastor of the
church — Rev. John Seward — became alarmed in
view of the danger of mob violence to the church
building and to myself personally.   Mr. Seward
himself, who was faithful in all the common duties
of his profession, did not think it wise to be present.
Mrs. Seward, however, a brave christian woman,
determined to accompany me to the church, and do
what she could, by her presence, to restrain the
mob.   As we approached the place of meeting the
crowd of determined and enraged men and boys
began a tumult of fiendish yells, and other inde-
scribable noises; and having loaded an old anvil
with powder, they fired it near us as we approached
the door, causing injury to the building, and nervous excitement and apprehension among the people.

When I began to speak some of the mob had
ascended to the belfry and hung out a black flag
and continued ringing the bell furiously. The anvil
and pieces of fire arms were loaded with immense
charges of powder, and discharged continuously
under the windows until the glass in every window
in the house was shattered to pieces. By the advice of the bravest who still remained, I descended
from the pulpit, which was a high one, supported

by pillars, and standing beneath continued my remarks on the value of Sabbath-School instruction.
Every woman left the house but Mrs. Seward. She
took a chair and sat beside me until violence outside
of the building could do no more. But the mob
was not to be foiled. They devised an expedient
that closed the exercises and cleared the house :
Mrs. Seward and myself withdrawing with a few
others that had remained. They got above the
audience room and broke the ceiling through in
several places. Through these holes in the ceiling
they poured down powder upon the church floor,
and upon this they dropped fire which produced
explosions, that would have ignited and destroyed
the building, had not those who took such dangerous measures to expel us suppressed the fire when
we left the house.

The church stood for at least six months in a
shattered condition before the damages were repaired. It stands there still; its former pastor is
still living. Since then, I presume, many of that
same company have heard valiant talk for liberty
in that pulpit; and no doubt after the battle was
over some of them became valiant anti-slavery men.
But we will not contemn the conservatives, some
of them were better men than the ultra radicals
whom they opposed. The only radicalism that can
be trusted in all cases and places is that which is
produced by faith in Christ which works by love to
men. Gospel radicalism is produced by love to
men, and love of right conjoined. Natural radical-

ism by love to self and love of right conjoined. In the martyr age of the anti-slavery reform John G. Fee was· an example of the one—Cassius M. Clay of the other.

CHAPTER XI.

AGENT OF THE AMERICAN BIBLE SOCIETY.

Before my term of four years at the college was closed, I was invited to become an agent of the American Bible Society to aid in an effort then being made to supply all the families in the State with the Bible. My field was the South-west half of the State of Ohio. My business was to visit every county-seat in my district, and organize a Bible Society in each county where none existed, and reorganize old societies that had ceased to act. In order to do this it would be necessary to ride continually from one county to another, and often to different portions of a county to visit prominent men and ministers, and get their assistance in the new organization. A part of my district was the North-west frontier of the State, where the inhabitants were sparce—roads were new, and agents for benevolent societies were unknown—or were making their first visits. The other portion of my territory included the oldest part of the State from Cincinnati to Steubenville. I commenced my work with a settled and prayerful purpose to do good as

I had opportunity. I do not believe that in a ride of two years, of the many with whom I rode in company portions of the way, or the multitude with whom I associated by lodging in new places from night to night, I neglected a single opportunity to speak on the subject of the Christian faith—not speaking as a task or a duty for them or myself—but introducing the subject in a way natural to the conversation, and rendering it easy for them to speak of things they had heard or seen or felt in regard to religious doctrines or practice.

A few incidents in this labor of two years have left their impress on my memory. The duty of agents in those days was more self-denying than now. I rode the two years without tarrying a day for rain or roads or weather; and often went without a meal in order to save expense to the society. I formed in the city of Cincinnati, the Young Men's Bible Society, which has done efficient work every year from the period of its organization till the present time. Salmon P. Chase we elected the first president of the society, and he continued to act in that capacity until called from the city by his duties as U. S. Senator. From then until the present time I have had some interest in his history; and at times some connection in a retired way with the political progress of Chief Justice Chase, until his elevation placed him above the range of my influence. He, however, did not forget his humble friend. After his elevation to the Chief Justiceship, I had some trouble with one of my publishers, who endeavored to appropriate the copy-right of one of my books. It was a book which Mr. Chase had appreciated and commended in public and private circles. When acquainted with the controversy, he procured an opinion in my favor from one of the best jurists in Washington city, and sent it gratuitously to me. May the influence of his lofty life abide in the Republic always.

With an excellent Episcopal clergyman of the city—the pastor of Mr. Chase—I had an interview which left a very different impression upon my mind from that produced by subsequent familiar intercourse with the same gentleman. I visited him in company with a young man who had been a college friend, and who was now studying medicine in the city. The clergyman had once been a student of medicine, and was very courteous and familiar with my friend, but said little to me, and gave me no encouragement in regard to co-operation in the formation of the Bible Society. Better success, however, was achieved in other congregations and the society was a success. I was not insensible to the slight of Dr. A., and in conversation with the gentleman who accompanied me to his study, I learned that the doctor had never lived or labored outside of cities. My apparel was that of a layman, adapted to my labor in the new counties rather than in the cities. Others understood this ; it is probable he did not. He had never probably seen a man who wore a cap and rough overcoat laboring for such objects as I proposed to accomplish. He therefore

made little account of my application, and was perhaps in doubt whether there were not some mistake
or imposition somewhere. Other circumstances in
other connections led me to suspect that my apparel, although just the thing for the country churches,
was in the way of my access and success in the city.
I rectified matters on this subject; and, although
opposed all my life to uniforms and ministerial garbs
for the clergy—I procured for myself a citizen's suit
of genteel quality, which I found aided my sense
of respect—and aided others to respect myself and
my mission. But my city suit I never wore in the
new counties. There the rough coat and beaver
cap, somewhat the worse for wear, induced familiarity at once, and seemed to them more in keeping
with the mission of one asking aid from laboring
men to give the Bible to the poor and the destitute.
There are extremes on this subject. I have made
mistakes in regard to it several times during my
life. Expensive and uncouth fashions ought to be
eschewed by people of conscience at all times, while
some regard to decent and becoming apparel is due
both to ourselves and to those with whom we associate.

With the excellent Dr. Aydelotte, I had subsequently much pleasant and profitable intercourse,
and as I never mentioned the incidents of our first
interview, I presume he never surmised that the
author, editor and minister with whom he associated, was the man who once visited him in behalf
of the Bible Society, and who was treated with less

courtesy than his mission deserved. The doctor is now an aged and venerable man. The years between middle life and age had passed without a meeting. Last year we took each other's hand, looked into each other's face as aged men, and spoke of the days of other years.

During my service for the society I met in two instances at least with Bishop McIlvaine, who is undoubtedly the best Bishop of the Episcopal church on either side of the water. In England it is not possible for a bishop of the Episcopal church to be a very good christian. In this country the temptation to eschew the self-denying and humble and laborious life of a christian minister is not so great. In two instances the Bishop held a confirmation in the same county-seat on the same day with my appointment for the annual meeting of the county Bible Society; on both occasions he made a speech for the Bible cause. In the county Claremont, as usual, I was to introduce the business—and make an address in connection with the acceptance of the report. I had prepared an address with care that I generally delivered at each county-seat. On this occasion, there were appreciative auditors present, the Bishop among others, and I hoped to leave thoughts upon their minds that would be profitable in furthering the cause. I had scarcely become earnest, however, in my discourse, before I felt my coat twitching slightly. No conjecture of the cause entered my mind. I adjusted my coat and went on. The twitch was renewed with more energy. I

turned to look and found the county treasurer, who
was likewise treasurer of the Bible Society, had
been laboring with the skirt of my coat, and when
I turned he mildly whispered to me that I had better be short, as the people wanted to hear the
Bishop. My enthusiasm was squelched, of course,
and with a few embarrassed words I gave place to
the excellent man who was to follow.

The address which I was about to deliver was the
substance of that printed in the first chapter of the
"Philosophy of the Plan of Salvation." It has circulated more widely through Christendom since
then than any other argument in behalf of Divine
Revelation. The Bishop did not hear it then, but
he read it at a later period, and unsolicited by me,
did much that aided the circulation of my little
volume:—and upon my first visit to England, he
sent me a complimentary letter to his friends that
I found more influential with the best class of church
men, and likewise with the best class of dissenters,
than any other introductory letter that I took with
me.

The last time I saw the bishop he presided at the
commencement exercises of Gambier College where
I was invited to deliver the address and the diplo-
mas to one of the literary societies. At the close
he gave me a cordial greeting and signified his
hearty interest in the things I had spoken. I believe in the parity of the ministry, but if some
denominations must have bishops, I hope the Lord
will send them many such men as Bishop McIlvaine.

Striking incidents often occurred in my visitation of different counties in my Bible work. I found in the interior of the State a family by the name of Boydenot—who claimed to be the nearest lineal descendants of Dr. Boydenot—President of Princeton College, and first President of the American Bible Society. The family were poor, and it was found that they had no Bible in their house. One was given to them as a gratuity. This was an incident which their pious and learned ancestor could never have anticipated. An incident too, which shows the working of free republican institutions, which makes nothing of a man's antecedents but everything of what he is in himself and for his own time.

Late in the autumn I was traveling towards Marietta,—in the poor and hilly region of the Little Muskingum. Inhabitants on the road were few and far between, and night was approaching; I came to a stream that was much swollen by rains that had recently fallen. It was a long distance back to the last house. I was lame with a severe bruise that my horse had inflicted while I was endeavoring to make him comfortable the preceding night. I needed rest, and hoped there was some dwelling near by if I were only over the swollen stream. But the stream was rapid—the bottom might be obstructed by stumps; and below were trees lodged in the stream, against which my horse might be carried by the current. It was a moment of painful suspense. I concluded to brave the danger; and having fastened my saddlebags, which contained my

few papers and wardrobe on my shoulders, I, with
difficulty, urged my horse into the stream. He
swam bravely; and, although swept some distance
by the current, we reached safely the other shore—
my saddlebags dry, but my person drenched nearly
to my shoulders. For three lonesome miles I had
to ride, chilled and in pain, before I came to the
first house. It was in another creek bottom, and
proved to be that of a good farmer,—justice of the
peace in his neighborhood. It was getting dark—
the sight of the house was a relief, and the kindly
reception which I met was more than comforting.
My horse and myself were soon cared for; and the
method by which I had my clothes dried I will not
relate. Suffice it, that after about an hour spent
under a bed quilt, during which my wet garments
were drying, we surrounded one of the most tooth-
some supper tables to which ever a hungry traveler
sat down.

Providence seemed to work all things together
for my comfort that night. The family expected
that on that night the Methodist circuit rider would
make his quarters at their house; and, as was usual
in such cases, the best arrangements were made for
his entertainment. Indeed it was an effort with the
families on the outside circuits in those days to
show their degree of temporal prosperity by the
richness of their table during the minister's visit.
The minister had, undoubtedly, been detained by
the rains and swollen streams. I sat in his place;
and the family seemed to be glad that their culinary

preparation was not made in vain. We had stewed chicken and dough-nuts, and ham and eggs and short-cake—mashed potatoes with butter on the top, and "store coffee," with other fixings and fringes which I have forgotten. A sense of propriety led me to restrain the eagerness with which I appropriated the substantial items of the farmer's table; but I have no doubt I manifested sufficient eagerness to indicate my appreciation of the repast.

This family lived on a "bottom farm" in the hilly and sparcely settled region of the Little Muskingum to which the old hunters had retired as population increased in the better portions of the State. The squire entertained me with a recital of some of the services he had performed as a magistrate. They would scarcely be believed in our time, and yet they were no doubt exactly true. The men who were married were usually those who had "voted for the squire," and whose finances were sensibly affected by the payment of "half a dollar in specie." One couple had been married, with no attendants—the man in his shirt sleeves, the woman barefoot. Another was unable to meet the expense at the time, but he had "squatted" on a piece of land and promised to pay the bill in pumpkins the succeeding fall, which promise was faithfully kept, indicating perhaps that he was satisfied with his bargain. I left the squire's hospitable home in much better condition than when I arrived. He refused any compensatiòn. My expression of gratitude for bed and board were hearty and sincere.

At the other side of the State before the white
people had settled on the Maumee river, an incident
occurred that left quite a different impression upon
my mind. I had rode through the Black Swamp,
which was then almost impassable, between Little
Sandusky and Maumee city. There I met Mr. Van
Tassel, missionary to the Ottawa Indians, at whose
invitation I rode to the mission station, some distance up the Maumee to spend a day or two, and
visit the Indian camps. During my stay the missionary and myself took a canoe and "paddled" up
the stream to the camp of the Indians in order to
witness the *pow wow* which they annually cele-
brated at the season of corn-gathering. Two long
rows of logs were on fire, and between these the
Indians were holding a dance, in which they leaped
and contorted and swayed their persons in the most
violent manner—some of them humming meanwhile
a low monotonous strain in accord with the noise
of a sort of drum which was shaken by an old man
sitting apart from the dancers. A prophet or
"meteer" was on a visit to them and sat near the
"music man." A portion of the Indians which had
previously left the region had returned, much dissatisfied with the treaty by which they had conveyed
their lands to the Government. After spending
some time witnessing the strange movements and
grimace of the dance Mr. VanTassel and his half-
breed interpreter with myself in company, visited
some of the tents or lodges of those with whom
they were well acquainted. I was reclining on a

raised seat covered with skins at the side of the lodge, when an Indian thoroughly intoxicated entered. He mistook me—I was afterwards told—for an agent of the Government, and proceeded to make an extravagant and threatening address to me concerning the alleged fraud. His gestures were violent, and performed in near proximity to my face. The interpreter and missionary made earnest efforts to appease him, but he seemed oblivious to their explanations, and they could only advise me to keep composed and his rage would subside. I felt uneasy; and when the drunken warrior proceeded to draw his tomahawk and flourish it to indicate how such men as me ought to be dealt with, I was thoroughly frightened, and although the interpreter seemed to be ready to seize his arm if he should make the movement to strike—I was chilled with apprehension; and I remember no time in my life when I felt a greater sense of relief, than when the wild Indian subsided into a quieter mood and returned his tomahawk to his belt.

I have known something of missionaries to the Indians since I visited the old station on the Maumee. To the christian colony which I aided to establish in the woods of Northern Michigan—three men with their families came to reside. They had gone out from Oberlin as missionaries, without aid from any society, trusting to God for sustenance and guidance. They labored at Red Lake, in the cold and distant region of Northern Minnesota. They were men of faith and prayer and labor. But after years of toil and self-sacrifice almost to death, they abandoned the Indians and returned poor in all respects except the life of God in their souls.

They were never able to make the Indians believe that they were disinterested laborers for their good. This, perhaps, is not strange; men who have no faith, whether savage or civilized, cannot believe that one man can seek the good of others as the end and aim of his life. Every man *naturally* seeks his own good as his supreme end; hence he can have no evidence from his own experience that such a state of mind as disinterested benevolence can exist. His experience is against it. Hence, the Indians naturally believe there is some selfish motive back of every effort for their good. These good men thought the providence mysterious that led them to the sacrifice which they made with but bitter fruit of their labor. They did the work of God which no other men probably would have done. The divine plan is to offer the truth in the gospel spirit, to a people,—then, if they reject it, their end will come by Providential Judgments. These men fulfilled the divine plan successfully and faithfully. God does not usually give heathen lands as an inheritance to his church by conversion of the people. The business of the church is to preach the truth—then, when truth is rejected Providence sends war—wicked men—or pestilence, or famine—to remove the heathen and give the land to his own people. Such will be the history of the Indians in America.

I left the Maumee mission which had been established by Western Presbyterians, and passed by an Indian trail fifteen miles through the Black Swamp to the nearest settlement. After reaching Columbus, Ohio, I proceeded by the Great National Road projected by Henry Clay, as a thoroughfare of traffic and travel between the East and West. The conception of railroads and their uses, was not yet developed in the mind of the great commoner. The bed of the road was thrown up east of Columbus, but not yet macadamized. I had therefore, often to leave the road-bed on account of the impassable mire and take a side path. In one of these circuits, in descending to a small stream, about eight miles more or less from the city I came upon what was called a sponge. It was ground that looked fair enough on the surface, but being saturated by springs beneath, my horse sank at one plunge to his neck in the mire. I succeeded in getting rid of the animal, which struggled fearfully, and finally actually rolled over down the hillside. Saddle, saddlebags and all things else were thoroughly covered with mud and water. I led the horse a short distance across the stream, on the farther bank of which stood a country tavern, where I gave the landlord a moderate sum to have the animal and his paraphernalia washed and dried for progress in the morning.

At this wayside inn, the Irishmen who broke stone on the National Road had their quarters. The boss of the stone crackers was the only man

in the mess who had a single bed. Other straw
beds or "shakedowns" all occupied by two or more
of the men. I was courteously invited by the boss
himself to share his bunk. He was a large Irishman and there was but little space for me; and
having refused to partake of a "jigger of whisky,"
I did not wish to offend a man so drunk and rude
and dirty as he was. Besides there was no alternative but to sit by the fire, lie on the floor, or sleep
with the boss. If I had had even a partial apprehension before undressing of the evil to come I
certainly should have preferred to have slept with
my horse in the stable. I have slept in some strange
places in my life by land and sea, but a night so
repulsive to my sensibility in all respects I never
passed. It seemed as though the fumes of whisky
and tobacco not only expired, but exhaled and ex-
uded from every pore of the Irishman's person. To
separate myself from the body of pollution was impossible, as there was no room in the bed by which
I could lie apart from my bed-fellow. How I longed
for day-light no mortal can tell. I always eschewed
tobacco, and since that night I have felt even more
disposed to eschew all chewers of the filthy weed.
Many years afterwards in endeavoring to establish
a Christian church and colony in the woods of
Northern Michigan, I had a clause inserted in the
charter excluding the sale of tobacco upon any of
the lots and lands of the colonists. The experience
of that night, no doubt, prompted to the exclusion
of the filthy narcotic.

During the latter portion of my term of service
as an agent of the American Bible Society, I was
married to a young woman from New England, who
was residing in the family of Professor Nutting, of
Hudson, Ohio. She was a student in the ladies'
Seminary, and taught school and labored as need
required for self-support. From the change of
mind when I saw God in nothing, to the time I saw
God in everything, I had prayed naturally, not at
stated times and places, but as a constant state of
mind, in regard to all things in which I took a personal interest. And now that I thought of uniting
myself with a life companion I prayed with great
earnestness for the divine interposition and guidance. I had no doubt that for the obedient christian
matches are made in heaven. The characteristics of
my wife supplemented those of my own. My weak
points of character were antagonized or strengthened by her different qualities, and I do not believe
there was any other woman who could have aided
with more skill and efficiency the accomplishment
of the various labors of my life. She still lives to
review in age and infirmity the arduous and diversified labors through which she has passed with her
husband. She knew that I unduly appreciated my
own efforts, and I never heard her utter a word of
praise in regard to any of my labors, either in business or in the pulpit; and, although a woman of
strong will, yet she never objected to any change
of residence or of labor which I proposed. She
strongly desired to attend church in all cases when

I was to preach, and did so when it was with the greatest difficulty that she could ascend the steps of the sanctuary. I have since been sure that she went to pray while I was preaching. Three separate attacks of paralysis have reduced her in all respects to a second infancy; yet, any attention from her husband is a comfort even in her second childhood.

Soon after our marriage one of the ludicrous incidents that sometimes befall public speakers, who commit their manuscripts, occurred at a time and place well adapted to abate self-complacency. I was invited to deliver a fourth of July oration in Nelson, Ohio, not far from Hudson College. Two speeches were to be made—one by Judge Hitchcock, afterwards of the Supreme Court,—the other by myself. The committee, perhaps, designed to arrange for something judicial and weighty, and something that might be more popular and exhilarating. The audience was large and contained the elite of the country round about. I had written and committed my speech—something I have never done since. But on this occasion the position of the associate orator, and the presence of the woman towards whom I had the feeling that I suppose men generally possess the first months of married life, led me to devote some time and study to make a good thing of my speech, which was destined to be eloquent and edifying, and good otherwise in a degree that would give my wife, and everybody else present, a proper appreciation of my qualities.

I stood up and "spoke my piece" about half through, when the chain of association broke, and what followed of the speech dropped entirely from my memory. To make the matter more perplexing I did not have my manuscript in my pocket but in my hat, which sat on a window-sill near where my wife was seated about the middle of the audience. The only alternative, however, was to ask for my hat, which was delivered to me; and the balance of the oration was read from the manuscript, and must have seemed to the audience very much like the notes of a hymn tune after a Christmas carol. I was pious and could see after reflection that I had been possessed with a selfish desire to distinguish myself; and I had grace enough to be thankful for the providence that caused the failure; and when I found that the misadventure had no effect upon my wife except to create sympathy and apparently more kindly respect, I drove home from the gathering a happier man than I was when I went. The admonition produced a wise caution; and subsequently, in all my efforts, I endeavored to master the subject matter of my discourse, and used copious notes of the train of thought, depending upon myself for words, and upon God for guidance in what I had to say.

There was not much time for literary labor while riding from one county to another holding annual meetings—adjusting accounts—and putting Bible Societies into working condition. I did not, however, lose interest in historic incidents; and sometimes riding alone through the woods, when I was not singing the 11th part of the 119th Pslam, as rendered by Watts, my mind gave poetical form to incidents learned by the way.

In the county of Tuscarawas, there is the little village of Gnadenhutten, where the first white man who ever trod the soil of the State of Ohio lived and taught the Indians. He was a Moravian missionary, and at the date of my visit the Moravian church still held the ground occupied by the old Indian Mission. A few Moravian families still remained at the old site. They were ministered to by a pastor of their own godly denomination. I had learned to reverence the Moravians for their missionary zeal, and desired to see some of the people, and to visit the locality of the fearful massacre of the missionaries and Indians which had occurred at this place. Returning I wrote the following verses:

I.

Throw up thine arms, thou sycamore tree,
For rich is the soil that nourishes thee;
And the vine that climbs round thy branches high,
Should yield its clusters of rubric dye;
For the earth which the fostering juice imparts
Is drench'd in the blood of the red men's hearts.

II.

'Tis a strange, wild tale that they tell of thee—
Thou clambering vine and sycamore tree;
They say that in time, long past and gone,
The red man rov'd in these wilds alone;—
That here, in the midst of this circling wood,
In the days of old, a village stood
Where the warrior Indian, wild and free,
Rejoic'd in primeval liberty.

III.

A man of God, from the rising sun,
Came to Gnadenhutten and Shoenbrunn;
And he taught the Indians to love the name
Of Him who on errands of mercy came:—
They heard his talk with rev'rent fear,
And leaned on their bows around to hear;
Then buried the hatchet, and tilled the sod,
And bow'd to worship the white man's God.

IV.

Thus far in the wilderness' solitude,
Midst the tall old trees, and the mountains rude,
In prayers and praises, the ancient race
Lifted their hearts to the God of grace.

V.

But cruel War seized his flaming brand,
And shook at heaven his bloody hand;
And the warrior Indian seized the bow
And lurk'd like the panther for his foe;
But the Christian Indians would not sing
The song of war in their council ring—
Yet Suspicion whisper'd the Christians prayed
And plann'd for their warrior brothers' aid.

VI.

'Twas Autumn, when Ceres fills her horn
With the ripen'd ears of the golden corn,
When a band of pale-faced warriors came
With words of peace, in the Christian's name,
But their words of peace were spoke in guile,
With a "forked tongue" and a siren's smile.

VII.

At even, about the close of day,
They took the Indians' arms away;
And they gathered them in that sacred place
Which their hands had rear'd for prayer and praise,
Then told their doom, as History saith,
Indians—an hour!—then meet your death!

VIII.

'Twas fearful tidings—the red man stood,
In the pride of their race, in solemn mood;
But their cheeks blanch'd not, nor a quicken'd breath
Betray'd the fear of approaching death--
All kneel'd in silence and rais'd their eyes
To the God that heard their suppliant cries.

IX.
An hour elapsed—The white men came
And with deadly rifle took deadly aim,
And they rent the breasts of the Indians there,
As they kneeled and lifted their hearts in prayer.

X.
Now far in the West the Indian sire,
As he sits by his wigwam's flickering fire,
Oft tells the tale of what things were done
At Gnadenhutten and Shoenbrunn.

For the past sixty years—each period of twenty years has been a cycle of speculation and revulsion. Property appreciates in value. The currency is expanded. Purchases of real estate are made for the purpose of speculation—that is, to sell at higher figures. The inflated currency encourages the borrower. The borrower becomes the speculator— and this continues until property in large amounts is held above its value for present purposes, and thus kept out of the hands of those who buy for use. This cannot last long. The borrower has to pay, and the property held by him at last reaches a figure that does not pay; hence, a reaction commences. A decline in prices toward its value for present use begins. When the decline begins each holder makes haste to realize in view of a greater decline, and a panic ensues that puts real estate, and, with it, the produce of real estate, down below their actual value. Wages fall, because improvements stop, and they continue until by emigration and the natural growth of our new country, an equilibrium again takes place, and a new period of speculation and expansion begins; to be followed by another revolution, when speculation again places property beyond its value for present use.

Such a period of speculation was passed between the years 1835-45. Having disposed of my printing office, I proposed to myself to invest the proceeds in lands or lots that would appreciate, and thus freed from the care of accumulation in the present, and the fear of want in old age, it was my purpose to study theology and devote my life to the gospel ministry. My idea was to invest my means in wild lands or lots in growing towns—and pay no more attention to worldly interests. I proposed, when prepared to preach, to labor where I could do the most good, irrespective of salary further than sufficient to furnish food and raiment for my family, which consisted only of three persons—self, wife and sister-in-law.

With this purpose I started on horseback with Frederick Brown—brother of John Brown, of Harper's Ferry—to invest my spare funds in new lands in Michigan, and lots in Chicago. It was early in March. The weather the first days of our journey was extremely cold, and we were almost frozen before we reached Toledo. At that time the question was where the great city at the mouth of the Maumee was to be located. There was Maumee city projected above, and Toledo in its present site, and another city farther down, towards Lake Michigan. There are at this day some old houses and frames of houses in the lower town still standing that were built about the time of our visit. Maumee city

above, is a small, dilapidated village. Toledo is a
thriving commercial city; and property which we
considered too high to purchase at a few hundreds
of dollars, is now worth tens of thousands; and
property in the other city, for which hundreds were
asked, is now not worth so many cents.

We passed on and made our next stop and inquiry for investment at a new city just laid out
where the road from Detroit crossed the St. Joseph
river. There was then a blacksmith shop, a tavern,
a grist mill, and perhaps one or two other houses.
·It was supposed to be the head of navigation on the
St. Joseph. We inquired for lots, and were told
that the business lots were mostly sold; but the
landlord showed us at the distance of about one-
half mile, on an elevation, the place where the first-
class dwelling houses were to be; and when he
informed us we could get lots that would, beyond
question, double in value in a short time, as the
business lots had already done. We believe not
more than two houses were ever added to the population of the place.

At the tavern in this place we met a gentleman
that had disposed of his stock of merchandise and
the good-will of a thriving business, and was on his
way to St. Joseph, the name of a city on Lake
Michigan, at the mouth of St. Joseph river. He
had bought for $20,000 a farm at the mouth of this
river, where he was about to lay out a city, and invited us to purchase lots, while we could get good
locations. He was willing to sell lots for one-half

what they would be worth so soon as the location was known? and one-tenth of what they would be worth in a few years.

Some years afterwards, while living in Chicago, we frequently crossed the lake at St. Joe. It being the end of the stage route in former years—before the railroad was finished.

There stands now on the old site a large three-story frame hotel, capable of holding hundreds of travelers; and scattered over a large area of vacant land are houses vacant of tenants, and falling to pieces. The hotel, we suppose, was built by the first proprietor to accommodate purchasers flocking to buy city lots. The deserted houses were built by the first or second purchasers of lots in order to begin the new city. Such was St. Joseph when we saw it twenty years ago; and such are multitudes of other projected cities in the West. Maps were made of the new cities—and lots changed hands by the map. One succeeded—fifty failed.

We could not see as the landlord did, the future city at the crossing of the St. Joe., so we rode on to Elkhart. Here speculators had preceded us, and the property on what was to be the business street had changed hands, and lots were held at a high figure. There was a projected water power on the river, a short distance above the village. We were shown how the dam was to be constructed across the stream, and the power was to be as valuable as that at Lowell. It was supposed too, that the manufacturing city would not injure the prospects of

Elkhart, but that the greatness of the one would rather be auxiliary to the greatness of the other. We had not means enough to invest in so valuable a location, and concluded not to buy.

By this time the weather was getting warm, and the roads were breaking up and becoming almost impassable for horses. My companion concluded not to go further towards Chicago. Speculation was at the advance state, and we both concluded that prices were too high to make profitable investments. We learned likewise that prices in Chicago were exorbitant; and ten years subsequently, when the reaction had spent its force, I bought a lot in Chicago for less than was asked for them ten years previously. Reaction had ensued.

We started on our return home unwilling to invest at the prices asked for lots in the prospective cities.

We concluded to purchase a lot or two of wild land and return home. To accomplish this we traveled up the St. Joseph river to a point where land was to be had at low rates—and some government-land still remained in the region. While examining a tract on which there was a "wet prairie," Mr. Brown's horse sank under him through the surface soil of the prairie, and horse and man came near going down. When extricated from his predicament he expressed disgust with the location, land and latitude, and determined to return home and save his money. I concluded to stay longer and make a purchase. Next morning we parted company. Subsequently I purchased two pieces of land, and exchanged the excellent horse which I rode for two village lots which some one had laid out on the banks of the river near by. The location was called Bristol ; there was but one house on the site of the new city—whether another was ever built I do not know. I think, however, there is a village of Bristol on the line of the Southern Michigan Rail Road which is probably the old location where I made my first investment in town lots.

On our return home the stage got fast in the road, at night, somewhere east of Sturges' Prairie, and some of the fastenings breaking, and no dwelling house near, we had to sit in the coach till morning. Other misadventures incident to the early times in the West occurred, but we reached home in safety; and having expended the little balance of our funds in the purchase of a dwelling house, we took several boarders to aid in paying expenses, and I commenced the study of theology preparatory to preaching the gospel.

I continued the study of theology, at Hudson, under Prof. Hickox, now president of Union College, Schenectady. After about nine months had passed, an incident occurred which hastened the event of my licensure. A young man by the name of Canfield, who had been suspended at some eastern institution, had been admitted to Oberlin, and after a short term in that institution he had commenced preaching in a neighboring congregation without license. The people were unwilling to dismiss him, and the dilemma came up for the consideration of the Presbytery either to license him, or lose the congregation. They concluded to license him, and in order to have an apology for the procedure of licensing an Oberlin student, preaching irregularly, with imperfect education, they concluded to invite me to secure a license at the same time; and the Presbytery was called to meet at my house, and Mr. Canfield and myself were licensed to preach the gospel. Neither of us having graduated in the literary course, and our theology being attained in a few months.

It ought to be said, however, that Bible studies in college—and Bible classes, and the discussions of doctrinal theories—and revivals of religion in which the theory of the Holy Spirit was taught, were so common in those days, that I have no doubt we were, both of us, better prepared to meet the practical requirements of the age—and lead a congregation in doctrine and labor, than the mere preaching machines made by literary and theological training usually are. Canfield, in order to licensure as I feared at the time, became quite conservative and orthodox, and passed his examination in form with the Presbytery—and the older pastors received and exchanged pulpits with him at once. I was known as an Abolitionist, and one inclined to favor the Oberlin movement; and then the remembrance of my newspaper management, caused some of the Presbytery to look with disfavor on my examination. They argued that I would not

co-operate with the Presbytery, and absented themselves when the vote was taken on the question of
licensing me to preach.

Canfield was true to the Presbytery. He subsequently repudiated Oberlin Theology, and wrote
a pamphlet against their doctrine of perfection.
He had talent and soon found a pulpit in a city
church. The slave received from him no aid. He
preached the Orthodox faith, and still continues to
get a first-rate salary in a first-class church.

I was licensed, and prepared to preach in a small
church in the neighborhood, but the Adullamites
of the Presbytery opposed, and I preached my first
sermon at Akron. The people heard me gladly—
urged the Presbytery to ordain and settle me with
them. They assented. I could pass no examination in the languages—having but an imperfect
knowledge of all from Latin to Hebrew. But of
the English tongue I had knowledge and command.
And I studied a little volume on theology prepared
for Bible classes, and had the happiness to hear
that a new member of Presbytery, a graduate in
literature and theology who had recently settled at
Franklin, said while I was retired after examination,
that he had never heard so satisfactory an examination before in doctrinal theology. The ordination dinner was eaten, and the brethren went home,
and I began my labors as pastor of the Congregational church in Akron, and member of the Presbytery of Portage.

CHAPTER XII.

EDITOR AND REFORMER.

The first religious paper published in the United States was published in the old town of Chillicothe, Ohio, by Mr. Andrews, a Presbyterian minister of the pioneer age of the West. Two or three had subsequently been established at the East, when the Ohio *Observer* was originated at Cleveland, by Hermon Kingsbury, Esq. It was patronized by the early Congregational families of Northern Ohio. After the Western Reserve College had been established at Hudson, it was removed to that place, but its patronage not paying expenses—I was invited to take charge of the paper, and continue, if possible, the publication. My wife had saved something by teaching school in Southern Ohio, while I had gained a little by the most rigid economy. Our means combined enabled us to make the first payment on the office, and to provide first things absolutely necessary for housekeeping, when we should arrive at our new home.

We started in the early spring to travel the length of the State, from West Union in the south to Hud-

son in the north of Ohio. We journeyed, as the
stages generally did, by day and night. The first
night our progress was hindered by a storm and a
swollen stream on the route, and we sought shelter
about midnight in a log cabin upon the banks of
the creek. A bed, with a bed-companion that need
not be described, was provided for my wife. I and
the other passengers lay on the floor. We were
drenched by the rain, and made up a brisk fire, and
our feet being wet and chilly I placed mine in closer
proximity to the hot coals than was wise. I had
on boots and rubber overshoes, and being weary I
soon fell into a deep sleep, which before morning
was broken by a sensation that my feet were in a
furnace. I started up to find my rubber overshoes
scorching hot—partly melted and partly indurated.
They adhered to my feet with a tenacity that my
strength could not overcome. And when I rose to
make the effort the heat seemed to increase to an
intensity that destroyed all calmness. I made an
outcry that was unseemly, but which roused the
other passengers, as though the house had been on
fire. There were some frightened and some ludicrous looking features, as all suggested and aided
in the effort to detach the melted rubber and
scorched boots and saturated stockings. After I
had been extricated I felt a joy in being barefoot
more than that experienced as country school boy,
when I discarded my shoes, in the first days of
summer.

When we reached the neighborhood of Mt. Ver-

non the roads became impassable in some places.
The male passengers had often to get out, and with
the aid of rails from neighboring fences, aid to extricate the vehicle. We had left the main road and
were proceeding hopefully on a side track not so
much gullied by travel, when an incident occurred
that we had expected hourly for some time—the
stage upset. The old coach went down slowly,
and the jaded horses made no disturbance. The
passengers were settled into a pile at the bottom
side of the conveyance. No harm being done except the slight contusions and inconvenience experienced by the undermost from the incumbent
weight of those above them. All righted themselves as soon as possible, and looked about for a
place of egress from the old coach.

The coaches in those days had sliding windows
in the sides, hence the one directly above us offered
egress into the open air. An invalid young man,
who had been suffering from jaundice and ague,
prevalent in the early times, was inspired by fright
and nervousness with extraordinary agility; and
leaping up to the window above, got his head and
arms through the aperture, while he had strength
to get no further. Thus he blockaded the passage,
while his nether extremities hung dangling about
the faces of those inside. In this situation the lady
passengers, in their haste to get out, forgot for a
time the extreme modesty in which there is no profit.
Before the gentlemen had time to make themselves
masters of the situation, one of the ladies had

grasped the invalid by one leg, while another seiz-
ing the other, they struggled womanfully to elevate
him through the passage of egress. The gentlemen soon rallied to their aid ; but I know that the
ludicrousness of the scene so affected some of them
that their aid in elevating the man with the ague
was not of much account. When the passage was
cleared one of the gentlemen passed out and standing upon the top side of the fallen coach aided the
passengers—ladies first of course—into the open air.

After the storm, one of those sudden changes of
temperature occurred which often takes place at
the West in the early spring. The weather became
quite cold. The surface of the mud was frozen,
and the horses "slumped"—*i. e.*, broke through the
crust of frozen mud, and sunk, often knee deep, in
the mire below.

To make rapid progress was impossible, and the
coach was an incumbrance. Some of our passengers were left at Cleveland. The few who desired
to proceed farther, were put into a strong open
wagon, into which passengers, mail and trunks
were packed, without regard either to care or comfort. In such condition, on a cold, bleak day, after
a ride of eight hours, we reached our destination at
Hudson. I have made many trips in the stage
coach, and had been capsized many times, but the
incidents of the trip across the State to enter upon
new duties in the printing office was a marked
experience.

Our first home was plain enough. We had proposed to live within our income. And, although since then we have resided in a villa residence, the pleasantest in one of the pleasantest interior cities of Ohio; yet, I do not think we were more happy in our mansion than we were in our first rented house. We began without carpets; we used large stones for andirons; our chairs were of the cheapest construction. My wife, for a time, did her own labor, and sometimes sat up until the middle of the night to prepare the necessary furnishing for beds and other first things in our humble home. I was publisher, editor, and sometimes printer. Thus we worked on, every month gaining more ease and adding comforts. We first spread a cotton carpet on one room. This after a time was removed to another room and a woolen one laid down. The stone andirons were removed to give place to iron ones, and these again to brass; and in every advance in any direction there was more real pleasure than when the rich man, who has no taste for art, adds some artistic ornament to the adornments of his mansion. Before we closed our connection with the paper we were as comfortably and as tastefully conditioned as the average of our neighbors. Every day grateful to God for his goodness.

The first newspapers in the West were usually managed by practical printers, and most of the type set by boys. I had been a printer boy myself, and could understand their wants and ways. Four young lads aided in the printing office. It was our purpose to train these boys for usefulness and

inculcate in their hearts the principles of the gospel. With a good common school education, the
labor of three years in a printing office will prepare
a good boy for any trade or profession, often better
than the same time spent in the colleges of the
country. The printer boys labored a certain number of hours and spent two hours each day in study
under the guidance of one of the college students.
They sat with us at our family table reciting a verse
of scripture each morning with the rest of the family. At night they sang with us and kneeled with
us in worship, and on the Sabbath, when there was
a contribution for any benevolent object, they had
their mite with the rest of us to cast into the contribution ; and in the evening of the Sabbath there
was a family talk suitable to interest and instruct
young minds. In such exercises, interspersed with
such amusements as boys need, passed the weeks
and months for two years in the office and in the
family. Then circumstances rendered it desirable
that I should sell the property. When the paper
was sold, although a christian minister was the purchaser, he was unwilling to make the conditions
which a christian man should have made with my
boys—and they returned to their homes or sought
employment in other places. They all professed,
during the two years, obedience to Christ, and two
of them were admitted to membership in the church.
We have noted with interest the history of our
printer boys. One of them is a Presbyterian minister—one is a successful lawyer—one became clerk

in a retail store, and finally succeeded to a share of
the business. The youngest is editor and proprietor of a successful newspaper in Illinois. Another
one, who was with us but a short time returned
home. We have not learned his history, but have
confidence that his life has been a success.

The anti-slavery sentiment was strong at the
periods of the Revolution and the war of 1812.
Franklin, Clay and Harrison were in their day each
members of Emancipation Societies. The men who
originated the anti-slavery discussion which terminated in the overthrow of the slaveholder's power
were western men. Foremost among them were a
company of Presbyterian ministers, settled along
the southern border of the State of Ohio. Some of
them had been driven from the slave States for the
offence of teaching colored children on the Sabbath. Of these, Rev. John Rankin was one. These
men preached against slavery — their presbytery
denounced slave-trading, and John Rankin wrote
his *Letters on Slavery*, which were widely circulated both East and West, before Garrison was im-
prisoned. The *Genius of Emancipation*, published
by Benjamin Lundy in the new region of Illinois,
was the first and truest of all the anti-slavery papers. From the Letters of John Rankin, William
Lloyd Garrison received his conviction of the evil
of slavery—a fact which he magnanimously acknowledged in public and private. It was from
these men that Thomas Morris secured his convictions—the first man that stood up to denounce

slavery and demand emancipation in the American
Congress. John Rankin is yet living, having
worked in the anti-slavery reform from its incep-
tion to the overthrow of the inhuman institution
by a war brought on by the force of truth and
prayer on the one side—and the insanity of the
guilty on the other.

When the anti-slavery sentiment began to extend
itself in Ohio, the churches and colleges were placed
on probation, as they are by every reform which
demands the suppression of evil and the advance
of righteousness in society. The Western Reserve
College was the first institution in the West to accept and advocate the doctrine of the abolitionists.
The three leading professors were active agitators
in the early years of the discussion. Greene and
Wright were men of unusual intellectual acumen.
President Storrs was a man of marked religious
character, commending his views to every man's
conscience in the sight of God. Arthur Tappan,
one of the best men that ever lived, had given of
his means freely to endow the college at Hudson.
But the wealthy churches and the politicians in
church and State, East and West, denounced the
anti-slavery men. This was true in a general sense
of all denominations. A few were faithful to Christ
—but those few found that what James G. Birney
said was true—"the churches were the bulwarks
of American Slavery." Very soon the determined
hostility of the professed Christian Churches, Colleges and Theological Seminaries made itself felt

at Hudson. The Board of Trustees opposed the reform in the college, and by a majority vote asked the anti-slavery professors, Greene and Wright, to resign their places. President Storrs continued at the head of the institution—faithful to principle; —but the hostility of the pro-slavery trustees hastened his death.

This was the condition of things when I took charge of the religious paper at Hudson. The old and able professors were removed and new men were in their places. A portion of the students had acquiesced in the new condition of things; some had gone home; others went to Oberlin. The few and faithful anti-slavery men were incensed by the dismission of the professors and the persecution of the president, so that the parties were personally and warmly antagonistic.

President Storrs had been my friend in business and in study. In impenitence and in obedience his kindness and courtesy never abated. Professor Elizur Wright was a scholar, and a man of unusual literary ability. Professor Greene was a righteous man, and his cutting logic convinced many of the sin of slaveholding. President Storrs was a good man, and gained to the cause those that Professor Greene convinced. I respected one, and respected and loved the other. Long after the decease of the good man—after the war of freedom was inaugurated, I inscribed to his memory the following verses addressed to those who with myself had received his instruction and accepted his principles:

To the early members of the Western Reserve College, in memory of our deceased friend, President Storrs :

Honor the good—bow down and bless
The pure in heart whose holiness
   Reached and enriched your mind;
The humbly wise are truly great—
Great in high thoughts which elevate
   The aims of human kind.

Honor the Great—the great of soul,
Who live above the mean control
   Of low and selfish aims;
Who see and dare maintain the right;
When cowards flee, they stand and fight
   In presence of the flames.

Honor the heroes, who will stand
For truth and justice in the land,
   Nor yield to selfish fears;
Who in the dark some seeds of light—
Germ truths which spring to moral might
   In minds of after years.

Honor the dead, whose lives were given
A sacrifice for truth—the leaven,
   Of martyr—blood has power:
If fal'ring in the fight with sin—
Storrs faltered not, remember him!
   'Twill help us in that hour.

Every new truth which Providence brings to the front and puts before men, challenging conscience and conduct on their part, puts them on probation for a higher or lower moral status. The ordeal through which I passed was not an easy one. I had not been the first nor the firmest in recognizing the righteousness of anti-slavery principles; but I accepted them at an early period, and desired to maintain them kindly and firmly.

When we had taken charge of our printing office and opened our new home, the pro-slavery members of the Executive committee of the college desired, of course, to conciliate the new editor, and influence the paper into the conservative side of the controversy. They made a concerted effort to do this. The new faculty were moderately conservative—the Executive committee of the Trustees were ultra conservative. The agent of the college had been to New York city and returned with the report, that the principles of Arthur Tappan, the philanthropist, were repudiated and even abhorred by the ministers and churches, and that the college would lose all patronage in New England, and at Andover in particular, if they did not recede from any avowal they had made of anti-slavery principles. The most efficient man among them, therefore, became my earnest friend at once. He brought and sent us choice items for our table—aided to get in and arrange our few articles of plain furniture—and tendered suggestions for himself and others of good will and wisdom in regard to the management of affairs. It would have been discourteous and heartless to reject proffered kindness and counsel, and yet it would be against conscience to suppress or deny anti-slavery conviction. What was to be done? The authority of Andover and New Haven, and all the churches at the East, and Lane Seminary at the West, were the crushing response to all suggestions of reason and right. It was vain to say that Andover was silent on the subject of masonry until the anti-masonic sentiment prevailed during the first discussions in New England; and

then its teachers bravely came in after the struggle
was over. That the temperance reform received
no aid till it needed none; and then an Andover
professor wrote ultra articles under the influence
of a narcotic stimulant refusing church fellowship
to any one who used ardent spirits. Andover de-
fended slavery from the Bible; so did the Colleges
and Theological Seminaries generally. The Methodist churches repudiated the sentiments of Wesley
and hugged the sin. Oberlin was just in the tran-
sition state, and after a struggle in the Board of
Trustees adopted the anti-slavery principles by
only a single vote. Everything seemed against
those who maintained the truth. But the few anti-
slavery men had confidence in the cause and in the
God of justice. They stood for right and liberty.
Lost some friends and gained a spirit of prayer
with courage and a good conscience.

When it was made manifest that my paper was
committing itself to anti-slavery principles the college authorities became alienated and averse; and
the presbytery, which included all the Congregational churches of the region were mostly alienated.
These were mostly good men, and they had power
to do the paper much damage. The agent for the
Foreign Mission Board, who visited all the churches
and was the most active of the college trustees,
did much to hinder the circulation of the paper. I
threatened retaliatory measures and proposed to
denounce all societies and agents that made active
efforts to injure the paper. There were men enough

in the churches who had embraced the truth to give effect to anything the paper might say in its own behalf. After a year of quiet struggle on both sides—during which the paper through the faithful labors of a devoted man who acted as field agent, continually gained ground,—a final and wicked device was conceived to get the control of the publication. The paper was originated at Cleveland by Harmon Kingsbury, Esq., one of the Trustees of the college, who had sold the good-will of the establishment with the type and subscription list to Rev. Mr. Stone, who had removed it to Hudson. The press upon which the paper was printed he had donated to the college, and rent was paid annually to the trustees for its use. The scheme was to claim the whole establishment on the plea that the ownership of the press included all the rest; and it was not purposed to repay me for my purchase nor for the material in the office. Strange as it may seem this dishonest trick was favored by all but one of the College Executive Committee. Mr. Kingsbury was absent at the time. I was willing to appeal to him in a joint letter for his construction of the case. But while the negotiation was pending a letter was sent to him without my knowledge, by the President of the college, (with the counsel⁻ undoubtedly of others,) adapted to draw from Mr. Kingsbury an answer that would favor the attempted fraud. Providence interfered to defeat the evil scheme. Mr. K. was detained at Syracuse some time. His letters were to be directed

to New York. When I learned that I was betrayed
in regard to the joint letter, I wrote immediately,
directing my letter as they had done, to New York
city. The detention of Mr. K. prevented his getting their letter before mine arrived. The good
man, who was an anti-slavery man, understood the
scheme and denounced it—stating to them and me
that their claim was invalid. Thus ended the first
chapter of the effort to get the paper back from the
righteousness of anti-slavery sentiments. The
effort, however, cost me anxiety and trouble, as
lawyers were consulted and a suit would have been
instituted, provided they had obtained by misrep-
resentation, an answer from Mr. K. favorable to
their claims.

Having failed in utterly improper schemes to obtain control of the paper, after a time propositions
were made to purchase the office, and as I had
grown weary of contention, and had little fear that
the anti-slavery sentiment could be set back by any
effort, I proposed terms which they immediately
accepted, and the paper was transferred to a gentleman whom the college men and presbytery had
selected as the best man to manage the publication,
which was a more powerful instrument in forming
public opinion in the churches of that early day
than it would be at the present time.

They did not have the paper a week before a sad
mishap befel the press upon which it was printed,
and with which they endeavored to obtain all the
little property I possessed. A prominent man in

the place had seduced his neighbor's wife, and a communication was admitted and published in the paper denouncing the act and printing the name of the lawyer who was the guilty party. This was published in the closing issue of my paper, although the contract had been closed and the transfer made. The irritated culprit threatened vengeance on all parties, and learning that he was seeking me with a cowhide, I learned at the same time I had no desire for a meeting.

The purchasing party were probably not aware of the difficulty which would meet them on endeavoring to make a conservative out of a reform newspaper. The soul knows what justice is, and in those who approve and those who resist, truth creates conscience. Those who resist are irritated, and those who obey grow strong within themselves. Hence, to repudiate the anti-slavery sentiment would cause a loss of subscribers. To maintain it would irritate the other party. It became, therefore, a mere go-between, manifesting neither conscience nor courage. We do not thus speak because we think conservative men are always bad men. Some of them are among the best men in the churches. But God constantly brings up moral principles to try us. Some men fear public sentiment or some other earthly thing; they close their eyes when the light shines, and cease to grow in grace; and often resist truth until they experience the divine displeasure in some form—not knowing oftentimes the cause of the adverse providence that strikes them.

It was so with the men of the paper and college. The newspaper was removed to Cleveland, but it failed to receive the patronage hoped for. It came back to Hudson, but succeeded no better. It lived a struggling and dying life for a number of years, when its subscribers were transferred to a religious paper which had originated in Cincinnati.

The college, largely endowed by self-denying men, has had but few students for many years. Its professors and Board of Trustees quarreled and damaged each other. At the present day it is rich, but still its influence limited. The money paid by Arthur Tappan in the beginning, and the large sums procured from industrious farmers by agents, are expended to support a cultured and easy-living class of christian teachers. Its pupils are few. Its societies are secret societies,—and its influence for the cause of Christ others may estimate.

After the sale of my paper I invested my money in western lands and devoted myself for a short time to the study of theology, and was licensed by a committee of the Presbytery to preach the gospel. The examination was held at my own residence; when the vote was taken two of the college trustees left the room, and the members of the Presbytery remained and voted me a license to preach the ever-lasting gospel of the Son of God. When the question of the Presbyterian Confession of Faith were propounded—whether I accepted the Confession of Faith as containing in substance the doctrines of the Bible, I answered that I did, interpreting it by

the Scripture quotations written under the articles.
The answer was new, but it was accepted at the
time ; and subsequently, when I was ordained by
the same presbytery, no objection was made to the
same form of answer.   So, subordinating human
tradition to the New Testament, I entered with a
good conscience upon my labor in the churches.

CHAPTER XIII.

FIRST PASTORATE AND PROFESSORSHIP.

We commenced labor in the church of Akron, with a spirit of simple devotion to the work which we do not now possess. The reason of the gospel is clearer now. We see that the fundamental principles of faith in Christ's life as a rule of duty, and in his death as a source of love, is true as a necessary condition of righteousness, benevolence and purity in men. But we think with less conviction from reason as to the necessity, the principles of the gospel and the benevolence and wisdom of the great plan of Jesus—the faith in the facts which we felt then was more efficient upon our heart and conscience than the clearer intellectual conviction of the facts which we see now. We think, however, that Christ as the manifested God is more to us now than formerly.

Our devotion to our work in those first years we think was sincere and active. An immense gathering to hear and see a presidential candidate in the village did not take us out of our study. We made efforts to instruct the people and awaken a religious

interest. We had heard Professor Wright lecture
on Geology; we had read on that subject what
books we could obtain, and in order to get the ear
of the people of the town, we delivered in a public
hall a course of lectures on the subject—making
maps and gathering knowledge as we proceeded in
the course. The people gave us credit for more
knowledge than we possessed; but we were better
informed on the subject than any of the hearers,
and hence our presentation of the facts of the new
science as then understood was a success and benefit. It awakened a spirit of literary interest in
the place, and gathered some additional hearers
into the church on the Sabbath.

Religious inquiry was soon awakened, and such a
state of things ensued that those opposed to the
religious life, as urged by the pastor, formed a new
society and invited a Universalist minister who
commenced service in the town hall. At the close
of a sermon, this gentleman being present, arose
and asked the privilege to give notice that he would
refute at his place of preaching the doctrine of
future punishment, which I had argued as a natural
effect of sinful character. Universalism did not
succeed. Its adherents built a fine stone church,
which subsequently passed into the hands of the
Baptists. But religious inquiry did succeed, and a
revival of religion in which I had the aid of Pres't
Mahan, then of Oberlin, was the means of gathering a large number of persons into the communion
of the church. The two first converts were two

lawyers of the village—one of them mayor of the town. Their conversion surprised me and all other citizens who knew them. One of them, Mr. S., I have lost trace of; the other, Judge B., still resides in the place—an exemplary christian man, as I suppose. A second ingathering filled our little house, most of the congregation now being professors of religion.

I now felt that my work was done in that field; and desiring to write and publish what I had written on the Plan of Salvation. Having an opportunity to consult Professor Storrs, of Lane Seminary, who spent a Sabbath at Akron, I asked a dismissal from the church, and removed my family to Cincinnati, with the purpose of prosecuting my plan of publishing my first volume.

Before I left the church—just at the time I supposed it had reached a high degree of prosperity and usefulness—a vision of the night perplexed and troubled me. I record it because it was among some of my most vivid mental experiences. One night in deep sleep I saw a stone church standing on the site of the church where I labored. Its foundation story seemed natural and firm, but another story seemed to be added upon the old structure. The stones were loosely laid together—and its top seemed open and enveloped in a cloud. It was firm below—but dilapidated and unsubstantial above. The dream affected me. It seemed to me to indicate future evil to the church; and yet I remember distinctly that I thought such an issue most unlikely—and set down shortly the impression I received as owing to some cause which indicated nothing in regard to the future.

But if there was no indication in the dream, the future history of the church filled the requirement of just such foreshadowing. After an absence from Akron of about two years, having visited the church but once in that period—I returned on the day previous to the one upon which the Millerites had predicted the end of the world. After I left the people they chose for their pastor an eccentric man whose name was Pickens. A man of talents and peculiarities. He embraced the theories of Mr. Miller—and some of the most influential members of the church, and some apparently the most devoted, embraced the same views, and looked for the end of the world the following day. The Adventists from the region around had assembled in convention in my old church, and Mr. Fitch, of Cleveland—a man of reputation and sincere piety was preaching to the people in convention assembled. His text was a passage of the Psalms: "O Lord destroy the wicked out of the earth." He taught the people that the succeeding day—or certainly in the immediate future, Christ would come and destroy the wicked and glorify His saints.

I sat until the close of the discourse, and then asked the privilege of addressing the people. I had come a long distance to save some of my old church if possible from the delusion in which they were involved. The convention would not hear my remarks; and the most affecting incident was, that my old friends, who had become Adventists, desired that I should not speak.

I failed in the public effort. I then called on Mr. Pickands, and sat at tea with him and Mr. Fitch and others, expecting the immediate appearance of Christ. They seemed sober and collected, and talked of the immediate advent as a reality; and replied to no inquiry or conversation on the great fatuity that filled their minds.

Mr. Pickands' child was sick unto death, but he left home to preach the advent in Canton, where he declared his purpose to be found preaching when Christ should appear. The next day, although a message was sent to him that his child was dying, he refused to return, but continued, as I was informed, most of the night in the pulpit preaching and waiting the advent of the Redeemer.

The world went on as usual. Mr. Pickands returned home. But he and a part of the church were demoralized. One portion separated from the other. The steadfast men and women built a new house in another part of the city. The Adventists, with the exception of a few persons who were restored to the common faith, lost faith in revelation, or they adopted some evil tenets that led them farther into evil.

Another singular episode occurred during my ministry at Akron. While agent for the Bible Society I became acquainted with several gentlemen who were engaged in founding a new college a

short distance from Lawrenceburg, Indiana—a village about twenty miles below Cincinnati, on the
Ohio River. They were mostly of the Protestant
Methodist denomination, in connection with a few
Presbyterians, who took an active interest in the
new institution. A large farm had been purchased
and a college building erected on the hills about a
mile from the village; and after I had labored about
six months at Akron, the agent of the Board of
Trustees presented me with an appointment as professor, and urged my immediate acceptance, as all
things were ready to commence operations, and the
president, Dr. Snethen, was already on the ground.
Influenced I fear by the desire for literary distinc-
tion, and the desire to publish my views on certain
subjects, I accepted the call—and against the prot-
estations of my people, I left them to enter upon
the duties of an instructor, for which I was in no
wise qualified. In the departments of Philosophy
or Belles-Lettres I might have been qualified for
duty; but, although the first Professor of language
at Oberlin was not a graduate,—a professor who
was scarcely prepared to enter college, would have
had hard work to learn what he needed to teach.
Notwithstanding all this I accepted, not doubting
from past experience but that I could keep in advance of the first students. But God did not favor
my project, and from the time I left Akron until
the time I got back again, I passed under the rod,
and the infliction was felt at every turn of affairs.

Myself, wife and sister started on a canal packet

for the Ohio River. It rained incessantly, and we found the canal broken near Chillicothe, and had a detention and a difficulty in getting round the gap. When we reached Portsmouth the river was flooded and the canal boats could not form connection with the boats on the river. After transhipment and long labor we passed Portsmouth, and took passage on a steamer to be landed at Lawrenceburg.

We reached the place in the night,—the river at high flood, and were set off by the steamer's yawl on what we supposed to be the main land below the town. The yawl returned and the boat steamed on, and we started to reach the town which was in sight. But to our surprise and the alarm of the women we found ourselves landed on a small island, or rather on a strip of land that the rising waters has surrounded and isolated from the main shore. There was no hope of extrication for us until morning, unless we could make our voices heard by some one who might bring us a boat from the main land. Add to this that the land was wet and the water of the river rising, and the night dark; and, although there was no immediate danger, the situation was not a pleasant one.

By loud calls long continued, we succeeded in arousing some one who brought a small boat from the main shore, and by whose aid we and our baggage were conveyed to the hotel, where rest and refreshments restored comfort of body and equilibrium of mind.

On the succeeding Sabbath we heard Henry Ward

Beecher preach his first sermon to a little Presbyterian church in Lawrenceburg. The church consisted, we believe, of about twelve female and two
male members. The young preacher held in his
hand during his discourse a small testament, and
preached an extempore sermon against the doctrine of Universalism. That afternoon he took tea
at the principal physician's of the village ; and we
remember forming a judgment from the manner of
his preaching and his easy social manner that popularity rather than power would characterize his
ministry. His history has proved that our estimate
was less than the measure of the man. Without
affirming for him the logical faculty in large measure—or an ability for accuracy beyond others in
analysis of any subject—it yet is probably true that
as an extempore preacher he is the first in the
world ; as much superior to Mr. Spurgeon as the
length and breadth of our country is superior to
that of Great Britain.

I never met with Mr. Beecher to have any personal talk with him but once subsequently. I had
for two or three years contemplated publishing a
hymn and tune book which I supposed was needed
to meet the wants of the western churches. I
had corresponded with Prof. Allen, of Oberlin, and
others East and West on the subject. But before
my material was prepared, the prospectus of Mr.
Beecher's book appeared, which promised to accomplish the plan of my collection so much better than
my own that I abandoned my work and called to

make some suggestion to him concerning what I supposed to be the wants of the new churches at the West in regard to Psalmody. I accepted his views on all subjects, except the size of the volume, which I would have had smaller by one-third, omitting the common place hymns and much inferior music; and in phraseology I thought the titles of endearment appropriate to demonstrative affection should not be used in application to Christ. The words blessed, gracious, merciful, and others which had no technical application to earthly love of equals, I thought should be, in all cases, substituted for such phrases, "my love," "the bosom of my God," "the arms of his love," and such like phrases. Mr. Beecher, as I understood him, was decidedly opposed to my views on the subject, and thought all phrases of domestic endearment, and appellations of human affection highly appropriate.

But to return to my first professorship. I found the affairs of the new college in quite a different condition from what I expected. There were no funds that could be relied on. The first building was not yet finished. It was expected that I would be a man of all work in teaching the first classes, and added to all this there were no first classes to teach. Some dozen of pupils were pledged and expected at the institution so soon as it was opened; but after a sojourn of a few weeks the prospects of the enterprise seemed to me so doubtful that I concluded to retire, and return to Akron, where my correspondents assured me the people were praying and hoping that Providence would send me back. Some weeks after I left, the college building was burned down and the enterprise abandoned.

Thus far everything in our journey had been disastrous and discomfiting. We procured a horse and conveyance and started for Cincinnati, on our return home. There had been another spring storm, and the little Miama was swollen to a flood. A man who had crossed with a heavy wagon told us he thought we could safely drive over the usual ford of the river. We ventured into the drifting water. It rose into the bed of our carriage, and the wheels floated in the stream. By an energetic movement of the horse we reached the other side in safety, grateful that we all escaped drowning.

By this time I had realized that my ways in the matter of the professorship were not God's ways. I began like Moses, when God met him at the inn, to fear that God would kill me before I got home ; and this sense of my danger and Divine displeasure was increased by another incident, which occurred in the afternoon when we were about seven miles from the city. Dark clouds had been gathering for some hours in the south-western horizon, and the heavy peals of thunder and swift drifting clouds indicated a storm at hand. We might have stopped before the storm struck us, but we drove on hoping to reach a more comfortable shelter; but no shelter offered in season, and one of those heavy thunder and hail storms which sometimes occur at the West, found us on the road some distance from a house. The din of the storm, and the hail stones falling in large size frightened the horse, and he ran at the top of his speed until he reached the first house by the roadside, when I succeeded in bringing him up by the fenceside, without overturning the vehicle. The women were able to get out and find shelter in the house. I had to stand in the storm and hold the horse, who was acting frantically, until the fury of the storm had subsided.

It was now getting late in the day. We had no time to dry our wet garments—my own especially thoroughly dripping with water—and in such plight we reached Cincinnati. The passage that the Lord met Moses at the inn and sought to kill him seemed verified in my experience, and I think I promised faithfully, that if God would forgive me for my folly, and not kill me while thus estray by the way, I would go home to my people, and make all literary ambition and personal desire subservient to the great aim of preaching the gospel, and personal labor for the upbuilding of Christ's kingdom.

We arrived at Akron in safety. A minister—a venerable brother yet living in the state had been engaged to preach for the church. He retired and I assumed again my labor, which continued through two years, at which time we removed to Cincinnati as before stated.

CHAPTER XIV.

AUTHOR AND PREACHER.

Having reached Cincinnati, we tarried for a few weeks, while I carefully examined the library at Lane Seminary to see whether the course of thought in my proposed volume had been anticipated by previous writers. The library had been purchased in Europe, by Prof. Stowe, and was full on all subjects of theological import. I likewise read some of the chapters of the MSS. to Doctor Beecher and his daughter, Catharine, then regarded as the literary Cynosure of the family. The doctor spoke words of encouragement. Catharine wisely suggested that books were not immediately successful in accordance with their value—that some of the most ephemeral, if introduced by a popular name, would succeed immediately, while books of substantial value, with an unknown name, would fail. I determined to revise and publish my book anonymously.

While engaged in the labor of reconsidering and re-writing I proposed to preach the gospel in some neighboring destitute church, and with this object in view I visited a little church on the Ohio river,

about twenty miles above the city. To this I retired with my wife and began work. Gospel ordinances had been suspended for some time; and
the few believers that remained had little hope that
their fallen tabernacle would ever be raised again.
But there were two or three of Christ's faithful ones
who sighed and prayed over the desolation of Zion.
One old man, whose wife was deaf, and who seemed
to be possessed with a spirit of prophecy, had just
before our unexpected arrival, invited his next
neighbor and some others of the little company of
believers, and assured them in words that seemed
the impulses of enthusiasm, that he was sure spiritual good was in store for them, and that the time
was just at hand. In the midst of this night, and
before the predicted morning had dawned, God in
His gracious dispensation sent us to New Richmond.

I arrived at the house of the elder, and on the
following Sabbath preached to them the gospel of
the grace of God. They were few and poor;—they
could give my wife and myself our boarding, but no
more. We concluded not to ask money from the
Missionary Society; but with the aid of a little
money earned by wife as teacher of a select school
in the village, and a little which I possessed, we
proposed to live with them and labor for them one
year, during which time I designed to finish writing
my book, while at the same time I devoted myself
to the spiritual good of the people.

On the first Sabbath but few of the seats were
occupied, but from that day thenceforth the congre-

gation gradually increased. The Methodist people had a class and a few good people; but the minister who visited them once in two weeks seemed to me to have little spiritual apprehension of the value of the gospel. In the evening I went in to hear him, and to some young girls who were whispering and unquiet in one corner of the church he cried out amid his rambling words—"I see you girls over there in the corner, turning up your eyes like a duck in a thunder storm." I retired, I hope, feeling some sense of the spiritual wants of the people of the town. The Baptists had previously had an organization, but it had been abandoned. The Unitarians had a good church building, but had no service, and expected none. Skepticism prevailed, and respect for religious services, except in the minds of the few whose faith had not failed, scarcely existed.

Some little knowledge of law and business, more than the little I knew of what is called systematic theology, aided me to get the attention of a portion of the people, and the number of attendants and the interest, especially in our afternoon prayer-meeting, continued to increase. Interest was soon apparent on the Sabbath in the fixed attention of some persons, and in their acceptance of the invitation to attend the afternoon prayer-meeting. The few faithful ones were wakeful and prayerful; and there were such indications that I appointed preaching every night for a week.

In this first season of religious interest a number of the church were renewed in the spirit of their

mind, and some of the leading young men of the
town were converted. There were three young
men, companions, in the village who were the most
influential—one of them a merchant, who was professedly a Universalist. The Sabbath after our
series of meetings began I preached from the text,
"he that believeth shall be saved." He was awakened and soon accepted the truth—became obedient
to Christ, and immediately was absent from town.
It was not known where he had gone; but he soon
returned with his aged mother, who soon rejoiced
with him in his new birth.

The effect of this interest awakened attention in
the community and revived the church. But we
had as yet no lamps for evening service; and the
Sabbath-school, which had almost ceased to exist,
was augmented in numbers, but with no regular
distribution of books or papers. Our singing was
led by a faithful old elder who could lead in but
three kinds of metre—long, common and short—
and who never attempted a greater variety than
two tunes for each metre. The congregation, old
and young, followed with good will, but not often
in good time or tone. And yet I am sure that this
service of song was more acceptable to God, and
did the souls of the people more good, than the
wicked exhibitions of organ and quartette in fashionable churches, which perform for the congregation, who often "know not what is piped or sung."

As the winter was coming in, it was thought
a good time to make an effort to increase our

facilities for all purposes; and to aid in the effort all
the people gave a little as God had prospered them.
We obtained lamps for evening worship. Bought
a new Sabbath-school library. Made a new confession and covenant for the church, and procured
a young man from Oberlin—now Rev. Mr. Edwards,
of Ohio—to teach a common school during the day,
and a singing school in the evening. The common
school did much for the rising youth of the town,
and the singing school did a great deal for the
churches, and in meliorating the manners of the
youth of both sexes, most of whom were yet un-
reconciled to the will of Christ.

The teacher was faithful as a christian; and
through him the young people learned to respect
religion, and were drawn into attendance upon the
services of the Sabbath. The religious people during the winter were humble and prayerful. Some
persons who had dishonored their Lord, publicly
confessed their sins—and confessed personally to
those who had been stumbled by their offences,
both in the church and out. These confessions did
good to the penitent and impenitent. The world
knows what christians ought to be, and when they
confess their sins, and reform their lives, many recognize this as the effect of the gospel on their
hearts; so that religion, instead of being disparaged
by the lives of worldly professors, has the honor of
their reform. These confessions, therefore, honored
the gospel; benefited those who acknowledged
their wrong-doing; removed stumbling-blocks, and

prepared the way for a further work of grace in the spring. The spring had scarcely opened when a revival of great interest began in the church, and for a series of weeks there was preaching on the Sabbath and at least two other evenings in the week. One evening was occupied by a conference and prayer-meeting, where were heard inspiring words from those who had recently believed, as also from christians who had made new attainments in holiness. During these meetings I procured aid from the city and seminary, as was needful. Rev. J. Blanchard, of the city, afterwards president of Knox College; Mr. R. W. Patterson, of the seminary—now Dr. Patterson, of Chicago—and Rev. Mr. Benton, of College Hill; and occasionally others spent a day or two in "the work at Richmond." Some incidents peculiar and striking will be mentioned at the close of the chapter.

Before the extra meetings were closed a choir was formed, mostly from the converts, who had been receiving instruction in vocal music. They sat in the two front pews, and the way in which they sung the songs of Zion, gave an impulse sweet and deep to the work, which often accomplished more than a sermon. What a mockery of God and a murder of devotion it is to introduce music that is harmony without melody, and sound without sense into assemblies that have professedly met to worship God. As in sentiment, so in worship. It is the sense of the song, set to a melody—a *familiar* melody—that aids to awaken answering emotions in the heart—

> What warm tears dim the eyes unshed;
> What wild vows falter on the tongue
> When "Scots wha' ha' with Wallace bled,"
> Or "Auld Lang Syne" is sung.

So it is—only with purifying instead of patriotic fervor,

> When Jesus who for sinners bled
> On Calvary, is sung—

One of the familiar hymns of the new converts I printed on the cover of the brief church confession, and it was sung with absorbing pathos, and sung so frequently that every one soon knew the hymn and joined in the service of song.

The special interest continued, with, little addition to the usual preaching service, except, perhaps, an additional sermon each week until near the close of summer. So large a proportion of the young people had been converted, and the reform in the town had been so general, that all the churches of the different denominations were revived, and those which had ceased to exist were reorganized, except the Unitarian, which included a good part of the wealth and intelligence in the region. At a revival subsequently most of the Unitarians believed in Jesus as God manifest in Christ, and united with us in the Presbyterian church.

The Methodist church was greatly strengthened in numbers and in faith; a Protestant Methodist, which had ceased to exist, was reorganized; the Baptist people became active and increased in number, and commenced regular worship in the Unitarian house; the Campbellites formed a society, and the congregations, especially the Presbyterian, Methodist and Baptist, were well sustained.

During all this time in New Richmond I had done but little work on my book. In addition to the labor in the town I had visited during the week, and sometimes on the Sabbath, a little church six miles distant, called the Scotch Settlement. Here, also, a revival had existed for some time, gathering in many of the unconverted families in the region. The two interests sympathized with each other, and I felt that my work was finished when the churches strengthened and instructed had grown to the full stature that could reasonably be hoped for at that time. I felt also that a man who could devote his time to pastoral labor, in which I always had failed, (although I had not failed to speak famil- iarly on religious subjects to every one at suitable times and places,) would do the work now needed better than I could. This was my sincere convic- tion, and I stated it to the people. There was no one that looked at the matter as I did, and parting with those who felt constrained to come and re- monstrate with me, especially the older people who always left me with tears and regrets, on this and a subsequent occasion, was one of the most trying incidents of my experience in New Richmond.

INCIDENTS OF THE RELIGIOUS INTEREST AT RICHMOND.

Going early to the afternoon prayer-meeting one Sabbath, before the people had assembled, (as I sometimes did,) I heard upon entering the door, an earnest—almost an excited talk among four old men who were in the habit of tarrying in the church during the interval between the morning service and the afternoon prayer-meeting. They were the oldest members of the church—so aged that it was pleasanter for them to remain in the sanctuary and converse of Scripture themes, than to walk to their homes and return.

As I approached the pulpit near which they were sitting together in a corner pew, the talk became lower, but the faces of all looked earnest and beaming, and it seemed as though the eyes of one at least, was still wet with tears. They seemed to have had an affecting disputation; but I found it was a disputation of an uncommon spirit. They appealed to me, and told me the subject of their difference:—Each one of the old men was sure that the grace of Christ in pardoning him as a sinner was more rich and conspicuous than in that of the others. They had been reciting the greatness of their unworthiness and the interpositions of Providence in their behalf, and each honestly felt that the mercy of Christ to them was the greatest. I could determine the question in no other way than that the truth was just what they felt it to be. It was the greatest in each case. The decision would have perplexed an angel; but I doubt whether any other would have satisfied them so well.

THE WICKEDEST MAN.

There were three men in the village, an old man

of seventy years and a young man of about twenty-
five, who were considered the wickedest men in
town. Father Emmerson, as he was afterwards
called, was professedly an Atheist. He was a man
of some means; was an invalid who had left his
house seldom for years; he was bowed together so
that "he could not lift up himself." He was quar-
relsome, profane, and terribly wicked in spirit.
Sometimes, in periods of anger, not being able to
wreak his vengeance on those whom he hated, he
would get his daughter's Bible, and blaspheme and
stamp upon it. The old man lived with his daughter, whose husband was a man of religious life,—
professing to have continually a sense of the presence and love of Christ. After the meetings had
progressed for some time—during the second period
of interest—the old invalid expressed a willingness
to "go and see." Accordingly he surprised every
body, by making his way to the church through a
back street, and appearing in a seat near the pulpit.
He continued to attend, and soon appeared at the
evening service when, as was usual in those days,
persons desiring special prayer and instruction,
came at the close of the service to the front seats,
as inquirers for the way of life. One night, after a
number had gone forward, I saw the old invalid
struggle to get up, but apparently unable in his
decrepit condition. I went to the pew before him
and gave him my hand when he seemed to rise
with almost superhuman agility, and walked over
the tops of two or three pews to the seats, where

those inquiring—"What must I do to be saved?"
were seated. From this time the old man attended
prayers in his son-in-law's family, and gradually all
things seemed to become new to him. Old things
had really passed away, and he was renewed not
only in mind but in body. Instead of being de-
crepid and bowed down, he became straight and
active for a man of his years. His pains and evil
passions left him at the same time. The healing
of the body seemed more strange to many than the
healing of the mind. Dr. Muzzy, the leading physician of the city, heard of the case and examined
into the facts as a case of the influence of the mind
upon the body.

The old man knew nothing of the Bible, and I
do not know that he had any example of christianity as he practiced it; but the first thing he did
after he awoke to the new life, was to go to a man
whom he had considered his enemy, and invite
him to church; and, as the man was poor—mostly
on account of a habit of occasional intoxication, he
proposed to aid in "fixing up" the family—children
and all, in order that they might attend church.
This he accordingly did. The children were naturally interesting, and soon appeared in school, and
the eldest daughter was subsequently the leader on
the ladies' side of the choir.

The old man united with the church, being baptized when almost seventy years of age, with many
others of the age of seventeen and upwards. He
prayed and uttered his pious thoughts in the lan-

guage of an alien; but he grew in knowledge; and his life, without any knowledge of the Bible, was better than those who know better than he what Christ required. He began immediately to labor for the conversion of others. He confessed his sin and made reparation in all cases where he thought he had injured others. He had been miserly in his latter years, but he gave of his means not largely but in fair proportion for gospel purposes. He had an experience that whenever he heard a passage of the Bible read that coincided therewith, he judged, as the best christian can do, the Bible by his own experience. Hearing the passage read—"I will take away the hard and stony heart and give you a heart of flesh"—he said, "that's true—it's a fact—I know it." He had been what is called a hard man. A son had died by violence. He had lost wife and children without shedding a tear or giving a sigh; but now the remembrance of those things visibly affected him. Without knowing any one else had ever done so, he made a list of about fifty persons of his old companions living in different places. For these he prayed, using other means as he had opportunity. As they were converted he erased their names on his list. It was said, which I hardly think credible, that all these men were converted. I know many of them were. But there was at least one very bad man in the town who was not con- verted, but who was suddenly killed by an accident in the street. The old man said he had gained much of his property by improper means, and it

would be right if he should lose it. This came to
pass by wrong doing of others; and he died a poor
man, faithful to the last, but dependent in his last
years upon others.

One of the other wickedest men was a young
man, Dave Putnam, of twenty-two or twenty-three
years. He was indolent, repulsive in manners and
apparel, and horribly profane. He was the only
son of parents that had fallen to the bottom of social life—utterly careless in habits and neglected
by all their neighbors. Nobody went into their
house except for some necessary business. I was
in once, the only time I ever saw the old woman.
Originally they were from New England, as was
Father Emmerson; but when people of good antecedents lose caste, and self respect and ambition,
they are likely to become more abject than others.
This wicked young man was converted. His father
and mother, who had once been professors of religion, were made aware of their debasement by the
new light which shone around them — and now
shone into their poor dwelling. There was improvement in habit, in house, and I hope in heart. David
maintained a reformed life for years. He subsequently married, and I have now no knowledge of
his later life. If he still perseveres in the new life,
the transformation of these two wickedest men was
miraculous. The other wickedest man never attended church, but opposed and blasphemed. He
was killed by an accident some years afterwards.

The man in the village to whom father Emmerson

had gone first to confess his sin and make reparation, and whose intemperate habits had kept
his family of interesting children in ignorance and
poverty, soon began to attend meeting.   At a conference meeting one afternoon, Rev. Mr. Benton, of
College Hill, near Cincinnati, was aiding in the
service.   He stood on the floor before the pulpit,
and was reading the twenty-fifth Psalm, when he
read the eleventh verse—"For thy name's sake, O
Lord, pardon mine iniquity; for it is great."   Mr.
————, who sat near the door, jumped to his feet
apparently under excitement.   He walked up the
aisle without apparently seeing any one, and stood
immediately before Mr. Benton, who was so non-
plused by the movement and the appearance of the
man that he ceased to read.   Mr. Benton looked at
me and I gave an indication that there was no danger.   He asked, "·what do you want read?"   The
man said—"Does that say that the man was pardoned because his iniquity was great?"   Benton
replied, "Yes, the psalmist prayed to be pardoned
because his iniquity was great."   "Pardoned because he had been a great sinner?" he replied.
"Well, yes; because he felt he had been a great
sinner."   The man replied loudly—"That's me—
I'm the man—does God pardon any one because
he has been a *great* sinner?"   "Yes; if they feel
and confess their sins."   "I do; I'm the man—am
I pardoned?"   I believe Mr. Benton made no further reply, and the man apparently overcome by
his emotion sat down.   The scene produced some

sensation; and there was prayer and singing—
some wet eyes and but few words, except those by
the leader of the meeting.

From that hour Mr. —————— was a changed man.
He worshiped God with all his house, some of his
children being already children of God by a new
birth. He was a reformed man in all respects. He
was never known to taste liquor again but once in
the city, at the solicitation of a friend. He was an
equable, peaceful and devout christian. Twenty
years after, when I saw him, he said he had never
known a day since his new birth that was not a
happy day. His children were among the respectable residents of the town; his son a faithful christian man, being postmaster in the place.

There was a colored family in the place; the
father, Lewis O'Banyan, being lame, intemperate
and cruel in his family. His wife bearing perpetual
abuse, and yet by her labor providing food for the
family. This man had his curiosity excited by the
general movement in the town. He did not go into
the church, but he frequently stood outside at the
window and heard the services inside. After some
weeks it began to be said that black Lewis had
stopped drinking and abusing his family. Little,
however, was thought of the matter, until the fact
of his industry and quietness and temperance became apparent to every one. Then some of the
christian people — myself perhaps — went to his
house, to inquire of his wife and himself concerning
the change of habits. All and more than had been

told concerning the change was confirmed. He
did not profess to be converted. He did not know.
He only knew "he did not feel as he used to;" he
hated his old habits; had no desire for whisky, and
felt happier on the Sabbath. After a long season,
during which he now attended church and sat near
the door, his life was so obviously a christian's life
that he and his wife became members of the church.
His children were clothed and in school, and all
things had become new both temporally and spiritually with the O'Banyan's. Lewis soon came from
the door and sat in a pew near the pulpit. He assumed the duties of sexton, and was faithful till
he died.

There was a large distillery in the place—one of
those immense establishments which produced
whisky by the hundreds of barrels. The clerk in
this manufactory of fire water, was an educated
Irishman, who was, in Belfast, a member of a Presbyterian church. He was a young man, and one
of the best specimens of an Irish gentlemen I had
ever met. He became, with others, a member
of our church under protest that his aid in such
business was wrong. All the christian reforms—
anti-slavery, temperance, Sabbath observance, anti-
masonry—were duly noticed and advocated in the
pulpit, as fitting occasion occurred to refer to them.
This gentleman left his place contrary to the wishes
of the owner, Mr. Atkinson. After a short time,
perhaps by continued solicitation, he returned feeling that he was too fastidious about the matter, as

he had no personal interest in the profits of the distillery. After a few weeks, however, his conscience
triumphed a second time, and he left the distillery
and purchased a farm on the Kentucky side of the
river, where, I have no doubt, God prospered him
as a conscientious christian man. There were
coopers in the place belonging both to the Presbyterian and Baptist churches. They refused to make
barrels for the distillery; took them by boat to the
city and sold them for what they could have had at
home.

Those who purposed to observe the Sabbath had
more difficulty, and failed—one of them at least—
after much expense and loss of time to obtain for
himself a day of rest. He was a river engineer,
and was receiving good wages. He left his boat
rather than labor on the Sabbath. He hoped to
get a birth on some packet that lay by on the
Lord's day, but failed to do so. For some months
he was out of employ, and his good christian wife,
who had been awakened to new life, sustained her
husband and herself by her needle. They however concluded, after self-denying effort, that Sabbath rest for the engineer could not be obtained,
and he took a place again on a boat with the purpose of so observing the day on the boat that,
although engaged in labor, his comrades would recognize him as reverencing the Sabbath day. Years
afterwards I saw one of the coopers, who was glad
he had made no barrels for the distillery.

The distillery was, by a providential accident,

destroyed by fire, and its owner failed in business. One man had prayed that a certain distillery might be burned down, (a prayer of very doubtful propriety,) and when the accident that fulfilled his desire occurred, he was somewhat startled and alarmed as though he might have had some personal connection with the disaster.

In the vicinity of New Richmond, at a distance of six miles, there was a little Presbyterian church, called the Scotch settlement. To this place I went usually once each week, and sometimes in the summer on Sabbath afternoons. A spiritual refreshing was vouchsafed to them, and most of those in the neighborhood who were not identified with other congregations united with the Presbyterians. Years afterwards, when those who were then children were settled in life, I met with some of them who remembered the days of other years. One old English gentleman, who was a man of very passionate temper, I met in his infirm age when he was quite deaf. He had fought a good fight against his propensity to passion, and had kept the faith that he professed with trembling.

One sad incident occurred during the year. The son-in-law of old Mr. Emmerson became insane and died. Insanity was hereditary in his family; and the religious interest he felt excited him. This, probably, occasioned an attack of the family malady. Great care had been taken in the Presbyterian church to prevent the interest becoming an excitement. The meetings were closed after an

hour and a half—sometimes sooner. Nothing was
permitted to prolong them. The people were advised to take their usual sleep. A meeting held in
the city by an evangelist, who prolonged his services sometimes from two to three hours, with protracted conference meetings every afternoon, had
occasioned brain fever in several cases, and the
death of at least two excellent men. Doing all we
could to promote "peace" of mind and body ; yet
nervous invalids would at times be unduly moved.
One lady, the wife of an excellent Baptist brother,
was the only one during all the time who interrupted the exercises by any nervous expression.
She spoke so excitedly, that the singers began a
sweet familiar hymn, when she gradually subsided
into peace. She had had nervous pains every day
for years. She was a member of our church ; but
her husband had created a doubt in her mind on
the subject of baptism, and her conscience was not
at rest. Every one was glad when she concluded
to be baptized by immersion in the Ohio. In connection with this baptism, the singular fact occurred, that the nervous pains (neuralgia, probably,)
that had afflicted her, especially in the night, ceased
from the moment of her immersion. Whether they
returned I do not know; but the healing at the time
was marked, and beneficent. The cold bath may
have had something to do with it—the relief of conscience may have had. The peace of mind from a
sense of duty done, may have had. A true faith
which works by love is better than medicine

oftentimes.   Of the two most nervous persons, excitement in one case produced evil, in the other
healing of soul and body.

During the time that I was editing 'and publishing my paper in the city, I spent a part of the time
on the Sabbath as minister of the Church at R.
The leading physician of the region, who was a
Unitarian, with some other men of like views attended the Presbyterian service.   The doctor's wife
is a faithful christian in word and deed.   One afternoon at conference meeting, unexpectedly to every
one, the doctor rose in the meeting and said words
of this import: His mind was not at rest;   if God
was in Christ, he wished to know it and feel it.   I
had preached Christ—not as God and man, but as
God in man.   Not as the second person of the trinity, but as God in his relations to the soul: That
He had power on earth to forgive sins.   "Christ in
the soul."   His omnipresence, as being with his
people "till end of the world;" and "where two
or three were gathered."   The true God revealed
only in Him.   No man knoweth the Father but
the Son, and he to whomsoever the Son will reveal
Him.   That the New Testament religion was to
believe in, love and obey God as revealed in Christ
—that God was in Christ, and Christ *is* in the Holy
Spirit.   The doctor believed; and not long after I
ordained him as an elder in the church.   He was
subsequently stumbled by the evil doings of ministers; but still hopes to be saved, and endeavors to
obey the Lord.   In connection with the interest

during which the doctor believed, many, but not all of the other Unitarians in the region accepted the gospel, and united with the churches. The remaining poor, likewise, came in; so that the little church contained the highest, as well as the lowest of the town, socially considered. One of the very poor was the wife of a blind wood sawyer, who had been a member of the Methodist church but was dropped for alleged immorality. Some of the alleged delinquences were, perhaps, too true. She attended church and professed to be a christian, but made no application for membership, and no effort to mingle socially with those by whom she had always been held as a pariah. Her life, however, was so exemplary that it was thought proper to speak with her of the duty and privilege which Christ offers to his people in church ordinances. When proposed as a member there were fears expressed of various kinds, but none of those fears were realized during my knowledge of affairs in the congregation.

When the work of conversion seemed to cease in some measure at least for want of material, those in the town being mostly members of some congregation ; and those not in attendance being more or less hopeless ; I thought it wise to endeavor to give some lectures, on literary and scientific subjects to increase the general culture of the people. They were a mixed multitude in the town from all parts of christendom, and most of them very deficient in general knowledge. I had a very imperfect knowledge myself of the things that I endeavored to teach, but I knew more of the subject matter than any one else that would lecture gratuitously, and with the assistance of books and maps I succeeded in interesting and profiting the people.

The time came, however, after I had spent some time with the church, (and my religious paper in Cincinnati was established and sold to Rev. E. Goodman, an excellent man who became my successor,) that believing my work in Richmond was completed—as did my brethren in the ministry,—I concluded to go and cultivate some other vacant field. Then came the only trial I had with the people. It may not be right for me to tell the story —but the old elders and members are still living, and some of them remember the scenes as vividly as I do myself.

When I had concluded to leave the city and the church at Richmond, my purpose was made known to the people. There was surprise and apparent sorrow, as they now were strong enough to give what would be moderate support to a minister. Some of the older people called personally to use their influence with me. The faithful ones who were there when I went to the village left weeping, and left me in a state of mind which I cannot describe. Then, by appointment, the elders called, when we had packed a part of our household goods. They talked earnestly and piously and soundly, and expressed their fear that I was resisting the will of God, and that some evil might come to me if I persisted. They were willing to take all the trouble of

unpacking my goods and to do anything I desired if
I would give up the plan. It was impossible for me
not to be affected by their solicitude, and I agreed
to refer the decision to my wife; but she refused to
take the responsibility. I then agreed to go on board
the packet with my goods, and if anything occurred
before I got to Portsmouth, I would return and
take my place again at Richmond. With sorrowful
faces we all aided to get the goods to the dock, and
we went on board the boat. I could not bid them
a courteous adieu individually, and they knew the
reason. I went into the boat, and the last man I
saw through the window as the boat left the wharf
was the colored man, poor Lewis O'Banyan, walking to and fro in a lot above the river. As the boat
passed he stopped and looked intently. I felt anxious to wave a farewell, but I did not venture out.
I really had some apprehension that I might be
fleeing from duty, as I had done once before; but
the boat landed us safely at Portsmouth, where we
took the canal packet for central Ohio, where a
ministering brother (Rev. Mr. Powell) had written
to me that a little church at Mansfield, which I had
aided to organize before I entered the ministry,
was destitute and somewhat desolate, and needed
a minister.

I went immediately to Marietta, where I preached
for a season to the oldest Congregational church
organized west of the Alleghanies; lectured in behalf of the Anti-Slavery cause to a small audience
in the church, where but two of the members were

willing to be present; aided to form a new Congregational church in Putnam on the opposite side of Muskingum river; and having received an invitation to establish a religious paper in Cincinnati, being urgently invited by a vote of the New School Synods of Ohio and Cincinnati, I considered it a call of Providence, and prepared to go to the city and accomplish the work if it could be done. I considered it a call of Providence, because I was sure such a paper ought to be established, and I was sure no one but myself could accomplish the object. I was a practical printer; had some experience as an editor, and could manage the concern with one-third the cost which would be incurred by men not understanding the operative part of the business.

CHAPTER XV.

AUTHOR, EVANGELIST, EDITOR AND PUBLISHER IN CINCINNATI.

We had gone to Cincinnati to revise and publish our first volume. For a few months we applied ourselves diligently, until the volume was about ready for the press. During a part of this time we were preacher to a small church at New Richmond, near the city, (of which more will be said in the next chapter).

A religious paper had been published for some years previous, and had failed. The Western pastors felt the want of a journal as a medium of communication with their churches,. and the three Synods of Ohio, Cincinnati and Indiana united in inviting me to establish and conduct such a journal for them. They pledged co-operation, and that they would procure by their own solicitation a certain number of subscribers. I have before me at this moment, the doings of a committee, signed by Rev. A. Benton, Chairman, and Rev. J. Blanchard, Secretary. It is written:

Rev. J. B. Walker proposes to commence a religious paper in the city, on condition that 1600 subscribers be obtained for him, and 400 more within three months from its first issue, the 1st of November. Voted that we undertake to raise the requisite number of names, provided Bro. Walker supplies the desks of such clergy as may be engaged in obtaining names. Voted that Bro. Walker be invited to come to the city by the middle of April, 1840. Pledges: Dr. Stowe, two weeks' labor; J. Blanchard, six weeks or 600 subscribers; J. Benton, labor as agent till the number is obtained.

The paper was commenced. What little means I had I employed in its establishment. My friends accomplished about as much as pastors and professors usually do in enterprises that require personal solicitation. Rev. Messrs. Bingham and Blanchard spent some time on the field and obtained a good list of subscribers. Prof. Stowe visited the Synod of Indiana, and made a speech in behalf of the enterprise. Dr. Beecher commended the new enterprise to the patronage of his people on the Sabbath. There was likewise a circular sent to the churches inviting subscriptions. All these efforts producing less than one-fourth of the number of subscribers promised.

The only alternative was, that I should give up the enterprise or obtain by agents a supporting list of subscribers, and support myself and family by other means until the paper gained a paying list. Within the course of one year this was nearly accomplished, and the *Watchman of the Valley* was generally circulated in Western Ohio, Indiana and

Northern Kentucky. But there were other difficulties in the way of its progress besides the effort to obtain subscribers. The anti-slavery question was vigorously agitated in the churches. The new paper was scarcely radical enough for the old men who had initiated the discussion, and it maintained principles that the opponents of the anti-slavery cause would not tolerate. Hence, many subscribers, especially the wealthy members of city churches, discontinued the paper as soon as they understood its sentiments on the central subject of the times. It was maintained the first year by sacrifice, and rejected by some and approved by others; it labored, under much embarrassment, for human freedom and vital religion.

Dr. Beecher and Prof. Stowe, of Lane Seminary, were personally friendly, and approved the sentiment of the paper; but their relations to the churches in the city were such that Dr. B. especially, did little openly to aid its circulation. He began a series of articles on the doctrine of Christian perfection—a subject much talked of, and more frequently exemplified in those days than at present. But the most influential family in his church were actively hostile to the *Watchman* and remonstrated against his writing for it. The good doctor after initiating the discussion thought best not to continue his articles.

It was a period of awakened interest on the subject of religion in the city. Protracted meetings were held in the Presbyterian churches. The doctor

invited me to aid him in a series of evening meetings. I attended the preliminary conference, and
during some remarks stated that christian parents
should, (if a series of meetings were held,) be
specially watchful in regard to their influence upon
the young people in their families who were unconverted; that a walk and conversation in the spirit
of the services should be maintained, or any conviction of sin which the unconverted might feel would
be dissipated by the apparent thoughtlessness and
apparent prayerlessness of those who professed to
love Christ, and who should at such a time be anxious that their children might be converted.

This preliminary admonition was appropriate to
the time, and the unthoughtful state of many whose
children were expected to attend the special services. I returned to my home that evening feeling
deeply the responsibility of the labors which I supposed would ensue. Before I retired, however, I
was called upon by Mr. Hicks—since then a well
known laborer for Home Missions—who informed
me that after the sermon closed, the elders had a
meeting and requested Dr. Beecher to inform me
that in the evening meetings ensuing they desired
that no reference should be made to the subject of
Slavery, and no allusion to the habits of family life.
These conditions, of course, relieved me from my
engagement; and on the invitation of Mr. Mills, of
the Second Presbyterian church, without conditions, (although his views on the subject of Slavery
differed more from my own than those of Doctor

Beecher,) I engaged to aid him in a series of meetings which were immediately commenced, and
which resulted in the salvation of many who attended the services.

Dr. Beecher labored in his church faithfully and
prayerfully and conscientiously for weeks. Others
aided his zealous endeavors, but no fruit crowned
the effort at this time. It is not for man to judge
whether the Savior was displeased with the inhu-
manity and inconsistency of his professed friends.

A wealthy lady defeated another plan which the
doctor had on his heart, and which would have been
accomplished but for her management. It was proposed that a new Presbyterian church should be organized in the audience room of the Cincinnati college, then under the presidency of the late General
Mitchell. The general, at that time captain of a
volunteer company in the city, a West Point graduate and president of the college, co-operated cordially in the movement. I had arranged for the
music, and the co-operation of a number of christian laborers in the work. There was a ladies' society connected with the Second Church, which
had a considerable sum in their treasury, which Dr.
Beecher had the privilege of expending, as he might
deem wise, for the promotion of the gospel. This
he pledged to the new enterprise. We had individual subscriptions, and other resources sufficient
to meet the expenses of the enterprise. The lady
referred to, president of the missionary society,
who was wife of the most influential pro-slavery

man in the city—heard of the project; and that I was to take charge of the new organization. She immediately called the ladies of the society together, (few, if any of whom knew the plan which we had matured in dependence upon the fund which the doctor had pledged,) and obtained a vote of the society to expend the funds of the society to procure new stone steps and better fixtures for the front entrance of the Second church. Our project failed, of course, and the wise woman no doubt congratulated herself on the defeat of a plan that would have opened a new church in the city where the condition of the bondmen would be remembered. The doctor seemed to be somewhat ashamed as well as grieved at the failure of the movement. But we understood the difficulty of his position, and those who had been urged into the effort by his advice and pledges, were careful not to manifest in his presence regret that he allowed the good he might do and that he desired to do, to be circumvented by those governed by a wicked hostility to truth and freedom.

The doctor seemed determined that I should be permitted to speak to his people on that subject, and a portion of his people were anxious to hear things said that he believed but did not say. During his summer vacation he had the privilege of selecting the supply for the pulpit, and his people were to pay for the services. I accepted the invitation to preach during his absence. The watchful men on the board of elders were alarmed, and an order was passed, that I should be requested not to read any anti-slavery notices in the pulpit, and if I would not consent to withhold such notices, a committee should receive the notices and send only such to the pulpit as they chose to hear. There could be no voice in that pulpit inviting to prayer or effort for the negro. It was further resolved that a contribution should be taken each Sabbath to pay the extra expenses of the congregation while the doctor was absent. My conscience reluctated against these arrangements and prohibitions. I had, however, engaged to supply the pulpit for a definite time, and I worked on under the cloud a few Sabbaths when, being thrown from a conveyance and prevented by my bruises from proceeding with my engagement, I thanked God, and freed myself from my bondage. The congregation had no difficulty in obtaining an eminent preacher to occupy my place, who could withhold in prayer, sermon and notice, all reference to the sin of slavery.

Since then the church has had eminent preachers; but the gospel has been dishonored, and the people humiliated by a grosser defection of one of the members from principle, than that of those who refuse to read a notice for an anti-slavery prayer meeting.

The hostility of the pro-slavery men did not make the *Watchman of the Valley* more conservative—perhaps less so—until finally a gentleman who deemed its opinions intolerable, and supposing

from his position that he could accomplish by men-
ace what he had failed to do by other means,
wrote me a note, which was handed me by Wm.
Persons, desiring to be informed when it would be
convenient for me to leave the city; implying, of
course, that means would be used to suppress the
Watchman and its editor, if I persisted in publishing an anti-slavery paper as the organ of the New
School Presbyterian Churches.

The *Philanthropist*, the anti-slavery paper of the
West, had been destroyed, and its press thrown
into the Ohio river a few weeks before. Lovejoy's
paper at Alton, for a similar offense had been destroyed, and Lovejoy himself murdered. The note
came from a source that was not to be despised.
The individual who wrote, had sufficient influence
to prevail on every paper published in the city to
discontinue exchange with the *Watchman*, except
the *Gazette*, then managed by the resolute veteran
editor, Charles Hammond. After an hour's reflection, I returned for answer, that if the writer would
call on me at a certain time and place, he would
learn when I would be prepared to leave the city.
He did not come, and I heard no more from him,
except that he refused to visit a friend who happened for a few weeks to be residing in my family.

The *Watchman* continued its issues; "the country people read it gladly;" and, meanwhile, my
Sabbaths and spare time were devoted to various
other efforts which I deemed adapted to promote
the triumph of truth and righteousness.

There were two classes of people in the city
which were doing mischief. They had been met
by Dr. Beecher in a measure by efforts which he
made to meet mechanics and all others who would
assemble in their own workshops to hear the gospel.
There were likewise efforts made for systematic
preaching in the market house on Fifth street, and
in the Bethel Chapel in the other end of the city;
but we found the parties most active in hindering
the gospel adopted the same means of out-door
preaching, and promoted hostility to holiness
when we hoped to counteract it. It was thought
best, therefore, by myself and a few others, that I
should meet the Atheists, or the Fanny Wright
men as they were called, in debate, when the Infidel people would be present, and those who were
being led astray. The Reformers, as the Infidels
called themselves, had a large room on the corner
of Main and Fifth streets. Mr. DeRusmont, the
putative husband of Fanny Wright, had his head-
quarters and library there; and the club assembled
twice a week for discussions and business. I proposed to meet them in their own room and discuss
the question, "Is there a Supreme Moral Personal
God apart from, or above the laws of Nature, who
rules and judges men?"

I invited only a single friend, Mr. VanBergen, an
elder of the 3d Presbyterian church, who was occasionally present at the discussion. The Infidels
and those who sympathised with them were out in
force. I remember only a few of the turning points

in the discussions, which terminated happily in de-
taching from the reformers some men and women
who were tending to irreligion and immorality.

The action of conscience was a main topic.
They argued that conscience was both light and
law to the soul, and all the light and law the soul
needed.

I argued that conscience itself needed light;
that like the natural eye, it was true in itself but
could not see in the dark. This was illustrated
one night at length by showing that conscience en-
forced the faith of the soul right or wrong; and the
more sincerely men believed error the more potential was conscience to enforce it. In dark ages and
heathen countries this was evidently true; true to
all believers, Catholic and Protestant. The point
was established and gained for truth. They con-
ceded that conscience needed light, and then argued
that they had the true light—but their strength at
that point was broken.

They insisted that all men were governed by
motives; that God foreordained whatsoever comes
to pass—good and bad alike. Mahomet and Jesus
—murder and mercy—and the penalty, all there was
for the wrong, was conscience and consequences.
I agreed in part, but argued that if good and bad
action were alike produced by a power independent of man, that power must be malignant; because,
to produce in man bad conduct and then punish
him for acting in a manner which he could not
avoid, was the character of a supreme devil. If

all action were alike caused by law without freedom, man should suffer no more for a good than a
bad act. A father who would cause his child, or
even a dumb beast, to do an act, and then punish
for it, would be a monster. And if we were in the
power of such laws, or persons, or principles, or
whatever they might call Fatality, we should all rejoice in annihilation, because to exist would surely
bring evil sooner or later.

If, as some argued, chance governed the world
instead of fate, the cause was still evil. Change
corrected nothing. It created disorder. We might
chance to be deranged; think we murdered our
parents; but chance could not correct the evil. In
the eternal future left to chance, we should look with
dread to the morrow—if any said there was no
future. We had chanced to exist once. We might
again; but not for the better. We are the highest
creature now. If change—not probably so again.
It is said we are spirit, and matter cannot give pain
to spirit. It does now and may again. The dread
of the future, if left to chance would be torment.

Some of the women were alarmed, and some men
never came back to hear the close of the discussion.

During my term as editor, and some months
thereafter, I labored in the neighboring churches
as an evangelist when pressure of other duties
would allow. In Madison, Indiana; in Columbus,
Ohio; in the 3d church in Cincinnati, and elsewhere. I witnessed the process of the revival
years from 1836 to 1840, and some marked incidents

impressed on the memory and certified by experience may be noted with profit. There were professional evangelists in those days, some of whom still live. The best of them all, Rev. C. G. Finney, of Oberlin, still lives; and Burchard and Littlejohn and the Footes, have ceased to labor; Mr. Avery, and Clarke, of Cleveland, are the only men now actively engaged in the West. Most of these men had a process and a method peculiar to themselves. Their method was true to the spirit of the gospel, and while it was vital with faith and devotion, it accomplished the end for which it was sent. The next general visitation of spiritual interest may be dispensed by a somewhat different method, but the spirit must be the same.

Another class of persons called themselves Universalists. Some of them upright and amiable, but teaching the thoughtless views of the doctrine of sin and holiness, that absolutely prevented repentance and faith in Christ as the Savior from sin.

They were deluding many persons by pretences which part of them supposed to be true—that the christian ministers of the evangelical denominations were unwilling to discuss the subject with them. They challenged Dr. Beecher, not supposing he would meet them, to vindicate the truth he taught in a polemic way. But the fact of the challenge, common in those days, and that no one like Paul in the School of Tyrannus proposed to meet them, gave them adherents every week. After consultation it was thought best that I should accept their challenge to discuss the question, Will all men be saved? The discussion was to be held in their own church. After consultation among themselves it was agreed that a discussion should take place first in a village church not far from the city; and subsequently in the city.

Mr. Pingree, who subsequently died in Louisville, a man of many gifts and unusual ability, entered the arena first. The discusssion lasted three days. The business was a new one to me. I had read Ely's debate and Dr. P. Cook, and I devised a new process of argument, which I was sure would convince an audience if not the disputant, of the absurdity of Universalism. On the appointed day we met and dined together, and with proper courtesy I was introduced to the people. Mr. Pingree argued from various scripture passages, that all would be saved. I rose and argued that all would be damned. I had collected a large number of scripture passages, and appealed to the audience if I had not, on their own principles of construction proved that none would be saved.

The method was a new one, and succeeded in upsetting all the old arguments by nullifying them.

When my opponent argued that certain words did not mean everlasting, I assented provided he would apply the same rule to the other side, everlasting life.

After two days I had succeeded in destroying confidence in the construction of scripture by which Universalists sustain their views in the eyes of the people. The third day the rational argument was appealed to,—the unreasonableness of eternal punishment was argued successfully by Mr. Pingree; and if I had contended for eternal torments, as the old divines did, I should have done something to diminish my success in the debate. But I declined to argue eternal torment for the impenitent, and argued that they would be punished as much as they deserved, and as long as they were sinful, and that they would either sin and suffer forever, or else suffer for sin and then be annihilated, which is the scriptural teaching; but that those who grew worse instead of better by their probation could never enter heaven.

The debate did good; the evangelical people in the neighborhood rejoice in the issue as a great deliverance from a boastful and injurious error, to this day.

The next debate took place in the Universalist church in the city. Every effort was made to get a change of terms as to the place of holding the debate. They desired that one-half the time it should be in some evangelical church, but I was unwilling to change the arrangement.

The debate in the city was with John A. Gurley— subsequently member of congress, now deceased. I would pursue no method but to oppose his argument by its opposite and to apply his definitions to both sides; I affirmed that sinning only increased the propension to sin; and that the second death by annihilation, or otherwise was as endless as the

second life. Dr. Beecher and the evangelical ministers, and many leading men on all sides attended
the debates. It had one good result. Previously
there had been in the city and region about, a constant urging for debate, and assumption that the
evangelical people were afraid to let the common
people hear the two sides compared with the Bible,
and many people were believing these statements.
Subsequently, till the present day, Universalism
has grown more orthodox and more modest in
that region. The truth about the matter was,
that the orthodox ministry, learned in tradition,
and pious as some of them are, with the exception
of Dr. Beecher and Mr. Burnett, of the Campbellite
church, were entirely unfitted to meet the Universalist preachers before a mass audience of the people.

This last discussion occurred about the time that
I closed my connection with the paper. I transferred the office of the *Herald of the Prairies*
to Rev. E. Goodman, one of the best men I ever
knew. I now had leisure, which I could not obtain
till now, to publish my first volume. I had delivered
some of the chapters as addresses at college and in
labor for the Bible Society, the last chapters being
the experience at New Richmond. I had preached
most of the book, and had re-written and arranged
the whole ; and now I proposed to print the work
with my own hands, and give it to the public that
it might propagate the truth, if truth was in it. I
believed in the book myself, but had no idea of
what its history would be. I felt that I had a

mission to publish it, and was willing to risk a part of what little money I had on the issue.

Dr. Bailey, then editor of the *Philanthropist*, afterwards of the *Era*, at Washington City, was a friend. We had issued our papers from the same office; saved some money by exchanging articles in both, and I felt confidence in his ability to judge of the value of the work. It was submitted to him in MSS., but after retaining it for a time, I called and he told me he could not possibly find time to read it thoroughly, and could not advise in regard to its publication.

I took the MSS. to Dr. Beecher, who willingly heard me read such portions as I desired to have examined. Miss Catharine Beecher was called in by her father. She was then considered the strong mind of his family. Mrs. Stowe had written only the Mayflower Stories, which were not appreciated at the time of their publication as her subsequent writings have been. The doctor expressed, without hesitation, his opinion that the book would do good,—dwelling with earnestness on some parts which others have not noticed so favorably. Catharine thought well of what she heard, but feared it would be a losing enterprise to publish it. She stated what abler writers than myself have found to be true—that a book may be original and of sterling value, but if produced by a man unknown to fame, as almost all original works are, it will gain little or no circulation, at least in its own generation. Her talk was honest and true, and led me to publish the book anonymously, hoping, as in the case of Walter Scott, Irving and others, that it might stand on its own merits; at least, that the unknown name of its author should not detract from its acceptance by the public.

I retired to my office and determining to make the loss as light as possible, I concluded to set the type myself. A needy Baptist printer, out of employment, I engaged to do the presswork. The proofs were read by myself, and Rev. J. Blanchard, then of the Fifth street Presbyterian church. Of the fifteen hundred printed only five hundred were bound, and I took my departure to introduce the book to the public.

After supplying personal friends, and leaving some with the booksellers in Cincinnati, mostly in exchange for other works, I took the balance of the edition with the unbound sheets and started for New York and Boston. In New York I left a volume with the religious papers and magazines. Two queer incidents occurred in this connection which helped and hindered. The editor of a prominent religious magazine, who had resided in Cincinnati, insisted on hearing the name of the writer as he was acquainted in that city. I gave the last name which proved to be that of a prominent lawyer of established literary reputation. He seems to have assumed at once that Judge W. was the man, and gave the book a very flattering notice. I took one to the editor of the New York *Observer;* and, although I desired to act *incog.*, he recognized me as the former editor of the *Watchman* in Cincinnati, and as I could not deny the authorship of the book, he gave the anonymous volume a notice that would have prevented any one from buying the work. Some years afterwards'when the book had succeeded he apologized in his paper for his unjust notice in the beginning: and not long ago I received a letter from the same gentleman, I suppose, stating that his father on his death-bed desired him to give his thanks to the author of the work for the aid it had given his faith in his last days.

A copy was presented to Dr. S. H. Cox, then in the zenith of his strength. He probably had seen the notice in the magazine, and read the book. He wrote, soon after, a notice of the work in the *Evangelist*, speaking of it as a rare book, the sentences, he said, were "clear as light and weighty as gold."

In Boston, Mr. John Tappan, then a bookseller and publisher, read the book and agreed to furnish it as anonymous to publishers, and endeavor to get a few reviews. He succeeded so well that the Boston press, with the exception of the *Magnet*, of which Theodore Parker was an editor, said nothing but good words for the volume. It was stated in some of the papers that it was, as they understood, the work of an eminent lawyer, who had been skeptical, and in this volume gave the views and reasonings which led him to embrace the orthodox faith. This reference of the authorship of such

a book to the bar rather than the pulpit, (although
with some experience in both; with the exception
of a few eminent men, I know that the average in-
tellect of the pulpit is in advance of the bar,) aided,
no doubt, in thê introduction of the work. A second edition was soon called for, in this country. It
was immediately issued in London, and in continuous editions on both sides of the water from then
till now. At the present time it is printed in most
of the languages of Christendom, and has a wider
circulation in the christian world than any American book.

While printing the book, and at other moments
of leisure, I preached at New Richmond, and as an
evangelist in many of the larger places adjacent to
Cincinnati. In the city of Richmond, Indiana—in
Columbus, Ohio—at Newark, Ohio, and many other
places, I aided the settled preachers at their own
invitation, and in all cases God favored the church
by converting many to the obedience of Christ.
At the city of Columbus, where I aided the late Dr.
Hitchcock, some time during three winters, I learned that God works by any process that is prosecuted with faith and spirit by the people, and no process without these will accomplish the end. For
two winters the people were humble, self-sacrificing
and dependent on God's mercy—the third, they
supposed the old forms would achieve like results,
and the forms were operated with a selfish aim and
little spirituality—hence but little good was achieved. Providence therefore introduces new men and

new forms to counteract the inveterate tendency to rely on forms rather than faith—on men rather than on God.

CHAPTER XVI.

PREACHER AND PASTOR.—MANSFIELD.

We had labored as an evangelist or rather as an assistant preacher in many of the cities of the West: and as our paper was read in all the New School Presbyterian churches, we were known to the religious communities generally. We had, therefore, invitations to churches and new colleges, where it was supposed our labors might be useful. A new institution was projected at Blendon, Ohio, near Columbus, in which we were elected professor, of which our former paper, after we left the city, made the following mention: "It will be with unfeigned pleasure that our readers will learn that the Board of Trustees of Central College have appointed Mr. Walker professor of Belles Lettres in this institution, and that Mr. W. has accepted his appointment. Eminent now as a writer, he is destined to be eminent as a teacher and professor. Central College is situated at Blendon, a few miles from Columbus, and is destined to be unsurpassed by any college in the state." We visited the site of the new college; but although its chief patron was

one of the most benevolent men in the state, and
its buildings were spacious and valuable, we doubted of the large success and usefulness of the institution; and admonished by a former experience of
the same sort at Lawrenceburg, and my purpose,
at that time, to hear the call of duty thereafter, was
why it did not seem to me that it would best promote the glory of God in Christ, for me to become
a professor at Blendon. We went on our way,
therefore, to Mansfield.

Myself and wife rode from Mt. Vernon to Mansfield, on a winter night in an open wagon. Straw
was thrown into the wagon, and my wife, self and
books were loaded in; and thence for thirty miles,
over a rough road, we were conveyed to our new
field of labor. The first Sabbath, the church presented a "beggarly amount of empty pews." The
congregation being more discouraging as to number
than a minister is usually called to meet. But the
history of the church and the character of the few
who belonged to it interested me more than others,
and I began labor trusting in Christ for aid.

The church had been organized several years
before, in a measure, by my own aid. When agent
of the Bible Society I had visited Mansfield, and
finding a few christian people in the Old School
Presbyterian church, persecuted for their zeal in
reforms, and their sympathy with the new institution at Oberlin, I advised them to form a separate
church, and drew up the articles by which the society was organized. They formed themselves into

a new society, and after worshiping for a time in the second floor of a warehouse owned by the late E. P. Sturges, they erected a small church building by personal labor and no small sacrifice on the part of most of the members. They had employed for a time several ministers before I came; but their abolitionism and the hostility of all the other churches turned away from their congregation those who loved the praise of men more than the favor of God. An anti-slavery lecturer had been assailed by a rabble while speaking in their church, and had to be accompanied to his room by friends lest he should be assailed by some patriots under the leadership of the late Major General S. A. Curtis, who was then a resident lawyer in the place. The general was subsequently converted to better opinions and principles, and during the late war for Union and Liberty made some atonement for previous errors.

There was in the little church two or three families that were wealthy, and by whose aid a small salary of about four hundred and fifty dollars and a free dwelling was made ours; and even this was quite an advance on what I had received at New Richmond, and was worth in provision nearly twice the amount at the present time. But I never felt willing to receive in my own behalf Home Missionary money; and with rigid economy on our part, we lived comfortably and received into our family one orphan child, besides my wife's sister whose home was with us.

It was not often that the prominent families in a village give their means and influence to spiritual, reformatory religion. But it was so in the early years of the Mansfield church, and to some extent it is still so in the same church; but they have recently erected an expensive and imposing church edifice, and may degenerate from early purity and piety. When a church that has a splendid house and contains an influential element in society, rises above odium, it is as it was with christianity in the early period, when the offence of the cross had ceased, worldly christians, who seek social position and association will seek fellowship in such a church, and an element of worldliness becomes intermixed with the good. I had some little experience of the sort before I left Mansfield. And previously, while in Cincinnati, a gentleman of means moved into the city from Rochester, N. Y. He professed to be an anti-slavery man. I used all the influence I had with him to lead him to unite with a church holding anti-slavery sentiment, which really needed his aid. But he could not be persuaded, and united with the Second Presbyterian church which did not need his aid. He subsequently removed to Brooklyn, N. Y., and united with a church which led him in his chosen way of worldly religion.

The little church in Mansfield succeeded abundantly—God aiding it. Every Sabbath added to its congregation, while still it maintained its purity as an anti-slavery, temperance and Sabbath keeping church. The odium gradually subsided as the truth triumphed, and we lost only one member, a merchant of wealth and influence, who rose in the congregation and walked out of the church never to return. He was offended by some remarks in regard to men at Washington seeking popular favor by the sacrifice of righteous principles. He died without a sign. Subsequently another gentleman, an attorney at law, supposing he was about to die, repented as he hoped. I baptized him in his bed, charitably endeavoring to indulge the same hope. He recovered, and took command of a company in the Mexican war, by which the South hoped to add more slave territory, but failed through the prayer and efforts of anti-slavery men and women. He united with the church on his recovery; but as we opposed the Mexican war, he withdrew when he took command of his company. He was subsequently Lieut. General of the State, and Colonel in the late war for Union and Liberty; and was more recently a successful attorney in Washington city, where he died desiring in his last hours to be taken back to Mansfield to sleep the sleep that knows no waking in the cemetery of that city. His action in regard to church matters was exceedingly peculiar. While he would not go into the church, because of the views which were held and preached, he subscribed more liberally than any other man in proportion to his means to support the teaching which he eschewed.

Temporal, intellectual and spiritual success was granted to the church. Series of lectures on

geology and other popular subjects were occasionally given by the pastor and resident gentlemen.
The Sabbath-School was enlarged and the increase
of children sometimes brought in the parents. On
the Fourth of July, we had, often in company with
the other schools, a procession—a repast—brief
speeches and dialogues by the pupils, which were
both amusing and instructive—amusement being
the principle aim. No pews were rented. The
little salary was raised by subscription. The congregation built in the second year a fine parsonage
on a large and pleasant lot of ground, which I orna-
mented for those that followed me with fruit and
flowers; and the labors and prayers of the church
were crowned with annual, sometimes semi-annual
ingatherings of a greater number into the fold of
Christ.

A weekly ministers' meeting was instituted, and
most of the evangelical ministers in the city attended; and thus a spirit of unity was obtained in
promoting the common interests of religion in the
place and the region round about. Instead of
bigotry, charity gradually prevailed, until the old
members of my congregation were filled with aston-
ishment, when the old minister who had disciplined
them for reform and revival utterances appeared
unexpectedly to them one Sabbath morning in my
pulpit to preach the gospel.

After a revival of religion which added a number
to our communion, and likewise to other churches
in the place, an association was formed including

the most influential men in the city, the object of which was to secure the better observance of the Sabbath ; to promote the cause of temperance, and to reform the vicious by whatever means and influence we might properly use. The association was · fruitful of much good. The Pittsburg, Fort Wayne and Chicago Rail Road, which was not then completed to Chicago, ran its cars through a portion of the corporation on the Sabbath day. We had the Sabbath train stopped for a short time, but it cost an effort; and the Marshal of the city, Mr. Gilkeson, who is yet living, and who was the first child born in the place, was baptized with scalding water from one of the engines while endeavoring to arrest the engineer. The management of the road, however, discontinued the working train and constructed a track outside the corporation. The Sabbath was for a season at least respected, and even those who had opposed the effort for cessation of the laboring train became grateful for the rest that was gained for themselves and others. Most of the reformers have entered into their final rest. Dr. Hildreth, one of the most active—then I believe, mayor of the town—has just deceased.

The ministers likewise, not only of the city, but throughout the country, formed themselves into an evangelical alliance, including at least seven denominations of evangelical christians, on a common basis of the essential articles of gospel faith. Our aim was to unite our efforts by which we would advance human interests by gospel faith. This was the first evangelical alliance ever formed in the world. It ante-dated by a year at least that subsequently formed in London, by delegates from all portions of Christendom. I still have its first record book. Sermons were preached alternately, and papers read in the different churches—no pastor preaching in his own pulpit at the exercises of the Alliance.

In my own church, I preached a sermon in the forenoon, endeavoring to lodge conviction of some one truth in the minds of the people. In the afternoon or evening, I gave a continuous exposition of a book or letter of the Apostles, from four verses to twenty or more at a service, till the book was finished. I preached once each quarter to the children, and usually made some remarks in the Sabbath infant class-room, to break the monotony for the little children. I had no differences with the people except in regard to renting seats and an organ. At the end of the second year, when the church became full—many of the new attendants, and some of the old, wanted the seats rented, about which I doubted, but which was accomplished by the congregation. The organ, I thought, would introduce artistic music instead of spiritual melodies sung by all the people with the spirit and with the understanding. A melodeon, I thought, would be all that would be necessary for an accompaniment. A compromise was effected, and a small organ procured, and although the effect was not so evil as if a larger instrument had been introduced, the people gradually began to listen to new tunes, instead of singing such as would make melody in their hearts unto the Lord.

The house being full and feeling that the work in the congregation was about finished, I acceded to a request that had been urgently pressed upon me by brethren in Chicago, to establish a religious newspaper for the North-West in that city.

CHAPTER XVII.

CHICAGO.

My Mansfield people were sorely tried when they found that I had engaged to go to Chicago. After my first installation at Akron, I had determined never to be installed again; but to be free to act on my own sense of duty to leave one field of labor for another, when my conviction and conscience determined. I therefore, on the invitation of the Presbyterian ministers in Chicago and some adjacent places, purchased a printing press of my old friend Harmon Kingsbury, and began the publication in Chicago of a Weekly Religious paper, which they had named the *Western Observer*, but which I changed to the "Herald of the Prairies." Its history was something similar to my previous enterprises of the same sort in Cincinnati. All the Presbyterian Religious papers then published in the free states of the West, had been established by myself: one in Hudson; one in Cincinnati, and now one in Chicago. (The one in Hudson existed before I bought it, but survived only by my efforts.) All were circulating at this time.

After renting an office for a few months, I purchased a lot and house on Wells Street, where the
Briggs House now stands, for seven hundred dollars, in which I lived, printed my paper and kept a
Sabbath School and Tract Depository; and fitted
up a room for a minister's meeting—where the
ministers of all evangelical denominations then in
the city assembled on Monday at 10 o'clock, to
state the form of their skeleton for the preceding
Sabbath, and discuss some religious text or topic.
There was more union in effect at that time than
now. We not only had a Union Bible Society, but
a city Sabbath-School Union, of which I had the
duty of being president, and a Union Tract Society
which aimed to put a tract each month into every
family in the city. William H. Brown, Philo Carpenter, and other leading citizens were engaged in
this work, and the women of the churches aided
efficiently. We had likewise an Anti-Papal Association, which told not only the good things in Ca-
tholicism, but the bad and dangerous things. The
popular ministry of our day have degenerated, and
through fear and favor are cowards, false teachers
or dumb dogs on the subject of the Papal super-
stition. Speaking only of its good aspects, (which
may be found even in the character of a felon,) but
withholding testimony against corrupting and dangerous errors.

Agents were sent over the prairies to the
churches in Illinois and Wisconsin, and a list of
some four thousand subscribers for the *Herald* were

obtained in about two years. Meanwhile I engaged
in the purchase of a lot on the West side for a
church building—a few wealthy men aiding mostly
in the pecuniary outlay. In this we organized the
Third Presbyterian church, and I—(a member of
the Fox River Congregational Association)—became its pastor, and aided to establish the congregation. The four youths working in the printing
office were converted. The enterprise prospered;
and not long after my departure the people divided
into two churches, the First Congregational and
the Third Presbyterian, which now have multiplied
into some eight churches.

I had chosen for my printer a pious young man,
Mr. B. F. Worrell, now preaching at Centralia, to
whom I gave an interest in the receipts of the
paper, and who aided faithfully in gospel work in
the city, and subsequently became a Congregational
minister. We cared for the Bethel cause in those
days. A lot was purchased near the river, and a
small frame church built. There was a chaplain of
little use to the sailors. Mr. Worrell managed the
Sabbath-School, and aided in the Sabbath services.
I occasionally preached on the wharf to sailors
congregated on the sides, top and bow of some
steamboat. We endeavored to have the Sabbath
observed; and, as farmers in those days came with
their wheat to market in wagons, and often passed
the bridges on the Sabbath, Mr. Worrell or one of
the printer boys occasionally stood at the bridge
part of the Sabbath and gave a tract on Sabbath

keeping to the thoughtless Sabbath breakers. The
temperance cause was not neglected in that early
day. I procured a set of wood cuts representing
the spider and the fly symbolizing the saloon-keeper
and his victim, and printed handbills setting forth
the aim of the illustration. These were distributed,
and some of our printer boys pasted them on the
public places in the streets. Useful and scientific
knowledge was not neglected. I delivered a series
of evening lectures in the city hall; and an annual
address to the Mechanics' Association, of which I
was a member; and in various ways we endeavored
to originate and aid right things in the new city,
while preacher, and editor of the *Herald*.

In those days we had no paved streets. Lake
street had been graveled, but in Winter it was a
deeper mire than some other streets. On Wells
street, near Randolph, where I had my home and
office, wagons sunk in the mire and the horses had
to be extricated from the vehicle in order to get
them out of the difficulty. I sympathized with the
dumb brutes, beaten often by intelligent brutes in
order to make them accomplish impossibilities. I
published several articles in my paper calling attention to cruelty to animals; and the papers in
the city noticed these articles and the publications
did good. I published the notice of the seceding
masons from St. Charles, who opened a lodge publicly in the court house, and gave them encouragement in my paper, which was not a very popular
course with some of my friends. The paper having

been placed on a paying basis, as was supposed, it was sold to Bross & Wight, (now Governor Bross, and Rev. Mr. Wight, of Sycamore). The cholera year impended. Scarcely anything but funeral wagons with a few followers were seen in the streets. I staid in the city and endeavored to do my duty to the dying. I, and Philo Carpenter, still living, stood by a dying man when wife and children had fled. On the Union fast day I preached the sermon in the West Side Methodist church to a few auditors so feeble that I steadied myself by holding to the pulpit.

My old people at Mansfield knowing I had closed my labor with the paper and proposed to leave the city, sent me an urgent request to return at once to them, which I thought it my duty to do for a season.

CHAPTER XVIII.

MANSFIELD AND ABROAD.

On my return to Mansfield I did not find the congregation larger than when I left the church; yet they were united and prepared for progress. After about a year of service an enlargement of the house was needed, and we built an addition to the church, and made much enlargement and improvement. Meanwhile I instructed an indigent and needy young man in Theology—now a Congregational minister.

While in Chicago I had formed the acquaintance of Alexander Brandt, a Scotch banker, who gave me the subject of a prize book, which a gentleman of Aberdeen desired to be written, the best treatise to secure the award. He asked me to write as one of the competitors for the prize. The number of competitors in England and Scotland was large, but he inspired me with a disposition to make the effort. He himself having accumulated a fortune in Chicago, returned to reside in the neighborhood of Aberdeen. Leisure to produce this work I hoped to obtain by a return to my old residence. Much

of my leisure for a year was given to the proposed
volume, and to the enlargement of our place of
worship. When the work was done I proposed to
take the MSS. to Aberdeen, and visit Mr. Brandt
and the relatives of a Scotchman in Chicago who
was urgent that I should report his prosperity in
person to his relatives still remaining upon the estate of the Earl of Aberdeen. In his early years
he had been servant on a farm which I visited, but
now he was a trusted and wealthy citizen of Chicago. Subsequently, however, by making haste to
be rich he lost his reputation and his wealth.

I went across the sea ; visited Scotland, high
lands and low lands, South and North, from Glasgow to the mouth of the Losey. At Aberdeen Mr.
Brandt was absent, but I had the pleasure of meeting the faculty of the Theological Seminary and
other persons of some literary note at a dinner
made in my behalf. Wine was freely used, and,
although I had not totally abstained from a glass
while traveling on the Alps, I maintained the American principle of "taste not," against the strongest
entreaty of both gentlemen and ladies to drink to
America. I remember that when I declined absolutely to partake of the exhilarating beverage they
asked me to pass the bottle, which reminded me of
the adapted passage of the Bible : "Woe unto him
that putteth the bottle to his brother's lips." I declined laughingly by uttering that passage ; but all
the others did not laugh—some looked embarrassed, and I had to make an effort myself to appear

as though I did not realize the import of the words.

I spent a night with a minister of the Seceder church in Elgin. In the evening a bottle of whisky was placed on the center table, and the servant brought in a kettle of hot water, and a supply of sugar and nutmeg. The minister and his wife drank freely and frequently, and their urgency for me to partake increased as the time came to retire. I was suffering with a severe cold, and the hot punch was known by them to be a specific. We retired, each of them taking what they called a night-cap, which is the technical term for a last full glass of hot punch. Next day I delivered an address at the annual meeting of the Elgin Bible Society. The ministers were there—one with red face and flaming nose. He was said not to be a drunkard, and "never went into the pulpit disguised by liquor." Such cases I met with in London among men officially connected with the church and the benevolent societies of the city. Even in some of the State churches not only the minister is marked with the wine color, but the man before the pulpit, who is hired to lead the responses has a face and nose aflame with the stimulus of brandy.

And not only in the State churches but among the dissenters as well, the drinking habit is prevalent. I preached for Dr. Raffles, of Liverpool, at that time perhaps the leading independent in England. On his table at dinner he had both wine and brandy, yet he was considered a temperance man, and was a member of the "Liverpool

Temperance Society—an association designed to discourage the intemperate use of distilled spirits.

In London I had the privilege of delivering two addresses in Exeter Hall, which were printed. The first, on the "Aspect of the American Anti-Slavery Question," was listened to with respectful attention; although the address of an American negro, which followed, received ten times the plaudits. The English people at that time were in a mood to be pleased with proceedings of any colored man who appeared among them, especially an escaped slave. This was not to be wondered at, so that the eclipse of my speech did not displease me as the colored speaker kindly informed them that my views were mainly correct. My address, however, was printed. Although Dr. Campbell mutilated that part which spoke of the influence of slavery in the Mission Board, the Quakers bought extras and distributed the full address in different parts of the kingdom.

My temperance speech was not so well received even as the anti-slavery speech had been. The audience was composed mostly of those in favor of moderation in drinking—but few, if any, held what was called the teetotal principle—which means entire abstinance. I was informed that there were but two ministers in London, Dr. Jabez Burns, of Paddington, and one of the ministers connected with the London City Missionary Society, that abstained habitually and entirely from all distilled and fermented beverages. In the audience were

many respectable men in the English sense.   Sir
E. Bass was there, who was one of the largest ale
brewers in London, yet one. of the most diligent
workers to prevent intemperate drinking.   He is
no doubt a christian of benevolent character who,
as all Englishmen, with few exceptions, looks upon
ale as a beneficial beverage.   I did not know of the
presence of any of the great brewers in the audience, and when a light gentlemanly looking man
rose on the stage and went out, at the utterance of
what I thought a most sensible remark, but which
the audience received with disapprobation, I was a
little perplexed.   The remark signified that we
Americans were surprised to know that many of
the large brewers in Great Britain were among the
active men in efforts to arrest the evils of drunken-
ness, at the same time engaging in a manufacture
which produced drunkards, and then using a portion of their profits to prevent the effects of their
own production.   The address was offered by the
officers of the Total Abstinence Society to all the
London papers that usually publish such matter,
but not one of them would insert it.   The objection
in each case was the improper disparagement by a
foreign speaker of some of London's most esteemed
citizens, the brewers.   The Quakers, however, have
courage as well as conscience, and they sent the
address to Glasgow in Scotland, where it was published as it was spoken, and large numbers of the
papers were circulated by them in London.   Intemperance is a principle source of poverty, misery

and crime in Great Britain; but until the English adopt the christian principle, which succeeded with the American population, they will never even abate the evil—the principle announced by Paul—"If wine cause a brother to stumble, or if it makes him weak, I will drink no more while the world stands." The moderate drinkers of the realm must deny themselves an indulgence that might not be hurtful to them, because their indulgence would encourage a practice that would be hurtful to others.

Introductory letters from prominent men on this side of the waters are influential in Great Britain. I had letters from Bishop McIlvain, Lewis Tappan, Governor Bartley and others. The Bishop's letter, which was cordial and complimentary, gave me access to the best people; and the letter of Lewis Tappan opened the doors of all the Quakers and Reformers that I met with. I did not use any other letters, except one to Dr. Campbell, and others from Dr. J. P. Thompson, then of the New York Tabernacle, and I never wrote but one letter from Europe to any American newspaper. I had read with a feeling of utter disgust the letters of Willis, speaking of the great ones he had called upon, and the book of Dr. Sprague, of Albany, and of the certain D. D's, of Boston, giving description of English families, evidently designed by the writer for the base purpose of printing their own name in connection with the well known names of England. Such things are humiliating to our national character. I had such a feeling of repulsion for such

writers that in the only letter I did write no single
name was mentioned.   This was the other extreme
—but a safe one.

The Quakers are really the only people in England who maintain the principles of reform as do
the christian reformers of America.   They oppose
slavery, tobacco, alcohol, seqret oaths of masonry,
deforming fashions, and maintain gospel principles,
together with some other views in a right direction;
and yet they have no appliances to propagate their
principles.   I found myself more at home with the
Quakers than any other people in Europe.

The Dissenters of England are no better than
the Establishment in their drinking and tobacco
usages.   I was invited to preach a sermon at a
dedication of a Baptist chapel.   The Baptist ministers from the whole surrounding region were present.   We had an out-door picnic, as we call such
gatherings, and a grand time socially.   After the
dinner I left the audience to speak to some poor
women and a company of Gipsies that were hover-
ing in the neighborhood of the company.   When I
returned I could not find a single minister of all our
company.   I inquired some time before some one
told me that I would probably find them in an up-
stairs room in the village, not far from the church
that had been dedicated.   I went up expecting to
hear some question of import discussed.   When lo,
I entered a room filthy with tobacco smoke and
tobacco stench—each man, with no exception that
I noticed, smoking a tobacco pipe, while the table

in the centre of the company, was loaded with ale glasses, and a bottle of brandy in addition. I preached in many of the dissenter's chapels in London—Congregational and Baptist—but with the exception of Dr. Burns, of Paddington, and Dr. Campbells, I was invariably offered wine in the ante-room after sermon, where a bottle was kept in a closet—and sometimes both before and after sermon, wine was urged.

On my return to Mansfield, the people of my congregation received me with real kindness and gratulation. Some of the expressions of regard on their part, I have recorded elsewhere. After remaining with them two years, I felt it was a duty to go to some other field of labor. The enlarged house was again full. The influential people of the town were professors of religion and not much material existed that was not in some of the churches, or in a reprobate state where no effort or truth could reach them. After I retired, the church was still prosperous, and it is at the present time the largest Congregational church in the state, except Oberlin.

CHAPTER XIX.

SANDUSKY.

There was a Presbyterian church at Sandusky city, which was one of the oldest in Northern Ohio. It had some members which were true to the principles of christianity. Some of them would pray for the slave, while others more wealthy and worldly, were hostile to any word of preaching or prayer in their behalf. The wealthy portion of the people withdrew and built a large stone edifice and organized a new church, leaving a few faithful ones poor and unpopular. There was a little church called the Oberlin church in the city that was likewise few and feeble. I went to the aid of the reformers. We succeeded in uniting the two churches into one Congregational church, and they called a minister from Washington city, who had made some stir as an anti-slavery man. They agreed to give him seventeen hundred dollars per annum, which was the largest salary paid at that early time out of Cincinnati. He proved a failure in all respects. For a few months a sort of declamatory verbiage of words about sacred things attracted

many people, and at the height of the popular
furor he was urgent for a new church building, and
got the best men in the church involved in the plan
of erecting a spacious and beautiful edifice—one of
the finest for church uses in the State. Before the
building was half completed the popularity of the
preacher had abated. The congregation had fallen
off, and the men engaged in building were left with
an unfinished church, and a debt of seven thousand
dollars upon their hands. Their minister resigned,
and the whole enterprise, spiritual and temporal,
seemed a chaos. They invited me to labor for
them, and I assented and began work in the hope
of saving church and property. They were in debt
for an unfinished church; in debt for a fine organ,
and in debt to the retired minister; but they were
a generous people, and agreed to give me twice as
much as they could afford to pay.

The first Sabbath some of the members were absent, in attendance upon a service held in another
church by the retiring preacher. They still sympathized with him, and it was several weeks before
a cordial union of all the good people was effected.
From that time, gradual but certain prosperity
attended the effort. We had a religious interest
that added some influential men to the church—
and others came to us by letter who were able to
aid in exigencies. There was a Wesleyan Methodist church in the city which had few members, but
they owned a good church building—I effected a
union with them. They took pews in our church—

became members with us—and we sold their house to enable us to liquidate in part our church debt, or rather to finish the building. The church was prosecuted for the debt due the preacher, and the organ and furniture attached. I bid in the property at a nominal price, and transferred it to the ladies' society, which succeeded in paying the pressing demand then pending. Other claims were pending, and at one time the whole church property was transferred to me as assignee for the creditors. I scarcely know all·the plans and subscriptions by which we saved ourselves; but we succeeded in paying the floating debt, leaving still about seven thousand dollars due upon the church building—not yet finished. The audience room, one of the most comfortable and tasteful in the State, was finished. The basement and spire were not; and the debris of the builders—stones, timbers and rubbish—were lying around the unfinished church. It stood on the public square on the same street with the Episcopal Methodist and Baptist churches—none of the lots of which were inclosed. The church buildings stood like neglected houses on a common. The whole was an offense to my sense of propriety and order, and with some effort I got all the churches to unite and fence in all the lots, and plant trees in them. The planting on the Congregational lot I did myself, with the aid of my wife; and the year after the rubbish was removed, and the trees planted, the churches looked as though christians cared for their sanctuaries.

It was not difficult now as the congregation was larger to procure funds to put on the spire and finish the basement for Sabbath-School and ladies' rooms. The ladies furnished means to procure the material; then, with the aid of a donation of some things from the car shop in the city, and the aid of young men in the congregation—with my own hands—we did the painting, and the scaling of the Sabbath-School rooms. When done they were tasteful and tidy, and the Sabbath-School and the ladies enjoyed their pleasant rooms.

We were now really prosperous in all directions. Many families came in who had not been identified with the congregation, and hence had paid nothing in the past for the house. The next year, therefore, we concluded to make an effort to free the church from debt, or at least to remove a part of the burden. The effort was successful beyond my most sanguine hope. The brethren who were personally responsible for the large share of the debt subscribed freely, so that more than one-third of the amount was assumed by them. From another I got a town lot, and from others subscriptions of five hundred down to five dollars. Our debt was paid. The house was full; and having meanwhile completed the MSS. of my volume in the Doctrine of the Spirit, I took a vacation of a few months in England in order to publish the work—telling the people to supply themselves with another pastor, if possible, as I doubted whether I should think it my duty to remain with them after I returned.

They had had several preachers while I was gone, but not being suited I continued to labor for Christ in the city during a year or more after I returned.

The finances of the family were managed in a good measure by my wife, while we were struggling to extricate and establish the church in Sandusky. We had concluded never to expend any year the whole of our income, whether four hundred or four thousand dollars. We secured a commodious house in Mansfield, and a portion of the time my wife took a number of boarders connected with the public schools; and, as in other cases, when my labor, many times almost gratuitously, did not pay expenses, she supplemented it by management, labor and economy. She has now done with labor —probably is a paralytic invalid—but in her day she did faithfully the part of a pastor's wife. Her last years are peace.

When the church was built up and the congregation filled up at Sandusky I again visited Europe to publish my third book—The Doctrine of the Holy Spirit. The English publisher took my MSS. and gave me compensation, although they could get no copy-right; and many more of my books have been sold in the old world than in the new, but in both they have had a constant sale. I do not know that this is decisive as to their merit, for many books by English authors of little or no value are brought out by American publishers that get little attention at home, and would never get any here if written on this side of the water.

I did not expect to remain longer with the church in Sandusky, but when I returned they were without a pastor, and I continued to labor with them for a season. In the meantime I made arrangements to sell my Ohio property, preparatory to removal to the wilds of Northern Michigan, to accomplish a project which I had cherished as one that I supposed would be the last work of my life.

CHAPTER XX.

BENZONIA AND THE COLLEGE.

From the beginning of my christian life I had an aspiration—(a selfish one, no doubt)—to accomplish some good in the world, not only as a writer, but likewise as a teacher and founder of a model christian college. I looked upon most of our colleges as rather abating than fostering a self-denying piety in students; and even in the case of some theological seminaries the students lost the fervor of their piety, and all their zeal for christian reforms, and became mere pulpit essayists, and in many cases mere preaching machines. I thought I could establish a school that would do better than this; and, as Oberlin, which had been the instrument of christian reform and piety, seemed to be determining to the forms of the world with others, (although, still the best of them all,) I was the more anxious to aid in establishing a school that would be in my view a true school of the prophets.

Two young men of Oberlin had a desire to found a colony and school, (a project common at that time,) and called on me to advise and aid in the endeavor. I was a trustee of the institution at Oberlin, and that institution had accomplished so much good in church and state that I promised aid and effort, if a good location could be found. The committee commenced their search for a location. (Mr. Fairfield grew dissatisfied with some of the movements of his companion and withdrew from the project). Rev. C. E. Bailey associated another gentleman with him, and they found a location in the Northern woods of Michigan, which was deemed favorable. No county was organized. No inhabitants in the region, except a few families living and fishing at points on the lake. The land was all government land. It was open for homesteads, and there was a certainty that the population of the Grand Traverse region would be a laboring, poor agricultural people. There were no schools in the region; and no academy or college to produce teachers within one hundred and fifty miles. It was an uninhabited wilderness country; but soon to be filled up with poor families on homesteads. The location suited me, as one to start a new christian enterprise. There was an actual want of the effort we proposed to make. There were too many colleges richly endowed in the older states; but here we could have a school to meet the actual wants of the church and the poor. I engaged heartily with Mr. B. in the enterprise. The agents and one other family of the stockholders went into the lands, and built cabins. I visited the location each season for three years, when others having gone into the colony, and difficulty arising between them and the agent, Mr. Bailey, I concluded to re- move to the new settlement, and devote my time and means to organize and develop in harmony the three great interests of Agriculture, Education and a pure Christianity. More than one-half of the colony had gone there directly or indirectly by my instrumentality. Some of them got up projects to leave the colony, unless I removed to the woods with them and gave my aid. We left, therefore, our pleasant villa in Mansfield; took with us a widow and five orphan children; left the most tasteful and pleasant residence in the city of Mans- field, and removed into a log cabin at Benzonia, the name I had given to our new town—(composed of a Hebrew and a Greek word). My wife never murmured,· although the change of residence and comfort was almost as great as possible—from a first-class home to a log cabin open to the weather. Every night during the winter when it stormed she shook the snow off our bed in the morning— and there was no bright night that we could not see the stars through crevices in the logs of our cabin.

I expended all my income annually in opening a farm—planting fruit and encouraging and aiding others to do so. I took to the region the best breed of stock; best varieties of fruit and fowls, and helped the settlers what I could in their endeavor to get homes and surroundings so that they could sustain themselves. Many of them needed frequent and energetic assistance, which I gave so far as I was able; in some cases furnishing food—sometimes clothing.

But I had gone there solely prompted by the motive to develop the country and locate a christian college. Our agent, in purchasing government lands and managing our finances, had acted for his own interest, perhaps more than was meet. So, after spending years of toil, a part of the time in colony matters, and two years as a member of the State Senate from the Northern District of Michigan; after organizing the first Congregational church in Lansing, the capitol of the State, and preaching for them six months in a hall which I built and gave for their use on the Sabbath, without charge; after seeing the school at B. in operation with two professors and an assistant; after erecting a mill and aiding in making roads, bridges, etc.; after seeing all the log cabins removed, but one, and many tidy frame houses erected; after success in a good measure had been achieved, I found the agent of the colony and treasurer of the college so managed the finances that, although there was no fraud, I utterly despaired of effecting any benevolent end in connection with the enterprise, or of preserving the lands of the institution: I therefore reluctantly gave up my cherished scheme and left the colony. I left, however, all the lands I had given, which was a large part of the whole five thousand acres, to be used for education in that destitute region, and by the school which

had been established, so far as it was established
at all, mostly by my personal means and agency.

The Congregational churches of Ohio had not
been organized when I returned to Mansfield. The
Oberlin people had what was called an Oberlin
Association, and there was an organization at Marietta of a few churches; but no state association,
and most of the Congregational churches were
independent or in the Presbytery. After some correspondence, it was agreed by the active men of
the state, especially the Marietta men, to hold a
state convention at my church in Mansfield, in
order to organize, if deemed expedient, a State
Congregational Association. Providence so ordered
that I was president of the convention. The great
difficulty was to harmonize the Oberlin men and
the Western Reserve college and Marietta men.
They have never acted together. Many of those
present had repudiated Oberlin. By thoughtful
arrangement of committees and subjects the two
parties began to fraternize with each other, and in
the end a State Congregational Association was
formed, including all the Congregational and Independent churches in the state—Oberlin and Anti-
Oberlin died—and the Congregationalists were
brethren. I have been thankful that Providence
gave me the chairmanship of the State Convention.

I was in the Senate, chairman of the Committee
on Public Instruction. A Common School bill had
been prepared by a previous legislature—but had
failed. I adopted the bill, and with modifications

put it through the Senate by an almost unanimous vote. I think it the best Common School law existing in any state. Attempts have been made to amend, but every amendment will be an injury. I did my share in the Senate—preached frequently in my own hall—and cared for Benzonia's interests so far as I was able. When I returned from the Senate the citizens of Benzonia assembled and gave me a reception. I was addressed, and I answered as greater people do. And the walls of the log school house were hung with evergreens and inscriptions. "Welcome to our Senator," and other devices were on the walls. I was more embarrassed for words than I had been in times of debate on bills of import in the Senate.

May God revealed in Christ bless this narrative so far as it is pure to the good of others—and lead the compiler to omit anything that would turn attention to himself, except so far as example may do good.

JAS. B. WALKER.

THOUGHTS AND INCIDENTS.

1830—1880.

From time to time in my reading and study some thought has impressed me vividly, or has been suggested in some new form or relation.
I have often written such thoughts in my diary or in a blank book
lying on my table. I have here transcribed some of these. They
have—many of them—been embodied in some of my sermons or volumes; yet I have thought it would be profitable for me, and it may
be for others, to read them here as they were originally set down.

Christians who live by faith in the Son of God have less to do with
the dispensation of Moses than they suppose. Christ's example and
precept is their *law*:—to please Him their *motive*:—and the love
produced by faith is their life. To the believer, "Christ is first and
last and 'midst and everywhere."

"Except ye repent, ye shall all likewise perish, as did those upon
whom the tower fell." Does this mean that the death of the body
is likewise the destruction of the soul to the impenitent? It cannot
mean that they would perish temporally by a similar providence.
But the warning may refer to the violent death of the great multitude of the Jews at the destruction of Jerusalem.

The peculiarities of evangelical labor in the revivals of 1830-1840
were the true methods of gospel progress.
The truths of the gospel were presented in a searching and unsec-
tarian form. Different denominations often united in the effort. The
preachers urged the people to turn from all sin and uncleanliness, as
necessary in order to communion with God. Sometimes weeks were
spent in preaching to professing christians, until they saw their sins
and confessed them *publicly* to each other and to God. Each then
felt free from a sense of condemnation. No intoxicating liquors were
used—tobacco was generally abandoned as a filthy habit—and believers attained peace and purity in believing.

1

Then the people were invited to work and pray—to speak kindly to the impenitent—confess to them—if they had misled them by living vain and worldly lives; and then invite them to the prayer meeting and to the sanctuary. In that prayer meeting and sanctuary were the believing people imbued with a sense of the Spirit's presence, and with the worth of the soul; and exercised with a deep and loving spirit of prayer—prayer that was not form but power. Experience meetings for christians; inquiry meetings for the impenitent—individual effort—all conducted without fanaticism, (except in occasional cases which will always occur in connection with any energetic movement). The means of grace thus administered were blessed of God to the conversion of hundreds of thousands in all the evangelical churches in America. Many neighborhoods were transformed. Many denominations rose from dead works and forms into spiritual life, and the foundations of the churches of the present day were mostly laid during the revival period from 1830 to 1840.

The form of revival effort without confession; without forsaking of sins; without the spirit of prayer and repentance, and without humble reconsecration to Christ, is a mockery, and will fail to accomplish good. Some churches afterwards endeavored to work in these forms without true confession and repentance. It was as beating the air: "the form of godliness without the power thereof."

What the world needs is more *love* in the hearts of men for God and for each other. So far as love is increased the world is saved, the law fulfilled and God glorified. Now, faith in Christ draws love from the Godhead into human hearts. Believers draw love from Christ into their own hearts by faith; and hence, as love seeks good of others and is diffusive in its nature, they disseminate love among men. Thus every one that truly believes increases the *love power* in the world. There can never be an item more of love in this selfish and corrupt world than there is to-day, except it be drawn from Christ by faith and then diffused among men, by believers.

Suffering has power above all other power to move the emotions, and thus induce activity among men. It was the sufferings of the Waldenses that moved Milton, Cromwell and all England. The recital of the sufferings of the slaves moved England and then America in the greatest reform the world has known. It was the sufferings of the settlers in Kansas that moved all the free States to move for their rescue. The atonement contains the love power developed by suffering in the highest degree; hence its power to move the world.

Sometimes there is interest great as the perpetuity of free institutions urging patriotic men to vote for men of moral principle, irrespective of party attachments. A professed christian that does not do this when the moral character of the candidates, or the moral principles of the canvass require, is derelict in duty.

The trinity of the New Testament is different from the trinity of the dogmatics. The New Testament is not irrational. Some of the creeds are. The Scriptures speak of the Father (the Unknowable substratum or substance of divine Being) as being revealed in the person of the Son, and both Father and Son as being revealed by the Holy Spirit, who comes in the personality of the Son.

When philosophers write about infinity of time or space, as being a simple innate idea, they use words without knowledge. The idea is nothing more or less than the finite indefinitely extended. It is a finite idea with limitation subtracted; this is all the infinity that the human mind can know. The perfect is the conception of character deprived of imperfection; and as the creation tends to this end, perfection in this sense will sooner or later be attained by those who are rising in moral attainment.

There are too many of our best hymns which express a desire to depart from this world. There should be few such hymns, because they can be truthfully sung in spirit by but few christians. It is not the state produced by the Spirit except in the case of those who are nigh unto death. Christian courage, love, hope, effort, experience, are better expression for hymns which are not praise and devotion in view of the providence and attributes of God. Most christians sing untruthfully, who sing hymns expressing a desire to die.

The gospel is the only remedy for the moral evils of mankind, because there is no religion which will work out the *good of the whole world* but this. No religion that will work all sin out of the soul of individual believers, but this. No religion that glorifies God by revealing fully his love and justice, but this.

Each new species in the natural world is evolved from old species by the process of gestation. So the new species of humanity of which Christ is the head. By faith the lineaments of the new species are begotten in the old. As a chrysalid in development here— perfected at the resurrection. The new species will then have its appropriate corporeity, "We shall be like Him," etc.

Decent, tasteful apparel is comely, but to me the professional badge in the apparel of ministers has always seemed undesirable; hence I have endeavored to counteract the tendency by wearing brown and

other Quaker colors—or part of a suit—in preference to a full suit of
black. I have, I think, accomplished the introduction of the *white
vest* into the pulpit. Ten years ago I wore the only white vest as
chairman of the convention that formed the Ohio State Conference
of Congregationalists. Every year since then the State Conference
has had an increasing number of white vests, until in the present
year, the spotless color predominated. The methodist brethren took
the reform more easily and more rapidly than the Congregational
and Presbyterian ministers.

Individuals in whom the Holy Spirit was consciously dwelling,
would probably not be displeased to see young people dance in proper
places and with proper associates, but would not themselves ordinarily be disposed to unite in the amusement, even for the benefit of
the excuse. It is probable that the friends of Christ danced at the
wedding feast; but it is *not* probable that he or his mother did so.

We should be guarded in the matter of old ecclesiastical institutions. If they accumulate wealth or character they generally become
time-serving and corrupt. They can bestow honor and patronage;
hence the venal will seek their favor and sacrifice to them as a fish-
erman of old sacrificed to his net.

On a certain occasion I visited, by invitation, a certain city and
found that the daily papers the preceding Saturday had published a
notice that "*the Rev. Dr. Walker*" would preach in a certain
church the following Sabbath. I was a stranger to most of the congregation; but reading the notice I thought they would expect something profound; or a discourse on some important subject, from a
Doctor of Divinity. I was tempted to select a subject of such
character; and not select under the influence of the true motive:
What will do this people most good! The title D. D. being contrary
to Christ's command, is of the devil. It does injury to those who
accept it, and to the cause of Christ.

Much of the dogmatism on the subject of imputed righteousness
has grown out of the wickedness of man's heart, which leads him to
devise schemes of hope that are in some cases preposterous, rather
than obey the example and command of Christ, to labor for the good
of men, with a loving and self-denying spirit.
Imputation is practically true in only one sense. It is the merit
of Christ; his self-denying life; his sacrificial death, which by faith
affects the human heart, and by producing the love and disposition
to obey which the law requires, makes the man righteous. Hence
the merit is in Him who produces the change in us—*but the love and
obedience is in us.* But to talk of imputed righteousness only so far

as we possess a loving and obedient spirit is a sham and a sin. As saith the voice of reason in the Scriptures, "If while we seek to be justified by Christ we ourselves are found sinners, we make Christ the minister of sin." Such dogmatism actually makes Christ's sacrifice an occasion to continue sin rather than a producing cause of holiness among men.

It cannot be questioned but that miracles were necessary to introduce the gospel dispensation. No truth could at that time have been received as from God without them. All men believed miracles were wrought by the divinities which they worshiped, and the nature of the human mind is such, that while men believed this it was necessary to credence in the Messiah to give them the evidences of miracles. After the descent of the Holy Spirit,—which was the great miracle,—the moral instead of the physical aspect prevailed more and more in the propagation of the gospel, until in the end an internal experience, and an intellectual apprehension of the ultimate spiritual character of the manifestations and precepts of the gospel becomes its witness.

The fact, therefore, that miracles were wrought of a striking physical character in the first ages of the N. T. Dispensation must be true. But how they were wrought, whether subjectively or objectively—in accordance with natural law, or above natural law, is not of so much importance. The effect gained was the end sought.

I have generally found that trained singers with no firm religious principles, whether they are professors of religion or not, are an evil, if they are members of a select choir in a congregation. They manifest selfishness—class feeling, and fastidiousness in regard to singing with certain persons, and with certain voices. Their absence from the choir, or their presence in it leads others to absent themselves. Then they introduce many new tunes which the congregation cannot sing; and which, being new to themselves, they sing like a man walking on a tight rope—hesitating, careful and balancing—without spirit or impression. Then they sing to make melody to the congregation—not to God, which is idolatry; and the congregation admire the artistic performance instead of feeling the impress of devotional thought. A choir may lead a congregation—and an instrument accompany the choir—but they should so lead that all the people could sing, and that persons of common musical culture and strong good voices should not be excluded from the singer's seat.

I sincerely believe that if I ever get to heaven, it will be by the immediate power and mercy of God, and I shall myself be without the least degree of merit—"a sinner saved by grace."

There is one man whose name is attached to an advertisement in my paper published at Chicago, and likewise in the *Independent*. I have never noticed his name in either of those papers without uttering an inward and sometimes a vocal thought of prayer for his prosperity, temporal and spiritual. That man's name is Lucius Harte, of Burling shp, New York.

———

Once when I was hard up (as business men say) for means to meet some indebtedness on my paper in Chicago, I sought advertisements from business men at the east, who I thought would sympathize with my endeavor to establish a new paper in the West devoted to reformatory evangelical religion in the churches. Mr. Harte received me very kindly; talked like a man and a christian, and paid me in advance a considerable sum for advertising for him in my new paper in a new city—Chicago. I greatly needed the aid; felt his kindness and the manner in which it was bestowed. I kept his advertisement in so long as I printed the paper; and have never since noticed his name without saying sincerely, *O Lord, bless Lucius Harte.*
P. S.—I visited Lucius Harte in 1848. Now, in 1866, I see by his advertisement that he prospers in business.

———

I don't believe in the change bearing law of Babbage's calculating machine. Either there is some provision made by the original designer by which the link in the chain after ten millions and its fraction is extended, or else some defect in the machine creates the variation. It is not possible that a machine fixed by a perfect material structure to progress by unity to 10,000,000, can change *unless the physical structure provides for it,* or produces it as a result of its operation.

———

Unless there are well directed efforts by wise and good men to enforce the great central doctrine taught in the precept and example of Christ, viz: *'that God is glorified only by labor for the temporal and spiritual good of man,* there will be a tendency in half a century from this time, to that contemplative self-enjoying state produced by faith in love, which is the tendency of the mind that shuns labor and does not love men as Christ loved them. The new commandment is: Love others, AS I HAVE LOVED YOU.
This world is a world of work and self-denial. In the next, it may be, our circumstances will be different. The holiest condition on this earth, and perhaps in all spheres, is to find happiness in *doing good;* not in *feeling good,* unless the *feeling* arise as it ought from *doing* for others from love as a motive.

———

Ministers who are not at home with common people—who know

little except the dead languages—and the things which relate to dogmatic and sectarian theologies, are not the best class of gospel ministers. They are not fitted for such work as that done by the apostles. Some godly men who were accounted peculiar in the seminaries, worked for the poor during their student life, and thus escaped the incapacitating process, as the first students at Oberlin; as Whitefield and Wesley. But a recluse seminary education usually injures men's spirituality, and tends to make them mere *preaching machines* (as the professors often are); fitted only for the worldly churches, where persons assemble as a form on the Sabbath.

Skeptics admit that the example and precepts of Christ, are the best rule of life that has ever been given to men. Now, reason as well as religion requires that men should conform to the best known and approved principles of duty. Hence it follows that God must judge skeptics as well as christians by the New Testament. The one acknowledges the rule as right, but is neither obedient nor penitent for disobedience. The other acknowledges the rule; seeks grace to obey; and when conscious of failure is humble and penitent, and as such seeks and receives pardon in Christ.

Wonder if those who believe in the development theory, believe likewise in moral development. If they do, then christianity is true; for the system of Moses was a development out of the patriarchal religion; and the gospel is a development out of the Mosaic dispensation. And the system is still developing itself into the image of the moral perfect. If development be true at all, (and I think there are sufficient data to prove that it is,) then it is true as a general law over the whole organic creation; and it is true likewise over the whole spiritual world; hence, the gospel which is developing the spiritual interests of men towards the perfect is true, because it fulfills the natural law.

Men have, by nature, a conscience that enforces the duties of morality up to the standard of the golden rule. We know without revelation what men ought or ought not to do to us; hence we infer what our duty is to them in like circumstances. *The sense of right in such cases is natural.* But conscience in relation to duties to God acts only by faith in revelation; and our duties to men become more consciously obligatory by recognizing God as requiring them. A sense of God in truth is the life of conscience.

The *I* of the mind is not conscious of itself. It is only conscious of its product or thought. Thought is the object seen by the ego or personality of the mind. Just as we are conscious of perceiving objects of sense but not of the eye which gives us the perception.

Conscious of seeing, but not of the eye that sees. Yet the perceiving *I* may know its own character, by perceiving the character of the thought which it evolves.

Sir Wm. Hamilton thinks that the EYE and the I, having the same sound in English, embarrasses the student in understanding the office of the eye:—but rightly understood the analogy aids the apprehension. Sir. Wm., like many other *professional* philosophers, writes many things that are hard to be understood, and writes them in regard to matters that need to be made plain by a true philosophy, rather than to be involved in a labyrinth of learned logomachy. True philosophy simplifies. *It is the province of a great mind to make things plain.* The idea of Hamilton, that we are *immediately* conscious of the external world is essentially unphilosophical. While it is true that *we have consciousness of the external world without being conscious of the medium through which we obtain our knowledge*, yet a *true philosophy gives the medium*, and in many cases corrects errors of the medium.

Very few nights during a whole life time have I been out of bed after half past nine o'clock. I have endeavored to *live in the light*— and hence, with a feeble constitution, I have accomplished an unusual amount of physical and mental labor.

In the worldly and wealthy churches are many good people, perhaps as many as in those churches which gather the poor alone. The churches should, if they are churches of Christ, embrace all classes of society. People will, from the nature of things, associate by affinity; but where true religion exists faith in Christ is the strongest affinity existing on earth. When a church has collected within its congregation those who associate by worldly affinity, only the fact proclaims it as one destitute of the Savior's marks of a true church, as given to John.

I have known persons convicted of the truth, who felt that they must do something—yet were unwilling to deny themselves and obey Christ. To escape the sense of obligation they bribed their conscience by associating themselves with some church of society, where they could serve the world and bear at the same time the name of Christ. Ministers in popular churches should be faithful to such.

I have just returned from a monthly meeting of Presbyterian ministers. A skeleton was read on the passage, "Ye are dead and your life is hid with Christ in God." It affirmed that the christian's joy and the christian's motive were drawn from Christ; that they were not of the world; that they had hidden sources of love, praise and duty, that the world had not. And the skeleton closed with an address to the impenitent to seek the hidden life of the christian. Such sermons describing christian character as it should be, and then appealing to the impenitent, as though it were true of all those in the congregation who profess religion, are an offence to reason, as well as to God. The impenitent present—many of them partners of professors—know that the description is untrue of the greater portion of those professing religion. They—if they think about it at all—either believe the minister is deceived, or that he is endeavoring to deceive them in regard to the mental joy and peace of professing christians. A few in our churches experience the grace of Christ taught in the gospel. The great body of professors, especially in worldly churches, fall far below the experience written in the text. Religion will make little progress until truth is preached by men who feel and do truth.

There is generally an emigration from old communities when the interests of true religion are to be furthered, as in the case of Abraham; the Israelites; the early Christians; the Puritans, and others. Old countries become so rigid in their dogmatic forms and creeds; there come into action so many monied interests connected with old forms and institutions; so many shibboleths; so many influential ecclesiastical bodies; so many doctors of divinity, that truth is cramped, and its life and light restrained, unless there be an emigration of godly persons into a far and free region. Hence, emigration is an act of Providence to preserve piety and liberty. It has followed, according to this principle, that while the older churches of the East yet maintain the truth, it is the truth in bonds. While those of the free West have less system, but more reform; more energy; more variety of means, and more conversions to Christ.

This is Sabbath, December 20th, 1859. I read yesterday a paragraph in the daily paper, stating that Mr. Moran, who receives the exorbitant sum of $25,000 per year for his services as President of the Erie Rail Road, has issued a circular asking the working men on the road to submit, without grumbling, to a reduction of their wages—most of them receive but the sum of one dollar per day—the mechanics something more; most of both classes having families. Now, it is my opinion that the man who will receive $25,000 per year for his own services, and then (in order that he may save the company in giving him his extravagant salary) will ask men who work as hard as himself to take less than $1 per day, is a selfish, heartless scoundrel. God forgive me for the denouncement.

There is a time when the soul or life principle of things begins to assimilate matter into the form of a body, which body changes its particles but not its form; hence, there is a life principle. *Forms* of matter have a beginning—perfect in its kind—hence, there is a God.

3

In a certain city in which there were churches of several denominations, there came at a certain time several naval officers, lieuten-
ants, midshipmen and others. They were lions in worldly circles,
and likewise with the churches of society. It was known that some
of them were like other officers of the regular army and navy—men
of bad habits; licentious men, excited often by brandy, and often
filthy with tobacco. The churches of society whispered to them that
the Congregational church was the "Abolition church," and the
whisper "accomplished the end for which it was said." The naval
officers attended other churches and were never seen at the church
that testified against prevailing sins. Thus the wicked were induced
to go where they could not be benefited. Worldly persons in those
churches, professing to be disciples of Christ, were gratified and rendered more evil by their association, and the church which testified
for truth was relieved from a malign influence—an influence which
in the end brought shame to some of the foolish families who had
courted it.

Ten years after writing the above sentences I visited the city
where the churches referred to are located. The Abolition church,
as it was then called, is now the leading church. The other is living a dying life.

The confessions of a contrite christian, which evince heart-felt sincerity are a sermon that reaches the souls of others, and convicts them
of sin, more certainly than any other expression of truth which men
hear. Men know what the gospel requires, and what professors of
religion ought to be; and when they see those that they know have
lived a worldly or unworthy life acting conspicuously without sense
and confession of past evil, they are stumbled. They know such
persons, in order to a good conscience, ought to first "confess their
faults one to another." Hence, when it is done sincerely they feel
it, and are convicted themselves of the purity and power of the gospel that thus reaches and removes sin.

Parents who attend prayer meetings and are at times *very much
engaged for others;* but who have unconverted sons and daughters
to whom they have never spoken on the subject of religion, are usually persons who do not exemplify the life of religion at home, and
who desire their children should have favor with the world. There
may be one good parent whose life does not avail against the character or moral evils of the other; hence, children are evil while one
parent is good.

The Logos; the Sent one—Messiah—is the highest conception and
the highest hope originated by the human mind. In the fullness of
the old world's age, God, who had inspired the conception in the
ancient world, and guided in its development, actualized it in the

birth of Jesus; and in the descent of the Holy Spirit in a personal form upon him at his baptism. The result was God manifest in the flesh. There is a prophetic element in the minds of all great and good men. Hence, this idea of a divine manifestation through man *to* man has been the final exposition of human wisdom in all the ages.

The best graces as well as the best forms of religion can be counterfeited, especially by men of sensibility and talent. Preachers who have little principle often do this. They know what they ought to be and simulate it; but hypocrisy is a cloak that sometimes becomes repulsive to its wearers; and those who feign godliness which they do not feel generally turn into sectarians, or formalists. They often oppose the reformed and spiritual movements which God from time to time inaugurates in the churches. And in such cases their formal godliness seems to many to be true godliness, and gives influence to their opposition to moral progress. So it has been in the anti-slavery and other reforms.

The word infinite, and all words of cognate import are words without meaning to the human mind only so far as they express a finite idea; and we conceive of that idea as *deprived of limitation.* The human mind is limited and cannot comprehend the infinite in any direction. The effort to do so produces an idea of a finite quantity with a suffix or prefix, depriving that quantity of conceivable limit. This is evident in the early forms of the Hebrew language.

The pure spirituality of the gospel dispensation was developed in the minds of the Apostles *progressively* even after the day of Pentecost. The christian system was gradually detached from Judaism; and Christ's character and his coming as the Divine Spiritual Redeemer, was better understood after years of thought and labor than at the first.

The doctrines of the New Testament are gradually developed in the world under the Divine Supervision. It is not quite time yet for light to be granted by providence in all places and cases in regard to the erroneous construction of future retribution, which taught eternal hell torment for all impenitents. Such a construction of the New Testament might be inferred readily from the prevailing interpretation of one, perhaps more, passages of the S. S. But the denouncements by the teachers of this doctrine in most congregations are less terrible than formerly. The time has come for the initiation of the discussion concerning the words *perish, life, death, hell,* etc., in the N. T. This initiation I have attempted from a sense of duty in the Oberlin *Evangelist;* a portion of which the good brethren there

have omitted.   They feared the influence upon the received views.
The result of the discussion will probably be that God is overcoming
evil, both physical and moral in his universe.   That the consequences
of sin here and hereafter are its penalty.   That no one not united to
Christ by the faith that purifies and draws life from him, will reach a
glorious resurrection; and that at the judgment, God will make an
end of evil by annihilating in the second death all reprobate spirits
whose trial proved a failure, resulting in deterioration instead of being rendered meet for the "resurrection of the dead."

It is a most striking and significant remark of Jeremy Taylor—
that an unjust acquisition is like a barbed arrow which must be drawn
backward with horrible anguish or else it will be the destruction of
the soul.

I am persuaded that the higher intellectual expressions of gospel
truth are not valuable to the less cultivated class.   I attended a
funeral to-day in a rude neighborhood; and as I have felt before, so
I felt to-day, that nothing but strong language and figures, and striking and moving illustrations, are adapted to awaken and interest the
great majority of such congregations.   The Head of the Church in
sending out the fishermen—the Wesleyans, and other teachers from
the populace, and in giving the *strong language of the New Testament*, and its awakening exhibition of love and penalty, has adapted
his providences; his manifestations, and his teaching to common
minds.

The literalists commit the same blunder that the Jews did in the
time of Christ, and that the disciples did in some measure before the
pouring out of the Holy Spirit.   The error of literalism is palpable
and hurtful.   Jesus especially spake in parables.   All his words have
a spiritual import, except in some cases where they relate to temporal
concerns.   Not a double sense but a spiritual sense.   The book of
John; the Beatitudes; the Revelation, especially are perverted if lit-
erally interpreted.   The language of symbols is a universal language;
and, although liable to misconstruction, especially by non-spiritual
minds, yet the import of Christ's words, and much of his own conduct have a spiritual sense.   As in the case of the barren fig tree
that was cursed.   The import is the same as that of his parable of
the husbandman who, seeking fruit, and not finding it, cast out the
occupants of the vineyard.   The tree is the symbol of the Jewish
church, which, bearing no fruit, was doomed to immediate destruction, which it experienced in the generation then living.   The with-
ering of the fruitless tree under the curse of Christ, was a visible
symbol.

Perfection of instinct in the beginning of life is not in accordance
with any possible theory of development by law.

The struggle between the animal and the spiritual in man indicates more than we see at first thought, in regard to man's moral nature and destiny.

The Holy Spirit was personally in Christ and Christ is personally in the Holy Spirit; and in that personality He is with the church to the end of the world.

I have had, since I hoped in Christ, four seasons of peculiar experience. Three of them were alike in my consciousness. Soon after I was converted I enjoyed a state of mind for many months that was a peaceful delight. The trees and the stars seemed to speak quietly of God, and I was not afraid to die.

The second, I was going to a meeting of days with a brother of peculiar rich and earnest experience. He had faith and hope and joy in his soul, and a spirit of prayer by which his soul seemed to reach and effect others. I slept, and talked with him by the way to the meeting, and next morning when I awoke my mind was in a sweet spiritual frame. I rose earlier than others and walked out into the orchard, and my heart and the trees and the heavens seemed lovingly to praise God.

Again in Cincinnati I slept and talked during a revival of religion with another brother of earnest, gracious exercises. He seemed "filled with the Spirit." When I awoke the next morning I had the same state of mind. I have no doubt these brethren prayed for me earnestly on those nights. But was there anything in the fact that they possessed the Spirit which by personal contact aided the impartation of the influence to me? Is there anything in the doctrine of the laying on of hands, (spoken of as one of the cardinal doctrines in Heb. 6,) which indicates that the Holy Spirit is communicated through persons? If so, what is the value of the ordination by formal and selfish ministers? If any Spirit be communicated through them, it is certainly not the Holy Influence indwelling by faith. I have had other deliverances from sin, not in such connections. In these two cases it seemed to be an impartation of spiritual life through others.

I just now found a black beetle which had been turned over on its back on a smooth surface. It seemed to be feeble, probably from long struggle to right itself; still it put forth efforts to get right side up, without success. I held out to it a straw which it seized and thus turned itself over. It felt better, and I felt better to see it released. I thus increased in some degree the sum of sentient happiness. My Father made the insects.

It is a remarkable fact, and one which repeated experiments renders indubitable, that one man can place his logos in another so

4

that the will and thought of that other will be his will and thought, while yet he retains his own logos in his own bosom. Who can solve the unfathomable mystery? That such things exist, (to which a better name should be given,) there can be no doubt. I have myself induced the magnetic sleep in those whose veracity could not be questioned. The susceptibility is not common, but it exists with some in a lesser, with others in a greater degree. In such cases some can read the thoughts in other minds.

Three several times in my life I have been sensible of power in the words that converted a sinner. I felt the power of the thought in my own heart, and I spoke it as though life was in it. The individuals afterwards repeated to me the *idea* and spoke of certain *words* as going *to* their heart and awakening them to feel their lost condition. I have no doubt that as a general truth individuals will feel a preacher's words in some measure as *he* feels them himself. And special instances as above often occur.

The holiness of the New Testament is the central evidence of its truth. Holiness of Christ; of the Apostles; of the doctrine. In holiness is the highest good of the human soul; hence, the New Testament is the highest truth.

Whenever an individual does any act that causes a great many minds to regard him with ill-will and indignation, some persons think that he may expect some evil providence to befall his person. Such an individual should pray without ceasing. He needs good angels to protect him. Observation has seemed to me to teach that such a statement has some truth in it, albeit it may not be postulated as truth. Evil wishes are prayer as good desires are prayer.

Present and perfect accordance with the will of Christ should be constantly the main point of christian purpose and endeavor. *I will be obedient and loving toward God every day and hour; and to please Him will seek and improve every opportunity to do good to man.* Purposes and rules for prayer, reading, etc., are well enough, but without the main purpose TO DO by faith the will of Christ daily and hourly, they fail of efficiency, and are often the means by which the soul excuses itself for neglect of duty.

When an individual feels wrong towards another, it seems as though some evil spirit ordered the words and conduct of that other so that the one with evil feeling could see what will enable him to judge according to his evil disposition. Occasion is given for the development of the evil exercises in the case of those who have the evil disposition.

The men who have changed the sweet *melodies* of old Sherburne and other like tunes, (melodies which were natural and easy, and hence delightsome,) into the forced and affected *harmonies* in some of the newer versions, ought to be damned, at least for a second or two; but not so long as they distress others by the disappointment and regret of hearing *artistic harmony* instead of the old *natural melody*. Why can't harmonists let the sweet melodies of the church alone! Make new, but spare the old. Not long since, in a large congregation, on a public occasion, the preacher gave out the hymn, "Shall Jesus bear the cross alone," which all knew was married to a tune they loved, written in the books. The fools in the choir se- lected another tune and disgusted and jarred the minds of a large share of the audience. No composer—Bliss excepted—writes more than from one to a dozen good melodies. Melody is the soul. Mere harmonies are body without soul.

There are passages in the books of Moses that are not in accord- ance with the New Testament view of God's character, except as we consider them judgments of God inflicted upon wicked nations, and inflicted by men whose own *natural* impulses (*i. e.*, the impulses of the natural heart,) were turned to account in executing those judg- ments. The slaughter of the women and infants by order of Moses; a like case by Samuel, and a worse case by the Levites, killing their neighbors who had transgressed by idolatrous indulgences. Great injury is done to the cause of Christ when men endeavor to render these cases consistent with the advanced light of our dispensation. The statement of David hanging the children of Rispah is probably an interpolation, as it is not found in the parallel record. But the preceding instances of cruelty are a true record; and even this may have been the act of a king jealous of the heirs of Saul. God permits similar acts of cruelty in wars of the present time. The Bible is re- sponsible only for giving a true record of such acts as were done in connection with Jewish wars. Such record could be made in our age; but the spirit of christianity is designed to change the charac- ter of the world so that the cruelties of one set of men inflicted on others as judgments for sin will not be continued. Such things, then and now, were seldom approved by the Almighty, except as judg- ments in which both the afflicted and the inflicter were guilty as to same extent in the war with the sleveholders. David, as a warrior, was a man after God's own heart chosen to scourge other guilty na- tions; yet he was himself called "a man of blood," and was not permitted on account of his blood-guiltiness to build a house of worship for Jehovah. And so far from being—as a common man— one after God's heart, the scriptures affirm that for his sins terrible judgments were inflicted on him, and the sword was not to depart from his house until he died. God is dishonored and the Scripture record misconstrued by making David a Saint, in any other sense than that of his sterling hostility to Idolatry, and his recognition of

God in all the providences that befel him. By deep repentance he received pardon, as it may be hoped, for his aggravated sins. Less aggravated in view of the darkness of his dispensation; but such as would have consigned him to destruction under gospel light.

Another evil more prevalent formerly than at the present time is that of endeavoring to make the local legislation of Moses, which was adapted to the children of a migratory nation, a rule of duty under our dispensation. Moses changed the legislation in accordance with the change of circumstances in the commencement. The penalty for theft was three times changed in Israel. Deuteronomy, the second law, was promulgated when the Jews were about to become a settled nation, and was changed and amended in various respects to suit the better circumstances of the people. The moral law, in the Ten Commandments, given on Sinai is immediately from God. It is the higher law. All legislation contrary to it is nugatory. It is the foundation of all legislation. The ritual and local laws of Moses were to last only till they were fulfilled. The Ten Commandments are to last so long as man lasts. Whosoever breaks one of them and teaches men so is the least in the Kingdom of God; and whosoever teaches the obsolete ritual is not instructed in the Kingdom of God.

The moral law is the law of nature revised and revealed with authority.

The first commandment with its introduction *recognizes the God of Providence as the True God*, and the only God to be worshiped. "I brought you up out of the land," etc.

The second forbids idolatry, because the worshiper will necessarily attach the attributes of the image to the idea of God.

Third, forbids irreverence and false swearing.

Fourth, appoints the day for rest and religious culture.

Fifth, duty of children to parents.

Sixth, protects life.

Seventh, chastity.

Eighth, property.

Ninth, character.

Tenth, makes all spiritual—forbidding the *thought* that prompts to wrong action.

———

"Male and female created He them." Man was created male and female. Juno sprang from Jupiter's head. Eve was from the side of Adam. Every head is male and female united in the cerebellum. The two sets of organs co-operate. But the organs in male and female do not seek like organs in each other. Nature seeks to balance herself. And that marriage is probably best if not happiest, when the organs of the male and female are the compliment of each other. That is, where a small organ in the male head is compensated by a larger one in the female, and *vice versa*. Similarity of organs does not produce peace and happiness, as phrenologists have taught.

Combativeness largely developed in both will be certain to produce collision—so in other cases. There is something in phrenology, but not all that phrenologists have claimed.

The doctrine of perfection is not so difficult, if there were discrimination. Whether men can be perfect or not, of course, depends on the standard they measure themselves by. To be perfect in love is a very different thing from being perfect in self-denial for the good of men. Christ was perfect in both.

There is evidence of the antiquity and genuineness of the Bible in that its early histories are not theogonies but homologies. Not the genealogies of gods but the genealogies of men. The puerile and impure tales of the Old Testament ought not to be read in families, although the parent ought to have them read by children, and explain that to the early men concubinage was permitted. That "old wives' fables," which the New Testament discountenances, were the staple histories of the old times; because the genealogies of families was the chief interest and the only history. That the deception of Abraham, Rachel and others were wrong then, but would be greater wrong now. That it was necessary for the Bible to give a true state of the low and beastly vices prevailing in early times, in order to give us a true record of the true state of the church and the world in that age.

In rejecting the Jewish view of their own Scriptures the Christians have erred in the past; but it was the error of the church rising from the dark ages to the more advanced state. It is now, or soon will be, a hindrance to the progress of truth to affirm that the minor histories and the hagiographa of the Old Testament were inspired in the same sense as the dispensation of Moses proper, and the preaching of the prophets.

Solomon's song is a love song; and in our age would be a lewd song. And while it may have been valuable to the Jews as an incitement to monogamy, or the love of one wife only, in our circumstances it is an excitement to lust rather than an inducement to virtue. The older divines, by making it an allegory, alluding to Divine love saved it from evil and used it for good. Inspiration relates in its most important sense to those scriptures which reveal the true character of God, and his true relations to man. Under the New Testament,—as God was in Christ,—through Him is revealed to us the true God and the true duty. *The Holy Spirit in inspiration produced ideas in the minds of the sacred writers in keeping with his own holy nature.* Where such ideas are not, the Holy Spirit is not. Providence guides in regard to other truths of history and hagiography. The books of Matthew, Mark and Luke are providential compilations of actual historical facts concerning the life, ministry and death of Christ.

5

The book of John and the epistles are historical and *spiritual* presentations of gospel truth and experience. All are inspired, but not in the same sense. One is by the influx of the Holy Spirit; the other by guidance and providence.

___

God of Providence and gràce who hath raised me up and guided me to do better than I would or could do, enable me to show others how much may be done by Thine assistance in a short life, for thy glory and the good of thy creatures. And help me to acknowledge kindly and gratefully, and to show others, that only those who are instruments in thy hands accomplish ends worthy of life's labor.

London, July 2, 1861.—Amen to the above, which was written in Ohio years ago.

___

Faith in the Gods of human invention is a natural state. The faith of the natural mind in its own creations. Faith in a character of God above and beyond human capabilities, is produced by inspired truth and supernatural influence—the Bible and the Holy Spirit.

___

The boy called the prince of Wales is a common lad, and he does not deserve so much honor as the self-supporting student in our common schools and seminaries. The Quakers, although ultra, were right in principle in refusing honor to hereditary place holders. Such usually deserve contempt rather than honor. Those who, like Queen Victoria, live a virtuous life, while they spend largely the public money, should be respected for being no worse than they are. But the Americans who, like Gorham Abbott, make asses of themselves by adulation of the prince of Wales, and do it in such connection as to pervert the principles of the young in regard to the worth of human character. Such men and women are sycophants and shallow hypocrites. Our contemplated college at Benzonia, I hope will never invite such mean minds to address any of our societies. There seems to be a hereditary taint in some families that causes some of their members to cringe and prostitute their conscience in the presence of factitious greatness or greatness in combination with crime—as witness the Life of Napoleon by one of the Abbotts—and the proposition to his pupils by another to demean themselves as menials in the presence of a boy, the prince of Wales. Such men fall little behind the eulogists of debased greatness—as Parton and other of like character, who eulogize mind or character without conscience.

___

In the coming ages the question of depravity will be resolved into development of the being by earthly, sensuous and evil surroundings, in which all are born. It will be admitted that man was created in adaptation to the imperfect conditions in which he was to live. That man's imperfection and Christ's perfection imply each other in the moral economy of the world, and that the last is designed by faith to counteract the other.

———

Jesus Christ is God projected into the objective, that by faith He might become subjective in man; or, Jesus Christ is the Logos, the intellectual objective in the divine mind, projected into a human nature, that He might become the moral objective to the human mind, and so by appropriating faith become subjective to the soul.

———

After all the discussions and doubts about doctrine in which Christians may be involved; after all the doubts about whether many in the church are better than some without, still it is pleasant to preach the gospel. The holiness of the gospel; the self-denial for the good of men; the practical character of its morals; the adaptation of its doctrine to benefit men; especially its power to produce love in the human heart, which is the thing needed—all these make it pleasant to preach the gospel.

———

A beautiful little bug has flown to the gas-light deceived, and has fallen in pain on my sheet of paper. Poor thing! What does such an incident mean in the system of creative nature? What does it indicate in regard to the rule of law—to the relations of Creator and creature? Lord, make us humble and docile by such inquiries. They are too deep for me.

———

It is not the *preaching* of godliness but the *practice* of godliness that convicts a household. Households that are externally fair but internally foul, raise those children which lead people to wonder how such good people could have such bad children. There are exceptions; but bad children generally are made by bad propensities in one or both parents, or bad management at home and home-life not known abroad.

———

Does Matter limit to some extent, and in some sense the exercise of divine power? There can not be two hills without a valley between. If a perfect level is raised in one place to a hill, it will from the nature of things and laws cause a depression elsewhere. So, if out of a perfect moral level God brings good, there will result its negative evil. Thus, out of nothing the eduction of good produces a residuum without the good; hence, if good agency be educed, evil agency remains and the progressive work of God in the world is by the good to work the evil out of the system.

There must be moral progress, or an eternal fixedness in perfection that resolves itself into an infinite and inert sameness. But progress implies immaturity; hence the creation is immature, but advancing to perfection in which memory of past history will destroy sameness.

The man whose heart is inclined to reform; to truth; to love, will be in favor of Christ and His gospel, and his mind will be inclined to confess the one and support the other—because Christ is the objective of his own internal state.

The words damnation and condemnation in the New Testament require a new definition in order to a right apprehension of their import by the common reader. The true sense is either self-condemnation felt in the soul, or the sentence of judgment dooming to penalty as the desert of sin. The words are generally understood as meaning the penalty itself as experienced after judgment instead of the sentence of condemnation before the judgment.

Belief in miracles is first, not last in the divine dispensations. When the reason of men shall be fully developed, so that men can see that Christianity is ultimate and perfect in truth, love and power, then the belief in miracles will not be necessary to the men of that age. But it does not follow that the belief was not necessary in the first ages of faith. Men then needed the evidence of sense in connection with the truth. The men of the last age need the evidence of reason, and reason will teach that miracles were necessary in the first, but not in the last ages of faith.

For the reader's sake I have endeavored in my published works to write in such a way that my readers may be drawn insensibly to a more liberal and rational and evangelical view of doctrinal theology in regard to points where the creeds limit the import of scripture.

We may be sure that a church or community that sins against the light of the age in which they live will not run on peacefully. Unless there be repentance there will be a · hardening in sin. Because, when sin is made manifest by truth, if men do not forsake their sin, they will seek apology and then justification of the evil; and hence, if they do not repent, they necessarily become blind and hardened in their guilt.

When the anti-slavery discussion first commenced in this country it was urged in view of moral considerations alone. At that early day, those who understood the retributive character of God's government over nations and churches, taught that God would visit the South with penalty unless they would hear truth and reform their wicked institutions. But the presentation of truth only rendered them insane in their sin. Rulers, priests and people have become hardened and aggressive, and the end will probably be penalty or destruction. We have already reached the beginning of the end. Why should good men wonder? God will reveal his attribute of justice and the future generations will understand that God is just, by his penalties which, perhaps, they would not learn by his precepts.

The first chapter of Romans seems to prove what sectarian selfishness has not brought out of the text—that, although the heathen are vile and desperately wicked, yet that those who conform to the light they possess with as much assiduity as the christian conforms to the light he possesses, will, *according to his degree of holiness*, be as acceptable to God as his more privileged fellow-man. The heathen cannot attain to the degree of holiness that can be attained by faith in Christ; hence, we are the happiest of the holy; but he cannot sink into such aggravated crime as those who have better privileges. It is wise to determine no more in regard to the future of the heathen than is revealed.

A proof that the Old Testament in its general history and its prophetic books was written by divine guidance, is found in the fact that the retribution of the nation from first to last, and the views of the prophets in regard to the causes of that retribution are in accordance with what must from the character of God, be the history of a people where privileges and tuition and transgression were such as that of the Jews. The attribute of justice, as it effects nations in this world being assumed, then the history of the Jews is a deduction.

The idea of a personal devil is necessary in order to lead the soul to hate sin. Satan to the soul is evil personified, and as such he is hated as an objective evil agent, and sin becomes odious as being agreeable to him and instigated by him; thus it becomes odious to the soul in view of its evil source and instigation. But if sin is considered an accident; a fatality; a human frailty, its odious nature is abated in the estimate of the soul. It is considering a character or quality objectively that leads us to feel most deeply its good or evil in ourselves. To hate evil personified is to hate sin.

There are some symbols in all languages which are derived from the grand objects and movements of the material universe; as light and darkness for truth and falsehood, and others that seem to all minds the natural figure for certain states of mind. Other ideas are the final results of human reason in all ages as that of the logos, or thought—birth of the mind. Now, suppose it to be shown as it may be, that the scriptural use of these and like expressions are derived from previous theosophies or philosophies, does that invalidate the

5

truth of scripture? Are not the ideas natural to man, and the symbols which all human languages produce most likely to be true, as
they are those that will be finally and universally accepted. Let the
New Testament be an eclecticism, gathering the gold from the dross
of past thought, and incorporating those ideas at which the mind ar-
rives as its ultimate deductions. Let Paul speak in the language of
the Rabbins, and John accept the phraseology of Alexandria, the
truth of Christianity thus proved does not lose its power. It only
takes on a form that will define it by the idiom of the times—that
will give it currency in its own age, and connect it with the matured
thought of all ages.

There are certain *ultima thule* toward which if the thought be
prone to run, the mind will find itself enveloped in shadows and
doubts. The future life in connection with the resurrection of the
body. The accordance of the old dogmatic teaching in regard to
the atonement with the views revealed in the New Testament. It
will be wise for most christians to accept the impression made by the
separate passages of the New Testament as they read them. Mental
effort to constrain them into accordance with the defined dogmatic
views of theologians, often hinders the impression of the apostolic
thought. It is wise for those who believe that love is life and heav-
en, to leave these speculations to those who like them, and look to
Jesus, believing in his life as the rule of duty, and in his death as
the manifestation of divine love for man.

The true and only true religion is that which being believed will
accomplish the most good in accordance with the laws of mind and
moral progress. No one can doubt but that in this respect the precept and example of christianity are perfect. But there is need, as
the soul is made, of something more than precept and example.
Love is life; it is the highest good of the human soul; hence, with
the perfect in precept and example there is the absolute need of the
love-producing power. This the Christian religion has in perfection to
those who believe. Further still, there is need that the love produced
should influence the will to work for the good of the race. No one
can doubt but that love to Christ does this perfectly. If, therefore,
the only true religion is that which accomplishes the best results for
individual men and for the race—the religion of Christ as it is revealed—not in creeds but in the New Testament—Faith in Christ,
as Lord, Teacher and Sacrifice, is the only possibly true religion—
and as human nature is constituted it is impossible for Christianity
to be untrue.

But what of the Old Testament? It was introductory and imperfect in many respects, because it was in the development before the
perfect. Yet, in the then state of human progress the religion that
taught the one God, Creator, and Controller of nature and providence—the religion that took the institutions produced out of the

necessity of the human heart and human circumstances and moulded them into symbols and into an introduction to the coming perfect, and gave them a moral significance, and at the same time connected God with the affairs of nations and men as the moral governor:—In this sense the Old Testament religion in that age and stage of development and in those circumstances was the best possible to be believed, and hence was the only possible religion as introductory to the perfect in Christianity.

Doubts connected with figures, as in Bishop Colenso, have nothing to do with the truth in the case. God's providence to 6,000, reveals the same truth as to 600,000. The fables and fictions of Jewish tradition and hagiography incorporated in the canon have nothing to do in the case. The nature of the Holy Spirit is such that his operation is only in connection with *holy thought*, and systems, and things necessary to human progress and human good. With this understanding of the plan where the divine connects itself with the human, in all dispensations, the truth-seeker will not be injured by such works as that of Colenso and other writers of the same class past and to come. There are figments and fictions, and old wives' fables in the old Testament, of course; but the plan and providence of God in the dispensation of Moses is above and independent of these.

This week Rev. Mr. C———, from Munson, Mass., is here. He preached yesterday, not as I advised him, but a sermon from the passage in Job: "Who by searching can find out God." His discourse was an abstruse attempt to show we could know nothing of God. "His centre was everywhere, His circumference nowhere. Infinity is incomprehensible; so omnipresence; so infinite power." The effort was to show that all reasoning in regard to God must be contradictory and absurd, and such was the God of the Bible. The sermon was in one sense true; but it was designed to accomplish just the opposite of what revelation and right preaching aims to accomplish. What a pity! God is revealed in Christ in order to be comprehensible to man.

Parents should be careful to be accurate in the use of language in the presence of their young children. The forms of speech settled in their minds from two to ten years of age, it is almost impossible to eradicate by later tuition. I learned from my grandfather's family to use the verb "to be" erroneously; and now, a Dr. of Divinity by the forced nomination of my brethren, and a Senator without asking the nomination, I still in senate and pulpit, and often in the first writing of a MS use *is* for *are*, and other less erroneous forms.

Christian people ought to cease praying for their pastor in his presence. I have always desired the people for whom I preached to

pray for me in private, but not in public.   Human nature is selfishly
good sometimes.   A modest preacher will not desire to hear prayer
frequently for himself if he can have it unheard.   And people, as
well as preachers, sometimes pray—as the politicians say—"for
bunkum."   A good brother is in the habit now of praying for the
young woman gone to teach, and for others in such a manner that
it reaches the *parent's* heart through their ears.   Pray personally
in private if persons are present.

Poets, and to some extent other literary men, who are merely men
of letters—those who have never associated with men or with nature
in the common walks of life—who have never labored with their
hands, and are conversant with ideas only, can never produce anything that will not be devoid in some measure of practical sense.
They may be brilliant and profound; but the clear, strong discrim-
inations of the practical mind will be absent.   Their verses may suit
mere students of letters, but the logic of Pope, the human nature of
Shakspeare, or of Burns will be wanting.   If such men, who are
merely scholars, espouse a good cause, as Sumner or Phillips, they
are heroes of the ideal rather than the practical.   It requires Garrison, the printer; Chase, the ferry boy and school teacher; or, especially Lincoln, the laborer, to maintain truth for those who would
practically apply it.   The simple anecdote of Abraham Lincoln, that
it is unsafe to swap horses crossing a stream, had more influence in
the general election of 1864, than all the able but glittering speeches
of Charles Sumner put together.   I knew this fact, because, in that
election I thought it duty to canvass my senatorial district for Lincoln; I could use his matter with the masses, but I had no use for
the expanded thought of Sumner.

Oberlin, more than any other institution in the land, has been
God's instrument in moralizing the politics, and spiritualizing the religion of the churches in the West.   Not because her doctrine and
action were perfect, but because they tended to perfection.
    The power was not so much in her professors, (except in the case
of Mr. Finney.   They were, most of them, pious men; but very
common men.   Mr. Finney has been the best, and some of her other
professors among the best christians in the land).   The power she
has exercised in the country has been in her principles and her prayers, and in the consecrated hearts of her first friends and her first
students.   She drew to her retired wooden rooms the spiritually inclined youth of the whole land.
    Her first school teachers, alive with gospel principle concerning
human freedom and spiritual holiness, felt within them a commission
to disseminate the light of truth.   They went by hundreds into the
school districts of Ohio and other western states and in the families,
quietly, (while the selfish politicians were scheming for themselves;

or while no political excitement perverted the perception of the people,) they enlightened and converted multitudes to righteous principle; established the truth in their conscience, from which scheming
politicians could not subsequently turn them. At the same time
Oberlin was doing this work State colleges, and other secular institutions, were preaching and teaching their orthodox heresies, and
sending out a class of lawyers and preachers and doctors, many of
whom resisted reform and were a bane rather than a blessing to both
church and State.

The fear now is, that Oberlin has fulfilled her mission as a power
of righteousness in the earth, and is falling to the level of rich, edu-
cational institutions; and at the death of Mr. Finney will pass from
being a spiritual to a secular religious power. Her halls are now
costly and large; filled mostly with worldly and wealthy rather than
poor and spiritual students. Her teachers who, in the days of her
greatest usefulness, did not get half the salary that other college
professors received, are now seeking larger endowment and salaries
equal with others. Thus, education for the people will end at Oberlin, and education for classes begin. The teachers will no longer
affiliate with the students in common; but will be more separate;
and Oberlin will rise in popularity, and sink from spiritual power.
She will regenerate no more States politically, and spiritualize no
more churches. Finney will be true till death, but such men have
no successors. May God give to Benzonia the spirit and the power
of Oberlin in the early time.

When churches or benevolent organizations become large and influential; when they have a name which is honorable; when their
managers are great and prudent men in the world's estimation;
when many praise and none can gain anything by dissenting from
their procedures, then arises the danger that men will begin to
regard the institution itself with improper deference. Its friends rely
on its name, its wisdom, its wealth to honor or promote themselves.
It may then begin to "seek its own"—its own growth, character,
interests, as an institution rather than the things that belong to
Christ. Great institutions and men of great *name* may do great det-
riment to true religion. With the prevalent desire to be esteemed
great in human estimation, to be a true minister, is scarcely possible.

On Dreams and Dreaming.—How mysterious and inexplicable
they are? Skeptical as we may be, and doubtless should be, in regard to any intimations of the future being connected with the common dreamings of the night, yet there are dreams that the mind
cannot dispose of as being the shadow of past thoughts. It is no
doubt true that the prevailing state of mind during waking hours
carries its hues into the hours of sleep, and these hues somber or
salient tinge the texture of our night visions. But is it not likewise

true that coming states of mind do the same—the one as much as the other? It is certainly true that the impress of the dream and of events which follow often force the mind to feel whether it will or no, that as shadow and substance the one is the complement of the other. There are visions that can be accounted for on no theory as yet proposed, and those who *assume* that such have no connection with the future are often egotistical philosophers like Merebaud, who seek reputation by negativing everything inexplicable. Dreams indicating the future confirm the hopes of a future life, and strengthen the testimony for the scriptures. My sleeping thoughts are often as distinct in the morning as my waking thoughts at night. The freed spirit expatiates in the past and future alike.

The symbolic representations of the future in dreams do not always nor often assume the shape of symbolic ideas, as we would conceive of them in waking hours—while yet in connection with the future they seem more striking and appropriate, than any which we could conceive of while awake. Take the following three instances among very many:

Before the principal revival of religion in Akron, I dreamed that the old meeting house seemed to assume the aspect of a dingy stone building. Its height increased; its tops surrounded with clouds, and apparently lost in the darkness of the clouds. The surroundings of the church did not seem inviting, but rather dark, and the enlargement seemed in some wise not pleasant to me. I had no anticipation except good for the church. The form of the church which I beheld in vision was something I did not anticipate and would reject. The impression was not pleasant, and yet there was extension. Now, while I remained in Akron the church prospered greatly. I left it a large and hopeful people. The revival then in progress greatly added to its members; but after I left Mr. Pickands went to that church. He was eccentric, and became a Millerite. The church was in the end divided, and its members scattered, and clouds and darkness were upon it, when the organization ceased and a new church was formed of its fragments.

In Chicago, during the progress of the revival in the First Presbyterian church, whilst I was laboring with them, I dreamed of seeing a field inclosed for cultivation. It had been used. It was elevated at its upper end and declined to the bottom. The lower part seemed rather barren and gullied by storms and strong currents of water which had passed over it. The upper part seemed more fair and fruitful, and I was engaged in setting out in it young fruit trees. Others were growing there, and the upper part of the field presented to my eye and left on my mind a pleasant impression.

That church was the first organized in Chicago. Old strifes and currents of public sentiment had separated and marred the minds of its old members. They were unfruitful for the most part. Church discipline of the most painful kind began before the protracted meeting closed. But there was a better class of members, who were revived and greatly advanced,--and to them were added, by my labors, a number of converts. These have since then been the hope of the church. The church has prospered, and a colony has gone out and formed a Congregational church which is likewise doing good. The reform element and self-denying spirit are mostly in the Congregational church—but both are prosperous.

A precious revival has just closed in this (Mansfield) church. The church itself has been more revived and enlightened than at any time before. With one or two exceptions, every member has made spiritual attainments. Now, in the midst of the revival I dreamed, and the dream greatly impressed and affected me.

I dreamed I was in a garden of fruitful plants and flowers; the buds on the trees which seemed like rose bushes were just developing, as the cabbage rose develops its flower. I thought that it was sunlight, but there was slight snow on the ground and it was cold and freezing. In looking at the buds I saw that almost every one had in its core a black worm; the head of the worm was visible, and it was moving and living—in some cases larger and more active than others. I stood and wondered in my dream how the worms could live in the freezing weather. It seemed strange to me but true. After contemplating the scene I took a stick and engaged thrashing the bushes and buds to knock out the worms and kill them. I thought I labored with some success, although not with entire nor general success.

Now the revival is over. It has been a rich blessing to us all. I have preached much to the church. Worldly and selfish aims were as canker worms in the developing christian character. The worms lived in the cold light of truth while there was little spirit or power; but by the grace of God something has been done to remove them in this revival. What do such dreams presenting unthought of symbols, which really do symbolize the future, mean? Do not beings that know the future commune with our minds in the night season?

OCTOBER 27, 1858.—Last night I returned from Chicago at nine o'clock. Slept soundly, as I was somewhat wearied. I dreamed, and in vision saw three scenes very dissimilar, and all seeming to purport the same thing. I seemed to be an observer rather than the subject of the dream.

I dreamed I was in a house somewhat old. By some force it was falling with myself and others in it. It fell and I awoke.

Asleep again. I saw a chestnut tree standing apart in a field. A crow hovered over its top. The bird seemed to alight on it as a dark cloud. A wind arose and uprooted the tree, and blew it down and along the ground.

Asleep again. I seemed to be on the second story of a house, and was pulling a rope to ring a bell. The bell, or rather steel ring, was cracked and gave out only the short, harsh jars of a broken bell.

All things seen in dreams are not the product of the law of suggestion, nor are they always originated by imperfect sleep, or by indigestion. These visions were very vivid. They are quite diverse in themselves, yet the same import.

OCTOBER 29.—This morning I received a note from a friend connected with a family in which in former years I had a deep interest.
One died insane; one is now insane, and I fear another is about to
lose her reason. I have not for years had any intercourse with this
family, they residing in a distant part of the State.

The letter just received is from Mrs. Harriet Emmerson, of New
Port, Ky. A passage of its doleful contents reads as follows: "With
one of my sons dead, and the other in the lunatic asylum, I find myself almost alone at fifty-three years of age, and dependent on others
for a living." This woman was one of the holiest members of the
church at New Richmond. Her husband died insane. She needs
help and asks for it. I feel deeply these afflictions, and will do for
the sufferers what I can and when I can. The dreams are being
fulfilled. The interpretation is by no possibility a chance similitude,
for every state of mind in view of these facts are the same which the
dream produced. The fulfillment does not always produce the same
state of mind—sometimes only it does. The cracked bell was a
symbol of impaired reason.

I have just heard a sermon on love. To me, although I knew it to
be sacred and vital truth, it was barren and empty. I am fastidious,
perhaps, beyond propriety in regard to preaching perfection, by those
especially who are known to possess only the ideal, not the actual of
their teaching. I would never give out even a hymn to sing if I
thought it overstated the spiritual condition of the singers. In that
beautiful hymn, "I love thy kingdom Lord," the verse containing
the imprecation,

> If ere my heart forget
> "This hand let useful skill forsake,
> "This voice in silence die,"

I have never given out for others to sing, and I have never sung
it when given out by another.

Worship ought to be the expression of the true emotions of the
heart. Reverence, humanity and utter truthfulness should characterize every word—or no word should be said or sung. It is somewhat different perhaps with preaching. But the common, formal
preacher who lectures on the life and power of love, which he does not
feel, does his duty while he is yet an object of pity. He may utter
the same truth, and yet the spirit of his discourse—its impression
upon the hearts of others will be very different from that of the man
who speaketh out of the abundance of his heart. Such discourses
usually affect nobody, except to repel or harden those who know that
the man's words are with him a mere theory, and to other hearers
they are as a "painted ship on a painted ocean."

A person that tells the evils that he knows to be true of another,
without at the same time telling the good that he knows to be true,
is a liar.

There should be some method by which omnibus bills in the legislature, appropriations of public moneys for improvements in States or in the Union, should be referred to an impartial committee of inquiry and determination, to report after investigation according to the need and value of each object asking appropriation. Experience in frauds upon the Government are constant, and interested representatives combine shamefully for selfish ends, to felch public funds. When in the Senate I found it difficult to resist combinations of this sort.

I am troubled with youthful feeling, as fresh as when a boy. An aged man, feeble in body—hair white as wool - and yet in style of intercourse with the young, almost the same as forty years ago. Others note the peculiarity. I shall surely soon get beyond this.

BENZONIA, August, 1868.—I have planted four orchards in my life, and these with words of mine have induced the planting of many others here and elsewhere. I have urged the people here to plant fruit trees and shrubs so soon as they had sufficient clear land. I have introduced good varieties of fruits, and tested them, and distributed them, from the strawberry to the winter apple; and by fairs and in other ways we have created a desire among the people of the whole region to cultivate good fruit. This we hope will be a blessing to their families. It will contribute to health, gratify taste, and make home surroundings pleasant and profitable. A gentleman who has been looking through my fruit yard and lawn seems induced thereby to remove here and devote his leisure to fruit culture. With industry, careful culture and wise selections, fruit growing—especially the best winter apples—may succeed as a business in our region. But, in order to this, time and skilled labor are necessary.

I have read the Bible of Reason in which the wise teaching of the ancient sages is compiled from Confucius to Lucca; and the statement affirmed that they are valuable as the doctrines of Jesus, if it were admitted that the excellence of the gospel is in its precepts—which it is not—but in the revelation of Divine Love in Christ. Yet, if it were admitted that the power is in the precept, then why did not Seneca conquer the world? Why don't Comte regenerate and transform men? Tell us, O ye men, who find truth superior to the New Testament, why does not the greater truth produce the greater effect? The power of faith on the conscience and heart is the central glory of the gospel—not its precepts.

There is a law which will operate to produce an increase of beauty in the forms and faces of the human family, especially in America. Persons who have a free selection of marriage mates—as the young

7

people of this country—will generally select companions of physical and mental qualities unlike their own. Those who observe will notice this. The selection in physical forms may grow out of the distaste one gets for his own uninviting peculiarities. A lean structure will usually select a round featured mate. A person with a long nose will never select a mate with the same peculiarity. The dislike they get to their own peculiarity repels them from it in another. So it is in mental qualities that are marked. Hence, this balancing and counteracting process goes on in a free society—crossing out peculiarities, and improving the forms and features and mental symmetry of civilized society.

Mark 11:24.—An excellent woman, Mrs. Huntington, is relating her experience. She had for months been prayerful and asking for the grace of love and faith. At length she experienced what is recorded in the 11th chapter of Mark, 24th verse—"What things soever ye desire when ye pray, *believe that ye receive them*, and ye shall have them." She says she came into the state of mind in which she felt—"*I believe these blessed things that I have sought* ARE MINE. Jesus has said, He will withhold no good thing—I have his promise. THEY ARE MINE. When I felt *they are* mine, my peace flowed like a river." The promise in the passage was verified to her just as it reads. She believed she had through Christ the promised good, and she had it. She is peaceful and useful. Is it not a law of the mind, that if we believe we receive spiritual good, we have it? Does the belief produce it?

It is necessary that we should believe that Christ suffered for our sins; otherwise the love of Christ would not lead us to hate sin. Love for a person will lead us to hate whatever causes that person to suffer—especially if the cause of the suffering be evil in its own nature—then both heart and conscience is opposed to it. Such is our nature, and the true gospel is so adapted to our nature that those who love Christ will hate sin.

Deacon Bailey has just said to me what surely must be a good quality in my pulpit labors. He said I "made everything so simple and plain that it seemed to him he knew it all before, and yet he didn't." I have rather desired that some one like the deacon who can appreciate truth when he sees it, would say just this of my preaching. The plagues of literature and of the schools are those who "see things through a glass darkly;" who have many words for few ideas; and who write in strained definitions, and talk profoundly about subjects that they cloud rather than clear to the apprehension of others. A great mind gives simplicity to profound ideas.

Is it a case of polygeneses? One of the first years of my residence in Benzonia a little brownish midge or fly infested the wheat stalks by the million. They seemed to suck the juices but not kill the stalk, as I feared they would. The succeeding year the woods and fields were alive with small, yellow butterflies which laid their eggs in the forest and orchard trees; and from these were generated the millions of canker worms—or inch or measure caterpillars, which destroyed leaves and fruit, and were the pests of the season, and continued in less numbers the second year. Was the midge the progenitor?

LIFE ATOMS.—What objection is there to the doctrine that God created life atoms? elementary norms of life which are latent until the adapted conditions develop them into active assimilation with matter as their specific bodies. A seed will lie hidden in the earth, below the search of air and sun, in a latent state, for ages; yet, when thrown near the surface it germinates. But life is not in the body of the seed, but a germule within the seed and within a cell. The qualities of things are educed by their correlation. The relative position of bodies or masses of matter develop their qualities and determines their form and motion—sometimes by contact, sometimes without.

Why not, therefore, suppose that life-atoms were created and mingled in the elements of matter, but latent till the changing and advancing conditions of the sun and the globe developed them? developed them in certain regions of the earth and at certain times. And thus from first to last stages of progress;—and that these atoms before developed had each the sexual constitution, and when they had assimilated to themselves bodies, had powers of adaptation to country and climate.

If God created molecules of specific life among the primary elements, the evidence of his wisdom and power would be as decisive as in the case of specific creations *per se.* In the one case He created the life principle subject to related and designed conditions of development; in the other case He created the animal when its adapted condition ensued. But as conditions are developed progressively, why not suppose the one to be conditioned with the other, and *all* by the immediate power and wisdom of God—the God who reveals His nature to men in the adapted personality of our Lord Jesus Christ, by whom alone God is known, and in whom alone He becomes personal?

The tenth and eleventh chapters of Daniel are undoubtedly an interpolation in the prophecies of Daniel, written and inserted after the time of Antiochus Epiphanes. The beginning of the twelfth chapter ought to be connected immediately with the close of chapter nine.

The Friend Quakers utterly fail in the matter of means and efforts
to propagate the truth in the world.   The Congregationalists fail in
spirituality and testimony against worldly conformity, while they
rigorously propagate the gospel as they understand it.   The two
qualities should be united.   There should be testimony and effort in
a spirit of love.

Against intemperance in drink and diet, and in favor of simplicity
and healthful variety in drink and food.

Against preposterous, injurious and expensive fashions; and in
favor of comfort, good taste, and economy in clothing.

Against amusements injurious to health, morals, and happiness;
and in favor of healthful and exhilarating recreations in proper asso-
ciations.

Against all oaths, especially oath-bound secret societies; but in
favor of legal *affirmations* for legal uses.

Against operatic and unintelligible singing in churches—which is
an abomination to God—and in favor of congregational singing in
familiar melodies and intelligible words, with light instrumental accompaniment.

Against auction of pews, and in favor of free seats—families taking their seats, but not excluding any one so long as there is room.

Against long prayers and long essay-like sermons; but in favor of
scriptural, earnest prayer and preaching.

Against all systems and persons who deny the Lord that bought
them, and for the evangelical faith that believes *"God was in Christ,*
reconciling the world to himself," and that these only obey the
Lord who labor for men.

Against all schemes which predicate the hope of heaven on forms
of faith and worship; and in favor of faith in Christ and prayerful
obedience by good works to his example.

Against the usage of making the Old Testament the religion of
Christians; and in favor of presenting it as the New Testament does,
as adapted to its place; but introductory and imperfect as compared
with Christianity.

Against all religious tests in political affairs; but in favor of requiring conscience and moral life in candidates for office.

WHEATON, Ill., July 29, 1875.—I am seventy years of age. The
good hand of my God having brought me to this birth-day in better
health than I had anticipated.   I have felt that God would now permit me to retire from pulpit duty, and devote my remaining strength
to the revision and publication of my books.   Of one thing, the
events of a life have convinced me, by experience, that good and
evil are inseparably connected with all things in this life; and that
there is a process going forward under the Divine Supervision by
which the good will eventually triumph.   In the balance of moral
good and evil the sacrifice of Jesus Christ is the cause that gives pre-
ponderance to the good.   The power of that sacrifice is increasing

in the world. The influx of love in my own time into the hearts of men is perfectly obvious by comparing the state of the churches now with their spirit a half century ago. That sacrifice is a part of the moral economy of the world, and is implied in the existence of darkness and evil and imperfection in the creation.

Carlyle – has become not only cynical and misanthropic, but bitter of heart towards his fellow-men. This is the natural result in the case of those who are gifted with a degree of mental acumen and discernment which enables them to see clearly the defects and selfish aspirations of men, and to discern the assumptions and selfish exhibitions of *medium* minds. No mere man with a mind superior to his fellows can observe the cunning –the weak presentments which some men make of themselves, and the selfishness which moves them, without feeling with the poet,

> " I sometimes wish that I could blot
> All traces of mankind from earth,
> As tho' 'twere wrong to blast them not,
>   They so degrade—so shame their birth."

Such men discern clearly the motes in the eyes of others, and unless they have the grace of God in their hearts, and the truth of God in their minds, they will in old age become unhappy and malignant cynics. He that believes the peculiarities of men are in a great measure natural—and that selfishness is in the nature of every one; and that he himself is one of the same family—and that a forbearing and benevolent spirit should be exercised towards those who possess a *lesser* and yet *assuming* mind—often without knowing their own obvious defects—such an one however gifted, may be happy in old age.

It seems to be the history of the different members of the solar system that from a state of igneous fusion they have advanced to -- or are advancing to a habitable condition, by cooling—then they continue to congeal until they become unfit for the residence of such beings as now exist. Assuming this to be true, then man is the objective aim of the creation. After him no intelligent being can exist in what will then be a frigid world. The coal or fuel supply is likewise limited—a thousand years more will exhaust the available deposits in the temperate zones—hence man is the ultimate of the Divine idea in the world. In the future this will be seen and the significance understood—but, the refrigeration proceeding, the planet will at length become unfitted for the residence of man as at present constituted. What then?

THE DEBTOR.—Jan. 1876.—This month I expected some three or four hundred dollars from those who are indebted to me. It is now the first day of February and I have not yet received a dollar.

Trusting to those indebted to me I let my arrears run low. There are several bills that I expected to pay during the month – of no great amount, but such as I always pay. I have been afraid for a week that some of these would send in a bill, and that I would have to refer them to another day—a thing which I do not remember ever having done in my life-time. I had promised to two or three that I would pay monthly as I always do, in their cases. What will they think? This day it is storming violently, and the storm is really a satisfaction to me, in this matter, that no one will expect me to go out of my house to day, and therefore will not feel disappointed in not getting the little sums due them. This is a new experience for me. How unhappy must be the poor debtor, who is always in such a case ; and how guilty such debtors as mine, who might and ought to pay their debts when over due, and do not.

———

THE SCIENTIFIC ULTIMATE.—The old questions of past ages are discussed with unusual interest, and deeper penetration by scientific enquirers of our time ; and the discussion has resulted as in the past, in a dead lock at the point of life and death. The contestants cover the entire field of inquiry; each student seeking the ultimate in his own department of study.

Learned men are agreed that the development or evolution of life-forms is correlated with physical conditions, or the environs in which the life principle or germ is located. The question is : *Is the life-principle a separate and substantial entity*, possessing peculiar specific qualities which are developed by conditions and subjacent surroundings? That while it exists co-ordinately with its environs and is dependent upon them for motion and development ; yet being thus brought to activity, it assimilates a body from its material surroundings, *by a specific power which is not of its surroundings*, but which acts upon them, and assimilates its body from their material ?

I can see no evidence in any case where life exists, that the *form-ating* germ and the elements from which it assimilates its corporeity are identical. There is evidence to the contrary. Every specific germ in creation produces for itself a body of a different form, yet all marked by adaptations to sustain and prolong its life. There is surely two separate entities in the case. The potency which forms the body is not in the particles or atoms of the body itself; but in the organizing germ of life which collects those particles into a form whose qualities are adapted to subserve the instincts of the vital ovum that produced them. Single germs assimilating various ele-ments into adaptive forms for life and reproduction—is a very differ-ent thing from the identical atoms uniting in prismatic forms. The one is an eclectic power exerted by one entity upon various elements which surround it ; the other is an adjustment of like atoms which takes place in the *eternal flow of all the atoms of the universe among themselves.*

And not only in the lowest, but in the highest being, man, the

germinal animalcule becoming attached to an ovary, a formative
process is begun which assimilates material from its surroundings
till the time of birth.   Then placed in new environs the testimony
of observation and consciousness is that the child, by its first movements, learns of the non-ego—the not me—the first consciousness
being that of its surroundings.   The first perception of the infant
is not self, but the surroundings which affect itself.   Thenceforward
the I—the self-germ—the Ego, lives in conscious contact with its
environs.   It—that is, the separate Ego, is conscious of thinking,
acting, feeling.   It is conscious of the ideas which are engendered
in the mind by its physical surroundings; but the Ego itself is as
separate from the idea in its own mind which it sees and judges,
and uses, as the agent is from the object.

I have had frequent attacks of what is called a cold in my life,
but for two years, while organizing a Christian school and colony, I
dwelt in the woods at Benzonia, Michigan, and lived in a log house,
through which I could see the light of the stars at night, and slept
in a room where the fine snow was often shaken from my bed and
the other beds in the morning.   In this open house not a member
of the family, so far as I can remember, had a cold.   All took out-
door exercise; all had good health, and good appetites.   My wife
here, in the third year, had an attack of apoplexy; rather as we
thought from excess of blood than ill-health.   We subsequently
moved into a closely sealed and plastered house, with close warm
rooms.   My neuralgia returned severely, and colds and complaints
were frequent.

I ought to be grateful—as I think I am—to the blessed Father in
heaven, that during a life of more than seventy-five years, I can remember but a single time of gloomy feeling, or blues, as we call a
despondent state of mind.   I have passed through trials of mind and
body, but always in hope and cheerfulness.   This is something to be
grateful for.   I have been reading of the despondency and peculiarities of authors.   I have known a little of authorship, but nothing of
the peculiarities mentioned.   At my advanced age I thank God for
a cheerful, and in a common way, a successful life.   I am sure this
has conduced to longevity.   The mind not only actuates but gives
form and force to the body.   I am not so strong to do and endure as
formerly, yet still my step is agile and my form erect, at the age
of seventy-five years.

In the little gifts which I have sometimes bestowed on others, unexpectedly to them, I remember those cases when a trifle seemed to
produce instant and marked surprise and pleasure.   Once, in London, passing up the Strand where many women were sitting selling
hogs feet and other items to appease hunger, I noticed among the

women, one pale and comely and diffident woman, not like most of the coarse women about her. I stopped and asked her the price of feet, and paid her for several. She presented them gladly. I gave her the money but refused to take the feet. She looked to ascertain if something was not misunderstood. I made her understand she was to have the pay and keep the feet ; a happy, grateful and rather wondering expression came to her pale face, and I passed along ; both of us happier than we were before.

Another day in London I noticed an affectionate looking little girl carrying a heavy basket. I gave her a shilling. She looked so surprised and happy, when I told her it was for herself, that I went to the same place afterwards hoping to meet and surprise the child again. I did not see her again, but I had left two adopted little girls in America, to them I wrote about the girl and the incident.

Once in New York on Christmas day, as I came out of a friend's house, Rev. D. F. Newton, I noticed a dejected looking woman, picking up old rags and papers. A lady, now Mrs. General Brinkerhoof, had given me five dollars, asking me to expend it charitably for her. I gave the woman part of the money. She took the money with an inquiring look ; and when she ascertained I had given it to her, with a happy surprise, she hurried—almost ran away. She probably had children at home suffering for food, and with a glad heart ran to their relief.

––––––––

The doctrine of evolution, which is true in the right sense, cannot be argued with one factor, as though an individual by its own force and nature alone, developed some new form and faculty. Varieties imply change of habitat and condition. And a new species implies a new environment coming in at the same time, and adapted to the qualities of the new species. Do progressive environs develop progressive faculties ? The earth has progressed from lower to higher conditions ; the species thereon has advanced from lower to higher faculties ; up to man. Will there be a farther advance ?

––––––––

I have often said that if it were appointed that I should live my life over again, I would not desire to change any material event of my history. I have been asked, was not the effort to establish a church, school and colony at Benzonia a failure that I abandoned as unfruitful of good. I am satisfied that it was not, and that it has and will accomplish, in a good measure, what I designed ; although, owing to providential circumstances, I withdrew from the enterprise sooner than I expected to do, when I removed to the colony. My design was to aid in establishing institutions in the woods of Northern Michigan, that would be a blessing to the poor people that would settle on the lands under the Homestead law ; to provide cheap education for their children ; and especially for the children of the colony that I should aid to collect there. All this was in a great measure accomplished. A christian church; one of the best and largest in the state, was gathered and organized at Benzonia. A school was started and endowed with land and money sufficient to support two teachers; the children of the colony and the whole region had opportunity for an academic education at a mere nominal rate, $12 per year. The best kind of fruits were introduced into the colony, and from it into the whole region. I aided to organize, beside the Congregational church at Benzonia, four other Congregational churches in the region, which are still living and doing some good; and aided in the organization of the Baptist church in Joyfield, besides helping in all reforms and institutions that I thought would do good. The region, in consequence, is right in politics; right in morals, and prosperous as a new region can be; and the influence of the district on the legislation of the state, which I represented in the senate two years, has always been good. If the country had been settled by another class it would have been different. The school and the churches which were first organized, invited in a good class of people, and they by affinity brought others. The part I accomplished in seven years in the Traverse region I accept as a part of my history, and do not desire to change the work. Selfish men worked in with the enterprise, but God does not design the good to exist without the accompanying evil. The preponderance of the good is what God and good men achieve. Thank God for guidance and success.

Is it unscriptural to suppose that man's body is an evolution from nature below him; that he is the highest animal of the chain; the end of the organic series, and that this animal nature was endued with a spiritual soul? *i. e.*, a spiritual nature superinduced upon the perfected animal form. Is not this truth indicated by the statement that animals were created of the dust of the earth, *i. e.*, that all organized bodies are formed of the elements of the material world; but to man, the most perfect of the animal forms, God added a rational soul, so that man is a compound nature, animal and angelic?

For the last month I have added a verse of praise at the close of my morning prayer in the family. I feel that to pray longer without praise would be wrong. God has guided my life so mercifully; so quietly through a wonderful variety of circumstances that I ought, before life closes and while it lasts, to praise as well as pray. Hence to our morning devotions we add the doxology:

> Praise God from whom all blessings flow,
> Praise Him all creatures here below;
> Praise Him above ye heavenly host,
> Praise Father, Son and Holy Ghost.

It is surprising that churches still rely on forms of worship as a passport to heaven. Forms, so far as decency and order demand are proper, but forms instead of faith, labor and self-denial for Christ is one of the delusions which cheat many souls out of heaven. Here is a Mrs. Bowler, of whom I have known something, as a weak, well disposed woman. She has just joined the Catholic church, as the best means of securing salvation. The idea of following Christ in labor for the temporal and spiritual good of men, has never been her conception of the way of life. Church rites and observances have grown in importance in her mind, until finally she has reached the Catholic—the church where rites are most relied on. Alas for her!

This week I have fitted out my youngest adopted child, James Benzonia Walker, for his trip to Nebraska. He was given an opportunity to learn a trade, or study for any useful profession; but, on account of weak eyes, and a disinclination to study, he preferred to work on a farm and own one in the West. He is sixteen years of age, and goes to work for some farmer for a time before he enters on his own land; if he ever does so. I have done all I could to train him in right principles and habits. I have expended thought and money for his good. I hope that he will be a useful man. If he fails it will not be because I have not done everything that a father could do for an adopted son. May God guide the boy. He is the tenth adopted child.

THE DOOMED MAN.

These lines have impressed me more than once by their solemn thought. If there be a point of doom often passed before men die, beyond which the truth and the Spirit of God fail to awaken the conscience, and to produce love in the heart, the solemnity of such a doctrine is awful. I have seen men that seemed to be doomed men. I have known when they saw the truth clearly, and rejected it intelligently. Some of them subsequently became skeptical. One, a successful lawyer, is living in Washington City—walking a dead and spiritually doomed man, without any apparent consciousness of approaching death.

> There is a time we know not when,
> A place we know not where,
> That marks the destiny of men,
> To glory or despair.
>
> There is a line by us unseen,
> That crosses every path,
> The hidden boundary between
> God's patience and his wrath.
>
> To pass that limit is to die,
> To die as if by stealth ;
> It does not quench the beaming eye,
> Or pale the glow of health.

The conscience may be still at ease,
The spirits light and gay ;
That which is pleasure still may please,
And care be thrust away.

But on that forehead God has set
Indelibly a mark—
Unseen by man, for man as yet
Is blind and in the dark.

And still the doomed man's path below
May bloom as Eden bloomed—
He did not, does not, will not know,
Or feel, that he is doomed.

He knows, he feels that all is well,
And every fear is calmed ;
He lives, he dies, he wakes in hell,
Not only doomed, but damned !

O ! where is this mysterious bourne,
By which our path is crossed ;
Beyond which, God himself hath sworn
That he who goes is lost ?

How far may men go on in sin ?
How long will God forbear ?
Where does hope end, and where begin
The confines of despair ?

An answer from the skies is sent—
" Ye that from God depart,
While it is called to-day repent,
And harden not your heart ! "

SATURDAY, June 28, 1879.—I have just returned from the funeral of my adopted daughter, Mrs. Emma Lincoln Moffatt, wife of Prof. T. C. Moffatt, of this place.

Emma was one of a family of orphans, left without parents in their infancy. We took her into our family, because she needed a home, and some family to care for and educate her. Her health was never strong, and she could not have borne hard labor. We educated her carefully, and she taught school for several terms. She came with us to Wheaton, where she was married in this house, by myself, to Prof. Moffatt. She had a kind, good, intelligent husband, with whom she lived just one year, having died on the anniversary of her marriage. She professed love for the Savior at an early age, and lived a consistent Christian life. Her religious experience was more marked than was known even to most of her friends. She leaves a little boy which is called Frances James. In reflecting upon my life in connection with her, I remember no word that I regret. May her death impress us and others with the duty to "work while the day lasts." Emma—farewell! "*Requiescat en pace.*"

I am an old man now, and no opportunity will ever again be granted me to travel extensively—but when a young man I traveled on horseback for two years through the west half of the state of Ohio, as Agent of the American Bible Society—forming county societies, collecting funds, and seeing that each county was visited and every family supplied with the Bible.   I do not remember that in that ride of two years I ever rode with a casual companion in the road without embracing some opportunity kindly to introduce the subject of religion, and endeavor to leave some good impression on the mind.   To-day in thinking of the past—this has been a consolation to me.   O how many neglected opportunities I have to account for! notwithstanding that some were observed in earlier years.   I think the early years of my religious life were my best years.